THROWING SHADOWS

Also by Claire Booth

The Sheriff Hank Worth Mysteries

THE BRANSON BEAUTY
ANOTHER MAN'S GROUND
A DEADLY TURN *
FATAL DIVISIONS *
DANGEROUS CONSEQUENCES *
HOME FIRES *

* *available from Severn House*

THROWING SHADOWS

Claire Booth

SEVERN
HOUSE

First world edition published in Great Britain and the USA in 2025
by Severn House, an imprint of Canongate Books Ltd,
14 High Street, Edinburgh EH1 1TE.

severnhouse.com

Cover and jacket design by Jem Butcher Design

British Library Cataloguing-in-Publication Data
A CIP catalogue record for this title is available from the British Library.

ISBN-13: 978-1-4483-1388-4 (cased)
ISBN-13: 978-1-4483-1391-4 (e-book)

All Severn House titles are printed on acid-free paper.

Typeset by Palimpsest Book Production Ltd., Falkirk,
Stirlingshire, Scotland.
Printed and bound in Great Britain by TJ Books,
Padstow, Cornwall.

The manufacturer's authorised representative in the EU for product safety is
Authorised Rep Compliance Ltd, 71 Lower Baggot Street, Dublin D02 P593
Ireland (arccompliance.com)

Praise for the Sheriff Hank Worth Mysteries

"An excellent procedural with the added attraction of a difficult, personally painful mystery"
Kirkus Reviews on *Home Fires*

"An outstanding police procedural . . . Readers of Steven F. Havill and Bill Crider will appreciate the novel's focus on small-town life and a local police force"
Library Journal Starred Review of *Home Fires*

"A fine novel"
Booklist on *Home Fires*

"Balances well-developed characters and dry humor with a solid police procedural"
Library Journal Starred Review of *Dangerous Consequences*

"Booth knows exactly what she's doing . . . a deeply satisfying conclusion"
Booklist on *Dangerous Consequences*

"Booth skillfully combines police procedural elements with a sharp focus on the families and professional lives of her protagonists. This superior regional series reliably entertains"
Publishers Weekly on *Fatal Divisions*

"Fascinating and complex"
Publishers Weekly on *A Deadly Turn*

About the Author

Claire Booth is a former crime reporter for daily newspapers throughout the United States. She's used this experience to write six previous Sheriff Hank Worth mystery novels. She is also the author of one non-fiction book, *The False Prophet: Conspiracy, Extortion, and Murder in the Name of God*. She lives in California.

www.clairebooth.com

For

Kenny
and
Aimee

ONE

The man ran, rabbit-fast and rabbit-scared, through the trees. His pack pulled on his shoulders as he scrambled over rotting logs and gouged the moldy sponge of fallen leaves with his boots. He couldn't hear what was behind him over his own frantic sprinting, the racket of an inexperienced fool. His foot hit a hole and he went tumbling down an incline, landing hard in the Ozark dirt. He got to his knees and tried to catch his breath. If he could only make it to the road. Maybe he could find help. Safety. He started to move, but his knees wouldn't stay steady enough for him to stand. He tried to crawl and got nothing but a few yards' progress and a stab in the thigh from a dead branch. He bit his lip to keep from yelling out as blood started to seep through his pants. He slumped down on his elbows and swore.

It was time to face facts.

He sat back on his haunches and shrugged the pack off his back. The wind hit his sweat-soaked shirt and sent a chill along his spine. He twisted around, searching for a hiding spot. Nothing. He forced himself upright and stumbled forward. He made it over the next rise, dragging the pack behind him, and saw what he needed. He concealed it as completely as he could. Maybe it would work. Nothing else during this whole calamity had.

He backed away and took in the lay of the land. He still didn't know where he was, but there were no longer sounds of pursuit. He chose to continue downhill. If he didn't hit the road, chances were good he'd at least hit a creek. That might lead to a lake, which might lead to people.

He limped along as quickly as he could. The puncture wound started to burn and he could feel the blood running down his leg and into his sock. The darkness was almost complete, and all the obstacles he'd been able to see and avoid were disappearing in the gloom. He tripped again, going down hard and cutting his cheek. He lay there inhaling the scent of fungus spores and animal piss and his own fear. He curled his hand over dry leaves, taking their last bit of sunbaked warmth and turning them to dust.

A nearby tree worked as support for him to regain his feet. He wiped blood and tears on his sleeve and pushed off. Then a glimmer of moonlight showed a sliver of flat surface, flat like a God-sent, man-made road. It was off to his left and he veered in that direction, heading past a stretch of blank blackness on the right. His step started to lighten and his lungs loosened with each breath. He quickened his pace.

He never saw them coming.

Hank Worth spread the paperwork out over his desk. There was a comfortingly large amount of it. It would take him a long time to sort through everything, which meant he'd need to stay here longer. And not go home. He didn't need to, not really. The kids were fine, on a back-to-school shopping trip with Maggie. They'd probably come home late with new lunchboxes and sneakers, and ice cream on their faces from the bribe their mother had to pay in order to get them into that last store for glue sticks and Ticonderoga pencils.

He'd be home in time to put them to bed. And then he could go work in the garage. And think about what to do about these catalytic converter thefts. He pulled the latest theft report out of the pile. A used-car dealership out on Highway 76 had had seven of the car parts stolen sometime in the past week. The manager wasn't sure exactly when, and didn't have any information about the lot's security measures. Only the owner knew that. Hank looked around the dreary office he'd been stuck with since becoming the Branson County sheriff almost two years ago, then out the window at the beautiful fall day. Maybe the owner was at work today. He grabbed his keys and quickly left the building.

Twenty minutes later he was walking through the not-so-gently-used collection of cars at Combs Car Emporium. A man built like a snowman emerged from the office and watched him approach.

'Yeah, I'm the owner. Wendall Combs.' He was wearing a polo shirt and slacks and had skin and hair so white he would've been impossible to spot in a blizzard. He shook Hank's hand and ushered him inside. 'Brian told me you all asked about my security when he filed the report.' He shut the door firmly behind them. 'The employees don't know what I got. Keeps them honest.'

'So what do you have, sir?' Hank asked. He hadn't been able to pick out any surveillance cameras as he walked across the lot.

'I got a camera in the light pole by the entrance.'

Hank waited. 'Is that everything?' he finally said.

'Well, yeah.' Combs shifted self-consciously.

'How much of the lot does that camera cover?'

'All of it.' Frosty was indignant.

'Excellent. May I see the video? You can orient me and then I can take a copy of the recording of the past week?'

The footage turned out to be even worse than Hank expected. A high-wattage security light washed out the view of most of the lot. The remainder was pockmarked with impenetrable shadows.

'It's real high up, now, so it's hard to see down in between the cars, like,' Frosty said defensively. 'I'm watching for thieves moving big-ass cars. Not small-ass parts. How the hell should I be expected to know they'd come for that kind of stuff?'

Hank gave what he hoped was a soothing nod, and made a few recommendations about camera placement and studies that showed visible cameras actually did act as a deterrent and perhaps Mr Combs could consider it? The owner grumbled a while before saying he would think on it.

'Do you have any idea when the converters were taken?'

'No, son, I don't know when. We just noticed it. The last time someone drove one of the cars was last Tuesday. So had to have been after that. But just 'cause I can't sell a 2003 sedan doesn't mean I want to offer it up for parts, free of charge.'

He had a point. They went outside and Frosty showed him which cars had been targeted. All were parked on the edges of the lot, where access was the easiest and the video's pockmarks were the blackest.

'So your employees don't know about the camera?'

'Nope.'

'And they've never seen video from it?'

'Nope.'

'Keep it that way. But add some more cameras, like we talked about, OK?'

He got grudging agreement and an icy handshake before Combs disappeared into his office. Hank thought for a minute and headed down to the next used-car lot, Briscoe's 76 Cars, where he ruined that manager's day in sixty seconds flat.

'What? Converters stolen at Wendall's place?' The manager hadn't heard and immediately sent his two hapless twenty-something salespeople crawling under every vehicle on their patch of asphalt. They found four missing. They also had no usable surveillance video. While they had three times the number of cameras as Combs did, it turned out they became ineffective when colonized by birds and covered in what birds tended to output at high rates.

The manager was furious and spent ten minutes stomping around before Hank could get another word in. Multiple swear words and a stale cup of coffee later, Hank had repeated his security improvement recommendations and gotten the list of Briscoe cars now missing catalytic converters. He left the manager dialing his boss with a look of dread, and walked back to his squad car, carefully skirting the cameras' drop zones on the way.

Chief Deputy Sheila Turley limped into the Pickin' Porch Grill, fingers curled lightly around the handle of her cane. She tried swinging it with a jaunty air, but her fifty-two-year-old body wasn't quite ready for that. She planted it back on the floor and made her way to the table. Her gait was slow but no longer torturous. Compared with her appalling wheelchair-bound immobility for the past several months, this stroll was equivalent to tap dancing into the restaurant and finishing off with a cartwheel.

A tall, trim white man in a suit and tie rose to his feet as she approached. He waited until she settled herself before resuming his seat. Wisely, he did not offer her any assistance. Their many phone conversations seemed to have schooled him on enough of Sheila's personality to know that would be unwelcome.

'It's nice to finally meet you in person,' Malcolm Oberholz said.

'You, too.' She propped her cane against the wall and eyed the prosecutor. 'You really are older than you sound on the phone.'

He laughed. 'I told you so.'

'I do wish you'd let me meet you halfway. There was no need for you to drive all the way down here from St. Louis.'

'Oh, I don't mind at all. It gives me an opportunity to see the area. Which is important.' He looked around. 'If I'm going to try to convince twelve Branson County residents that Eddie Fizzel, Junior, is guilty, I need to not seem like an outsider.'

Then the man needed a cheaper suit. She'd save that advice for later, though. Instead, she asked how they could possibly get an unbiased jury in this county.

'That's a very good question. I'm going to assert that we can't, and ask the judge to change the trial venue entirely. Move it to my county, ask the good people of a nice big metro area to decide.'

'Will a judge go for that?'

He shrugged. 'It depends on who we get. It will be a while before we know who it'll be, since it has to be someone who also has no connection to this county.'

Sheila nodded. It would be just semi-complicated if it were only her, Branson County's African American chief deputy sheriff, involved. But the man who assaulted her – in addition to being an unemployed, entitled little shit – was the son of a county commissioner. Edrick Fizzel, Senior, had been in office since God was young and the devil just fallen. He knew everyone. Half of the electorate loved him, and the other half he had dirt on. Combine that with people's strong opinions of law enforcement – both pro and con – and this citified white boy had his work cut out for him.

'So that's going to be one of my first moves,' Oberholz said. 'But it's a motion that's going to need to be argued in your courthouse, even if it is in front of an out-of-town judge. So I'd like to get my feet under me, so to speak.'

'A good place to start is with a fried chicken sandwich with extra chipotle aioli,' she said. Oberholz ordered two at the counter and had the waitress come back with their drinks. Sheila took hers, shifting slightly to ease the ache in her torso. Thankfully, Oberholz didn't notice.

'No matter where it's tried, though, we're going to have a problem with the ER doctor's report of your injuries.'

Or maybe he had. She sighed.

'That ER doctor is a friend of yours. They're going to allege that she's biased in your favor.'

Sheila snorted with laughter. 'The only thing Maggie McCleary is biased toward is an accurate diagnosis.'

Oberholz's lips turned into a thin line. Sheila looked straight back at him and calmly put her napkin in her lap. 'I'm not making light of how hard this is going to be. In Maggie's case, there are multiple surgeons and specialists who back up her initial opinion about all of my abdominal injuries. And the broken ribs. And the concussion. And my lacerated hands and knees. I know you like those.'

The second time they'd talked, he'd asked specifically for the photos her husband Tyrone had taken the night of the attack that showed her raw and bloody palms and kneecaps. Now he shook a straw at her before plunking it into his iced tea. 'Those two things tell a story. The story of a woman who had to crawl four hundred yards through the woods at night in order to save herself. Jurors will see your X-rays and it won't matter. To laypeople, that's just a bunch of shadows on a screen. But everybody can relate to scraped and bloody hands. And they only got that way because you knew you were going to die if you stayed there lying in the dirt. So you dragged yourself to the road in order for paramedics to find you. You saved your own life. Your palms might've been beat all to hell, but Edrick Fizzel, Junior, is the one with blood on his hands.'

Sheila sat back like she'd been smacked. Oberholz took a sip of tea. 'The facts matter. I'm not one of those lawyers who pretends they don't. But a trial usually comes down to who's the better storyteller. And ma'am,' his voice suddenly slowed and rounded into a drawl, 'ain't no one can tell a story like me.'

TWO

The Bronco wouldn't start. Sam Karnes swore to himself and shifted into neutral. He'd have to push it off the roadway. He'd just replaced the alternator a month ago, and it had been running fine until five minutes ago, when the engine let out a horrible gurgle and then quit on him, right in the middle of Gretna Road. He hopped out, and with one hand on the wheel tried to steer the damn thing out of the traffic lane. Cars were starting to back up behind him.

'Hey there, son. You could use a hand, I reckon.' A middle-aged man with an impressive pot belly climbed out of his pickup truck. 'You steer, I'll push.'

A second man, tall and much thinner, jogged up from a car farther back. 'This is one mighty old Ford. Has it died on you before?'

Sam shook his head. The two men leaned against the back and Sam guided the Bronco onto the shoulder. He wasn't appreciating this switch in roles – as a sheriff's deputy, he was usually the one helping other poor souls with broken down cars. Once his own was clear of the roadway, he shook both their hands. The one with the paunch gave him a pat on the arm.

'Don't forget to put your hazards on.'

'Oh, yeah. Thanks.' His hazard lights hadn't worked in years. He nodded in agreement anyway and gave them a wave as they both pulled away. The bottlenecked traffic started to move again, with some sympathetic driver waves and a few rude gestures. He chuckled. That was Branson. Two helping hands for every one middle finger. Usually.

He turned and looked at his poor Bronco. Then he took out his phone. Fifteen minutes later, a little red Toyota hatchback pulled up behind him. His girlfriend got out and gave him a look that perfectly hit the knife's-edge balance between empathy and *I told you so*.

'Was it making those funny noises again?' Brenna Cassidy asked.

'No. Honestly. It was absolutely fine. Until it died. Boom. Right here.' He pointed into the street as cars whizzed by. 'No funny noises.'

She eyed the Bronco skeptically. 'Have you called a tow truck?'
He had not. He didn't want to. His bank account absolutely did
not want him to. He tugged at his ear. 'I thought I'd get my dad
out here, we could take a look at the engine and—'

'You can't fix it on the side of Gretna Road. You have to call a
tow truck.'

He thought about his credit card balance. 'We could push it farther
up, into a parking lot. Then we'd be out of the way while we fix
it.'

Brenna glared at him. He fidgeted and thought about his father
giving him the same sort of frown if he suggested repairing an
engine outside some random business. He sighed and started
googling towing companies. An hour later, the Bronco sat in the
driveway of his little rental house and the tow driver was running
his Visa. Brenna had parked on the street and disappeared inside.

'You two have a nice evening,' he said. 'And good luck with that
thing.'

The driver nodded at the Ford and ambled back to his rig, which
sat there taunting Sam with its healthy diesel rumble. He gave his
poor baby one last look and trudged into the house. Brenna met
him at the door with a hug. They settled into the couch. 'Do you
think it's fixable?'

He shrugged and stretched out his lanky frame, staring at his size
fifteen shoes. 'I don't know. Most of the time, I catch stuff before
it gets bad. This time, I got no idea what's wrong.'

She snuggled in and laid her head on his chest. He ran his hand
through her dark blonde hair, breathing in the lavender scent he
loved. And things suddenly didn't seem so bad. She laced her fingers
through his. Definitely not so bad.

'You can use my car tomorrow. I'm sure Felicia can take me to
work.'

Brenna's roommate did photography for many of the local theaters
and could set her own hours. Brenna, who was a barista at the
downtown Donorae's café, could not.

'That would be great. I have to go in tomorrow. We're surveilling
that mechanic out near Kirbyville who we think could be dealing
in stolen catalytic converters.'

'Oooh, big-time crime.' She poked him teasingly.

'Ha. More like the opposite. But we have to watch it. And I drew
the short straw.'

He felt her smile against his chest. 'So my car gets to go on surveillance? Maybe it'll tell me all the exciting things you don't.'

'Hey, I've gotten better. I tell you stuff. I told you all about the mess with Hank's mother-in-law being murdered.'

She poked him again and sat up. 'That's because I'm the one who figured out in the first place that he must have something personal going on, because otherwise he wouldn't have been ignoring work like he was. Although, God knows I didn't expect the personal thing to be that somebody killed Mrs McCleary two years ago.'

They both reflected on that. The poisoning had only just been discovered, when some shoddy investigative work was exposed and old cases reopened.

'How is Hank, by the way?'

Sam let out a long, slow breath. 'Not great. He still walks around in a daze. Not like he's not paying attention to work – he is. But like he's numb.'

'It's got to be painful. I'm sure it'll take time.'

'I don't know. It doesn't seem to be grief that's causing it. Not grief for Mrs McCleary anyway.' He was trying to pick through thoughts that refused to form into words. 'That sort of grief wouldn't make things bad at home. And I think things are. Bad. And I don't know why.'

She rubbed her fingertips along his palm. 'I'll bet it's hard for Hank and Maggie to take care of the kids without her dad around. He's been gone quite a while. It'll probably be better when he gets back into town.'

Sam wasn't so sure about that.

The house was quiet, empty and cold. Except for the dog, who greeted Hank with his usual overheated exuberance. He locked his Glock in the gun safe and changed out of the shirt that now had grease and dirt spotted on the sleeves, the consequences of looking under vehicles at the car lots. He walked back toward the kitchen, averting his gaze from the stairs that led down to the basement. He started a simple pasta dish for dinner and turned on Monday Night Football. Two play drives later, his own linebackers burst into the house.

'Daddy, we got backpacks. Mine has a matching lunch bag. See?' Maribel shoved a shiny purple thing at him and ran back into the garage. Her five-year-old little brother took her place, practically vibrating with excitement. He clutched a bag full of school supplies.

'We got everything on the list.' Benny waved a crumpled paper. 'Everything a kindergartener needs. That's what it said. Mommy didn't want to, but we did anyway.'

'That isn't what I said.' Maggie, who could glide home calm and composed after a fourteen-hour shift in the ER, had been done in by a shopping trip. Her long brown hair was falling out of its clip and her jaw was clenched tighter than the hold Benny had on his Target bag. 'I said that we already had colored pencils and didn't need to buy more.'

Benny scoffed and dumped the supplies on the kitchen table. Hank looked at the pile, which included two of the same pencil packs currently in their art drawer, and then dared to glance at his wife. She mutely held out the rest of the packages and he quickly took them. She disappeared down the hall without another word, reemerging only when he called out that dinner was ready. A quick meal and two cursory baths later, both kids were in bed. Hank and Maggie sank wearily onto the couch, all the school purchases in a mound between them.

'How many places did you go?'

She rolled her eyes. 'I don't even know. The damn unicorn backpack was the killer. It took her forever to find exactly what she wanted.'

He picked it up. 'I can see where this spoke to a six-year-old's sense of taste.'

'You always did strike me as a unicorn type of guy.'

He put down the backpack and reached for her hand. They sat there quietly for a while, staring at the big stone fireplace. And the empty recliner right in front of it. So he wouldn't have to discuss that, Hank told her about his trip to the used-car lots.

'See any good minivans for sale?'

'We have a perfectly good minivan.'

'With a dented side panel.'

'It's toward the back. It's not that noticeable.'

'It's about to fall off.'

'It is?'

She sighed. 'Yes. It started rattling on our way back from Target tonight.'

'Shoot. I thought we could keep getting away with ignoring it.'

'Me, too.'

That statement sank in, and they sat there, carefully not looking at each other. Because they both knew how good they'd become at ignoring things, and this was how they did it. Silence and no eye contact.

'I'll call around to auto body shops in the morning,' Hank said.

She gave him a tired smile. 'Thanks. I'd be able to drop it off somewhere at the end of the week.' She rose slowly to her feet. 'What time is our appointment tomorrow?'

'Three o'clock.'

'OK. I'll see you there.' She kissed the top of his head and headed off to bed. He sighed and turned the football game back on. His team was now losing. Badly. He knew the feeling.

THREE

He didn't know where he was. The woods looked the same in every direction. He'd gotten so turned around that he couldn't even backtrack, retrace his steps. And his leg hurt like blazes. Limping along at this rate, he'd be here for days, even if he did know the way out. Which he didn't. He hobbled toward a fallen tree and found a branch long enough to use as a walking stick. He cautiously tested it and the wood held his weight. Small favors. The bark scraped against the dirty canvas of his pants as he moved forward. He tried to pay attention to the foliage, to keep his mind off the pain. It didn't much work.

Should he just stop? Wait for someone to find him? It would have to be a stranger. His friends didn't know where he was. His friends didn't know anything. Which made them not truly friends, he supposed. And whose fault was that? His. It hadn't mattered before. Now, as a low-hanging twig lashed his cheek and his stomach twisted with hunger, it mattered very much. He sank wearily onto a fallen log and looked around. This should've been the easy part. Easier than this, at least. The map with the graceful topographic lines looked so easy to follow when laid out on the table at home. It was once he found the spot that he expected difficulty. But no. The map turned out to be useless, and the difficulty had started too soon. He toed at the dirt and wiped at his watery eyes. It must be pollen in the air that was making them prick.

He sipped the last of his water and randomly picked a direction to walk. He made it a hundred yards over rocky ground before his stick let out a loud crack and split in two. He pitched forward and landed on his face. A group of chickadees took indignant flight and then all was still.

'Sammy, I gotta pull you off that mechanic surveillance.'

Sam blinked himself to full wakefulness. He'd been sitting in Brenna's car for hours with nothing to show for it except confirmation that the auto-repair shop did not do a booming business. Or any business. He rubbed his eyes and answered Dean Collins.

'Why? I'm five hours into this, man,' he told the department's dispatcher. 'If I leave and something actually happens, that is a lot of boring time gone to waste.'

'You're the closest deputy. Some idiot just walked out of the woods down south of you. Off Highway G. Dehydrated and raving like a lunatic. A motorist found the guy and called it in.'

'That sounds more like a job for the paramedics.'

'I've already requested them,' Dean said stiffly. 'But the motorist is getting more and more wigged out by this guy and doesn't want to stay. So.'

Sam straightened in the driver's seat and started the car. 'Sorry. You're right. I'm going.'

He headed south as Dean rattled off exact details. Six minutes later he turned a curve in the two-lane road and saw a Chevy Tahoe with Louisiana plates parked on the shoulder. He pulled up behind it, made sure the badge on his belt was visible, and got out to introduce himself to the couple standing by the back bumper. They looked from him in his T-shirt and jeans to the little red Toyota and frowned.

'This state is something else. The minute we cross into it we get lost, and this happens – and then what do we get, some kid on his day off?' The middle-aged man, beefy and sunburned, glared at him.

'I am actually on duty, sir. I'm Deputy Karnes with the Branson County Sheriff's Department. You called in about finding someone? A hiker?'

'We didn't "find" him. He walked into the road right in front of us. It's a miracle I could stop in time. He's staggering around, spouting nonsense. Wouldn't move out of the way. We had no choice but to pull over.'

The woman, teased blonde hair and plump cheeks, patted the man's arm. 'Of course we stopped. He was obviously in trouble. So we called 911 and gave him some water.' She paused. 'I thought that would calm him down.'

'It didn't.' The man put his arm around the woman Sam assumed was his wife. 'He kept ranting. About people wanting him. About everybody being after him. And about a dead man.'

Sam's attention, directed around the Chevy to try to see the hiker, snapped back. 'What did you say?'

'Are you deaf? I was perfectly clear.'

'George, don't be rude.'

'I wasn't being rude, I was just—'

Sam interrupted with a thanks and walked away quickly, rounding the big SUV until he found the hiker sitting on the ground and leaning against the front bumper. He was maybe thirty years old, with dark brown hair studded with twigs and leaves. Tear tracks cut through the dirt on his face, and his clothes were filthy and torn. Beside him sat a large backpack with a spade and a hatchet lashed to the side. Even with all the dirt, Sam could tell the equipment was new. In fact, nothing about this guy seemed broken in. Just broken.

He stood back several feet and introduced himself. 'How long have you been out here, sir?'

The man stared at him. 'Um, two . . . no, three days.'

Sam looked again at the expensive pack. 'Did you bring enough provisions for that long, sir?'

The man waved his hand weakly back and forth. 'It wasn't supposed to be that long. I got lost.'

That would explain a lot of things. Except how somebody could get that lost when a couple mile hike in any direction would bring him to civilization. Sam tried to keep his expression nonjudgmental. 'So you found this road this morning? Did you flag down these folks here?'

The man looked dazed. 'I didn't see them coming. They almost hit me.'

So the belligerent Louisianian hadn't exaggerated. 'I need to ask you about what you told them.'

That focused the hiker's mind. He staggered to his feet and clutched at Sam, who took a wide step out of his reach. 'Somebody beat me there. I was supposed to be first. But then it would've been me.' He swayed a little and went for Sam again. The blip of an ambulance siren stopped them both. It rolled to a stop next to the SUV. The paramedics knew as well as Sam that there wasn't enough traffic on this road to worry about blocking a lane. Two men hopped out of the rig. Sam had to hurry.

'Look, they said you told them something.' He pointed at the couple, now peering around their vehicle at the little crowd. 'Did you say you saw a dead body?'

'Yes. The one who beat me. The one who won.'

One paramedic was guiding him to a gurney. The other was

readying an IV. Now Sam was the one grasping for things. He grabbed the gurney. 'You can hook him up, but he's not going anywhere.'

'Bro, he needs to go and get checked out.' The paramedic, Wally Turber, was a friend of Sam's from high school. Sam ignored him. 'You have to tell me where you saw this body. Which direction?'

The hiker shook his head and started to cry as the medics belted him to the gurney. 'I don't know. I don't know. I couldn't find it and he did, and then I found it and he was dead.'

This was incredibly not helpful. Sam held on as his former classmate tugged at the gurney. 'Can you at least tell me which direction you came from?'

'I don't know,' he yelled, and started to struggle against the belts. His gaze hit on the backpack. 'Give it to me. Give it to me. You can't steal it. I won't let you.'

Wally's partner grabbed the pack and put it in the truck. They slid the gurney and its hysterical occupant in next. The partner got in the driver's seat. Sam stopped Wally before he could climb in the back. 'Do me a favor. See if you can find an ID in that pack before you get to the hospital. I need to know his name.'

'I'll try, man. He might not give me a chance.'

The yelling had increased in pitch. 'I found it. I'm the one who found it.' Over and over. The two Branson Valley High grads looked at each other.

'Are you thinking what I'm thinking?' Wally said.

'I'm praying that what you're thinking, isn't what it is.'

Wally nodded and got in the rig. A parting blip and it pulled away, leaving only Sam and the out-of-staters. When he turned around, they were already in their car. He motioned for the man to roll down his window. 'I need your information, sir. You're a witness, and we might have to contact you again.'

'A witness to what, a nutter in the middle of the road?'

'George!'

Sam stood there silently until the man finally pulled out his license. He copied the information and asked for a phone number. George spat one at him and pulled away with a flourish, calling out a parting shot as he went.

'I'm not spending any money in your town. I'm not even slowing down 'til I get to St. Louis, you crazy-ass Ozarkers.'

Sam watched the Tahoe's dust settle on his boots and then pulled

out his phone. If his and Wally's thinking held true, crazy Ozarkers
were exactly what these woods were about to get.

Sheila still wasn't great with the driving, so she rode down to
Highway G with Hank. He'd suggested she stay at the office and
continue to let her injuries heal. Her response had been both creative
and profane. So now she was struggling to climb out of the squad
car as Hank and Sam stood on the side of the road and averted their
eyes.

'Do we think this guy is telling the truth?' she said when she
finally made it over to them.

Sam tugged at his ear. 'I think that he thinks it's true. That he
saw what he thinks is a dead body.'

'Just somewhere out here?' Hank swept an arm out toward the
trees. 'How the hell are we going to find anything when he couldn't
even say which direction he'd come from?'

He thought of the extra personnel he'd need to search these damn
woods and groaned. His budget didn't have that kind of extra cash.
Or any cash at all. Maybe he could get a human remains detection
dog. Because the short leaf pines on both sides of the road looked
the same, and spread unbroken for God-knew how many miles in
every direction. He was starting to spin in a circle – very symbolically
apt – when Sheila elbowed him and gestured slightly toward Sam,
who looked about to pull his ear off.

'You need to tell us what you're thinking before you hurt yourself,'
she said.

'I think I know where we should start.'

'Great. Let's go.'

Both men stared at her. 'Um, it'll be a hike through the woods,'
Sam said slowly. 'Uneven ground and um, trees and stuff.'

'I am well aware of what "woods" are, don't you think? I'm also
not an idiot. I'm not coming with you. I'll set up at the closest
access point. And if you ask nicely, I'll even give you the water
that I thought to bring. Unless you remembered to bring your own.
No? Hmmm. That certainly speaks to who the foolish ones are here.'

She led the way back to the cars, and Sam guided them farther
down the road to a nearly invisible turnout. They parked and Hank
and Sam got out. Hank leaned down to say something to Sheila and
straightened to find Sam already a hundred yards into the trees. He
looked quizzically at Sheila. She shrugged. He started after Sam,

but the younger man was going too fast for him to catch up. He started to jog. Sam somehow stayed the same distance ahead, flitting in and out of view among the trees.

'Good grief, Sammy, will you stop?'

There was no response. He could barely see his deputy through the trees. He sped up. He had no idea what was wrong. Sam seemed edgy and uneasy, which made no sense. He was the one at home in this terrain. He was the one who camped and hunted all over Ozarks. He should be happy as anything right now, getting to hike while on duty. Hank was the one struggling to find his footing and unsure whether he just stepped in poison ivy. He put that out of his mind and concentrated on the flashes of movement up ahead until the little he could see of Sam disappeared. Hank scowled and tried to keep going in a straight line. He did well until he hit the incline at the same time Sam shouted at him. He jerked to a stop.

The ground sloped down about twenty feet and then flattened out for another twenty before climbing again on the other side. Sam stood on the flat but was off again by the time Hank descended. The gully curved gently to the right. Hank followed it to find Sam stopped, arms tense at his sides. Up ahead, a group of massive sandstone boulders rose out of the earth. Hard against the right embankment, they threw a shadow even at midday.

Hank drew even with Sam and didn't bother keeping the exasperation out of his voice. 'Are we there yet?'

'Yeah.'

'And where is that, exactly?'

'This,' Sam said with a great puff of breath, 'is Murder Rocks.'

FOUR

'Excuse me?'

Hank stared at Sam. The younger man was scanning the top of the slope above the boulders. Hank tried again. 'Do you mean rocks where you think a murder happened?'

Sam finally turned and gave Hank his full attention.

'No. Murder Rocks.' He flung his arms out. 'That's what it's called. What it's always been called. For forever. Murder Rocks.'

'And so that's why you thought it would be a good place to start looking?'

'No.'

If the poison ivy didn't kill him, the frustration certainly would. Hank tried again. He got half a sentence out before Sam walked away. He went to the nearest boulder and toed the dirt with his boot in a few spots, then came back to Hank.

'So then why are we here, Sammy?'

'Because of the other stuff the guy said. That someone else found it. That he should've found it.'

'Found what?'

'Yeah.'

'Karnes.' His voice echoed off the rocks. Birds took flight and beetles scuttled for safety. Sam didn't even flinch. He just shoved his hands in the pockets of his jeans.

'Do you want the story, or do you want to look for the body first?'

What kind of a question was that? The kind that could only have one answer. 'I'm really not appreciating you right now.' He stomped toward the rocks, Sam trailing slowly behind him. He walked around the flat section first, then scrambled up the incline on one side. Pausing only to glare at Sam, he went around to the other side and climbed that slope, as well.

'Nothing.'

'We should check the crack, too.'

'What crack?'

Sam walked up to the two biggest boulders. And vanished. 'Take one step to your left and two forward and then look right,' his voice called from inside the boulder.

Hank followed directions and suddenly there was a thin gap between the rocks that wasn't visible from any other angle. Skinny Sam slipped inside perfectly.

'Anything in there?'

Sam stepped out and shook his head. 'Empty vape cartridges. Some snack food wrappers. That's it.'

Hank added those two items, divided by his locally raised deputy and decided it could equal only one thing.

'This is a high school hangout, isn't it?'

'Yep. Come out here, light a campfire, chill.'

Hank scoffed. 'Translation: come out here to drink beer, smoke, and hopefully use protection for those other co-ed activities that go on in the dark.'

Sam laughed in spite of himself. 'Yeah. That's it exactly. Although in my day it was cigarettes.'

'You're too young to use the phrase "in my day."' Hank stepped back so Sam could get out of the cleft in the rock. He pointed to where Sam had scuffed at the dirt. 'Is that where they build the fires?'

Serious again, Sam nodded. 'It doesn't look like anybody's been out here in a while. Or at least nobody's lit a fire in a while.'

'Surely there have to be more accessible boulders for high schoolers to use as a hangout than these here.'

'There is a little bit shorter route if you start from the other direction. But that's not the point.' He stopped his study of the ground and looked straight at Hank. 'The story is the point.'

Hank bit back a sigh. He was about to hear a silly teen-generated ghost story, passed down from campfire to campfire. He hoped Sammy didn't believe it was true.

'This used to be a road – *the* main road from near where Harrisonville is now in Arkansas all the way north up to Springfield.' They both looked down at the still mostly flat ground that stretched like a wrinkled ribbon in both directions. 'And during the Civil War, things got ugly.'

Gangs of thieves roamed the Ozarks, Sam said, and one band in particular laid claim to this convenient bend in the road. They'd hide amongst the boulders and ambush travelers. They were led by a man named Alf Bolin, the terror of the Ozarks. Barely older than today's high schoolers, he took advantage of the chaos of the war and bushwhacked his way along both sides of the Missouri–Arkansas

border. He robbed and stole, assaulted and attacked. And killed. A
lot. He once boasted a count of nineteen dead, but folks think he
likely killed many more. Many of them right here where they were
standing.

Sam fell silent. Hank stayed silent. Not a silly campfire tall tale
after all. Sam scuffed at the dirt for a minute.

'So that's why teenagers come out here. I guess it's like choosing
to hang out in a graveyard. That same kind of creepy factor, you
know?' But that wasn't why he'd dragged Hank all this way. 'The
second part of the story is the important bit. The part where Bolin
hid his treasure.'

Pieces Hank hadn't known existed suddenly clicked into place.
'Oh, fuck.'

Sam nodded sagely, a teacher pleased with his student. 'The first
part of the story is legit history. The second part has always been
rumor. Or legend, more like.'

'Nobody's ever found anything?'

'Nah. But when that guy on the road today kept wailing that
somebody "found it," what else was I going to think?'

Sheila was alternating between watching a large bird ride the air
currents far above her and scrolling through Instagram when her
phone vibrated. She turned off a clip of Rachael Ray EVOO-ing a
pasta dish to death, and answered.

'Hi, Cindy, what's up?'

Her favorite nurse from the Branson hospital's emergency
department asked how Sheila was feeling before getting to the point.
'The paramedics said you all wanted an ID on this guy they just
brought in.'

'Yes, please.'

'Mingo Culver. Illinois driver's license.' Cindy listed the date of
birth and home address without being asked. Sheila decided to
forgive her for asking about her health.

'Did you find his ID in the backpack?'

'Yeah.'

'Did you find a phone?' They might be able to use that to reverse
track where exactly he'd wandered through the woods.

Cindy told her to hang on a minute, which Sheila was glad to
do once she heard a thump that had to be a heavy pack hitting the
nurses' station counter. The zipper sound confirmed it. 'Little

notebook. Pocket recorder-type thing. Computer cables. Wait.'
Another zipper. 'Here it is. Oh, damn, it's dead.'

Of course it was. At least that explained why the man hadn't
called for help once he figured out he was lost.

'How's he doing?'

'We're pumping him full of fluids right now. You know I can't
tell you anything beyond that.'

'I know. Can I talk to Maggie?'

'Trying to get around me, are you? Well, joke's on you. She isn't
working today.'

Sheila sighed. Cindy laughed at her.

'I'm trying to find an available deputy to come keep an eye on
him,' Sheila said.

'Why? I thought he was just a lost hiker.'

'He also said he found a body in the woods.'

'Oh, goodness.' There was the sound of something heavy sliding
away from the phone. Now Sheila laughed.

'I didn't say he had a body in the backpack, Cindy. Calm down.'
She tried to talk the nurse into searching the bag's main compartment
but was cut short when Hank called. She said goodbye to Cindy
and clicked over.

'We haven't found anything. We're going to keep looking in this
area, but I think it's also time to call out the fire district's search
and rescue. Get them out here to help. Can you—'

She interrupted to say she'd start making calls. Then she read
off the man's name and address.

'Oh, good. The paramedics found an ID?'

'No. Cindy in the ER has the backpack. She found it in there.'

Hank went so silent Sheila thought the call had dropped. 'You
there?'

'I gotta go.' He hung up. Sheila stared at the phone in surprise.
Then a slow smile worked its way onto her face. Now she couldn't
be accused of deliberately not telling him about the other thing she
planned to do. She slowly got herself out of the squad car's passenger
seat and walked around to the driver's side. She gingerly maneuvered
herself in and turned the keys handily left in the ignition. It was
time for a chat with Mingo Culver.

Sam watched his boss's face turn white. Then he hung up on Sheila
and walked off into the trees without a word. Sam had no idea what

the hell was going on, but he did know it wouldn't be a good idea to follow. So he occupied himself with a closer examination of the ground around the rocks. There might not be fresh signs of a campfire, but there could be traces of other activity. And he was good at that. He hunted turkey and deer and could follow the path of most any game. He'd also tracked his share of humans.

That was what he looked for now. Signs of at least one, if not two, people who were outdoor idiots. Shopping at Bass Pro didn't magically qualify you to hike into the backwoods. He chuckled. And this wasn't even the backwoods. Not really. There was a road nearby, and houses within a mile. Real houses. Not the ramshackle trailers and cabins with moonshine stills and meth labs, guard dogs and shotguns, that made up the real backwoods. If that man had gotten lost there, no one ever would have found him.

He moved methodically away from the Murder Rocks, finding nothing in the flatter portion in front of the boulders. He got to where the tree growth thickened and slowed even more. He continued to find a whole lot of nothing until he stepped over a fallen oak and saw it. The handle was coated in rubber, as most were nowadays. To give you a good grip. And someone must have done just that to this hatchet. It lay as if it were dropped headfirst, with the handle then toppling to the side against the rotting oak. And the blade was covered in blood.

Sam stepped carefully away and started taking pictures. He moved in a circle, further and further out from the weapon – it certainly wasn't just a tool anymore – until he finally saw what he was looking for. Footprints. Just two, headed east. He snapped more photos and then hollered for Hank. He got no response. He shrugged, unworried. He knew the guy would come back eventually, if for no other reason than he couldn't find his way out of the woods without help. Finally, he heard a shout and walked back to the flatter ground to meet him.

'Well, shit,' Hank said when Sam led him to the hatchet. 'Is this Mingo Culver's, do you think?'

'No. I saw his. It was still strapped to his pack.'

'OK, then.' Hank folded his arms and contemplated the hatchet. 'Well, this definitely supports the claim that someone else was out here.'

'And it looks pretty fresh.'

'Fantastic.' Hank ran a hand through his hair. 'Let's just pray it isn't a murder weapon.'

They looked at each other. Neither of them had much hope of that.

FIVE

Cindy clucked over her until Sheila wanted to scream, but she also brought a comfortable chair into the little curtained-off area. Sheila sank into it gratefully and eyed the haggard young white man in the hospital bed. She knew from his DL that he was twenty-eight and lived in Petersburg, Illinois. She knew from Cindy that he'd been carrying around a bunch of stuff that didn't make much sense for a hike. And she knew from experience that she could get a young person to talk.

'We're concerned, Mingo. About you, of course, and also about what you told those folks who stopped to help you. You said you saw a body?'

Mingo fidgeted under the thin blanket. He didn't look scared or confused, either of which would have been reasonable. He looked reticent and stubborn. Sheila settled in for a long chat. Where did he see the body? Did he know who it was? Man or woman? Could he tell how they died?

All the boy did was press his lips together in a good imitation of a clam, until the last question. That one made him flinch. Sheila pounced. 'How? What did you see? You need to tell me, young man. I'm responsible for people's safety in this county, and I need to go find this person. Find out what happened.'

'It's different than in the pictures.'

Sheila counted to ten in her head. Why couldn't people just give a straight answer? 'Could you explain that a little more? I don't understand. What's different than in pictures?'

'Bodies.'

Oh. 'So you saw a body. Just one?' His use of the plural had suddenly made her nervous.

He looked at her as if she'd suggested he didn't know how to tie his own shoes. 'Yes, just one. What the hell? Are there more? Those woods, man.'

'You tell me, kid. You're the one who was out there traipsing around. What were you looking for?'

'Nothing.'

'That's not what you told my deputy. You said the dead guy found it. Found what?'

Mingo fiddled with his IV and avoided her gaze, the wheels in his Gen Z brain clearly whirring. 'If he found something, I wouldn't know. I didn't search him. I didn't touch him.'

'But you took pictures?'

'What? No. My phone was dead.'

Sheila pinched the bridge of her nose. If this boy weren't already in the hospital, she would've gladly put him there. She made sure she could manage a friendly tone before she spoke again. 'Did you recognize him?'

'Not really.'

'It's pretty much a yes-or-no question, Mingo. Did you recognize him?' At least she now knew it was a man.

'He was kinda lying turned away. So I don't know. I didn't walk all the way around.'

Another twenty questions and Sheila knew that the man was in the trees and not a clearing, was wearing hiking boots and a windbreaker, was white – or at least not Black, and smelled bad.

'How bad did he smell, exactly?'

'About a couple of days' worth.'

Sheila sat back in her chair. That was a very interesting way to answer that question. Although if he was a true crime fan . . .

'Why were you in those woods, Mingo?'

'I, uh, just went for a hike.'

'Just a hike? With all that equipment? What'd you need the shovel for?'

He shrugged and stayed silent.

'What about all those cords and things?'

Now he stiffened, outraged. 'You went through my stuff? You could see the shovel on the outside, OK. But you went into my pack?'

'Me? No. The nurse was looking for your ID. While you were still . . . incoherent.'

That answer didn't mollify him. He looked around the curtained area in vain.

'I can ask the nurse to bring it in,' she said.

He nodded. She pulled out her cell and called the nurses' station. No way was she hauling her aching body out of this comfortable chair and leaving him alone, much to his obvious disappointment.

Cindy lugged the pack in and left it with a clunk on the hard-backed
visitor's chair next to the bed.

'Did you need anything out of it? I'm happy to help you.' She
started to rise. The dirty look she got in return was worth the stabbing
pain in her torso.

'No. Thank. You.' He tried to cross his arms like a petulant child,
but was stymied by the IV. She wondered how long they could keep
him here under the guise of medical necessity. So far, there was
nothing to indicate he'd done anything wrong, so they had no
justification to hold him. But she had a feeling that if she let him
walk out of the hospital, what little cooperation she'd gotten so far
would vanish completely. Hell, he'd probably vanish completely.
And she was in no condition to drive to Illinois to track him down.

'Let's go back to the area where you saw the—'

Her phone buzzed, startling them both. Sam had texted both her
and one of the department's evidence technicians. Just found this.
Plus footprints. Need you out here Alice. Will share location. And
Hank wants to know if somebody's been able to pull off patrol &
go babysit lost hiker.

Next came a photo. She didn't know what she'd expected it to
be, but it sure wasn't that. She took a deep breath.

'Let's go back to the body. You said it was turned away from
you. Did you see anything on his back? Any torn clothing? Any
injuries?'

He started to look a little nauseated. 'There was a lot of blood.'

From the look of the hatchet in that photo, she would expect so.

'His, um . . .' Mingo closed his eyes. 'His sleeve was ripped.
Yeah. And bloody. Like, soaked.'

'What about his back? And his head?'

'His back was OK. His hair was bloody, though. And his neck.'

'What caused all that blood? Where was he injured?'

'Man, I don't know. I didn't get close enough.'

Things weren't fitting together quite right. 'You didn't want to
look, but you would've taken pictures if your phone was charged?'

He looked away, down at the floor. Almost embarrassed.

'Is that why you said that pictures are different?'

'Yeah.' He still wouldn't look at her. 'Looking at pictures of
bodies. You know, of whoever, like in the true crime shows. That's
fine. But seeing one . . .' He screwed his eyes shut and held his
hands out as if he were using a phone to take a photo. 'If I could've

taken a picture and looked closer at it that way, that would be fine.'

Sheila was tempted to set him straight – there were some things you couldn't unsee, no matter how cleverly you tried to filter them. Instead, she swiped at her phone and looked at the hatchet photo again. The pit of her stomach told her this search was going to turn into something she'd want to unsee, too.

They were looking for more tracks leading away from the hatchet. Well, Sam was looking. Hank was trying not to get in his way.

'How often are people out here treasure hunting?'

'No idea,' Sam said without looking up from his examination of the ground. 'But I bet Leo Fackrell knows. He owns most of the acreage around here.'

'You mean we're on private property? I thought this was state park land.' Hank was horrified. They didn't have a search warrant. Or even verbal permission. And Sam didn't look at all concerned.

'Right here where we're standing, we're on state land. To get here, that's when we were on Fackrell land. There is another way to the Rocks that keeps you on state land, but you can't use it from where we parked.'

Hank looked back toward the Rocks, now out of sight and hundreds of yards away. 'So we totally trespassed?'

Sam came to a stop and looked up from his search for footprints. 'Eh, yeah.'

Hank looked at his young deputy and pictured him eight years earlier, a gawky high schooler traipsing through these woods with a group of friends and a six-pack of beer. It must be the most natural thing in the world for him to just pick up right where he left off – on a single-minded, damn-the-consequences journey to these horrible rocks. Hank's irritation evaporated. 'You keep at it. I'll get a hold of this Fackrell guy and see if he'll grant us access.'

Sam, his eyes back on the ground, barely managed a nod before heading off to the left. Hank decided to backtrack toward the hatchet and wait for the evidence technician to arrive. He found a semi-sturdy log to sit on and pulled out his phone. A few minutes of web searching and he had a phone number. The voice that answered was old and deep.

'The sheriff? You mean you're the actual sheriff? That young guy came from out of town?'

'Yes, sir, and I'm calling because I need to ask you a favor.'

If Fackrell had been younger, Hank might've played it differently. Presented it less as an option and more as an obligatory civic duty. But his gut told him that this voice had a very personalized definition of duty and wasn't about to be coerced by some questionable outsider. He explained what was going on, omitting only the bloody hatchet and which route they'd used to get to the rocks.

'Those morons. They think they're going to find something that ain't been already found in the past hundred and fifty years? There ain't anything there. Not a hundred and fifty years ago, and not now.' The voice rumbled to a stop.

'Yes, sir. We're afraid one of those treasure hunters has . . .' Been hacked to death, he thought but didn't say. 'Has . . . come to harm. If we could have permission to search your land around the rocks, it would be very helpful. And much appreciated.'

'So you're sure somebody is out there?'

'Not really, no. The man found this morning was very confused and disoriented. He might be completely wrong about what he says he saw. But I've got to take it seriously and look into it. Because if there is a body out there, I need to find it.'

A harrumph came through the phone. 'Someone who got lost that badly in an area not more than a mile from the nearest road? My money's on him being as wrong about a body as he is about directions. But I do see your point. If he's right, I don't want someone left out there rotting in my woods, either. So go ahead and search wherever you need to.'

Hank let out the breath he hadn't realized he was holding and thanked him. 'Before I go, can I ask you how often you get people like this? Looking for Bolin's treasure?'

Fackrell sighed. 'Too often. And there's probably plenty I don't even know about. I can't see that area from my house. The ones I do know about are folks I catch when I'm out hunting or chopping wood. A few actually come up to the house and ask permission. I got to tell them no – that I ain't stopping them from being at the Rocks, 'cause I can't. But I'm not giving them permission to cross my property to get there.'

Hank looked guiltily back the way they'd come. Then he thanked the man again and promised to keep him updated on the search. He hung up and contemplated the hatchet until he heard Sam returning.

'I lost the trail. There's nothing. We're definitely going to need dogs. See if they can pick up a scent.' He shoved his hands in his pockets. 'Sheila texted to say she's taking care of the search and rescue folks. And Alice Randall is on her way.'

The petite evidence technician showed up promptly, comfortably carting bags of gear that had to equal her minimal body weight. 'Yeesh. That's wicked looking.'

She pulled out a camera capable of much better close-ups than Sam's phone, twisted her Royals baseball cap backward, and got to work. 'You guys want to stick around for the blood test?' she asked as she clicked away.

Hank scoffed. 'There's no way we're going to be lucky enough for that to be animal blood.'

Alice, down on her haunches in front of the hatchet, looked up at Hank. 'I know. We haven't been lucky on anything lately, have we?'

'No, we have not. But yes, we do need to confirm that it's human blood.'

She nodded. 'I've got HemaTrace test kits with me. It'll be fifteen or twenty minutes before I'm done with the whole process.'

Hank told her they would keep searching and to text with the results. Then he turned to look for Sam, who was wandering away through the trees while staring at the sky. He hustled to catch up and realized they were headed back to the Rocks. Sam picked up the pace and then skidded to a stop once he hit the open area that was the remnant of the Civil War-era road. He kept looking up, spinning around to take in as much cloudless expanse as he could. Hank had no idea why. What they were looking for was on the ground and—

'Oh. We're looking for vultures, aren't we?'

'Yeah,' Sam said.

Hank groaned. He'd rather wait for the dogs. But he knew Sam was right. So he forced his gaze skyward. And wished he'd never heard of Murder Rocks.

SIX

Sheila commandeered a wheelchair and was using it to cart around the heavy hiking backpack that belonged to her suspect. Mingo Culver had become one the minute she saw the hatchet photo. And that was what she was explaining to a judge as she stood at the nurses' station.

'He's refusing to let me search it, so I'd like a warrant. Also, there might be something in there to help us locate the body he says he saw. We want to charge his phone battery, see if that helps.'

Sheila could practically hear the judge thinking on the other end of the line. Delia Havish was brand new, a former corporate attorney with little criminal law experience, and not Sheila's first choice for this kind of request. But Hank was on an anti-Marvin Sedstone kick and had asked her to avoid the county's senior judge whenever she could. So now she was having to both sweet-talk and educate at the same time.

'That ax could be something dropped by a hunter and just have animal blood on it,' Havish said.

'That's a good point, Your Honor. And something we wanted an answer to as well. A presumptive field test showed that it is indeed human blood, not animal.' Thank goodness for Alice's quick work. 'So when you take that, along with the potential help that Mr Culver's charged phone could give us, we believe a warrant for all of his belongings is necessary.'

She idly spun the wheelchair in a circle as the judge thought some more. She heard the rapid turning of pages and then finally got a response. 'OK, I'll grant it. But I want an, um, a very complete return with everything listed that you take.'

Sheila rolled her eyes at Cindy, promised the judge she would, and gave her the hospital's emergency department fax number. The signed warrant came through a minute later. Sheila placed it on top of the backpack and started to wheel quickly down the hallway. She'd been standing for too long and desperately needed to sit down. But she froze at the sound of her name.

'You look like you should be in that thing, not pushing it.' Maggie

McCleary walked up to her with an expression that mixed reprimand, exasperation, and sympathy in a way only she could. 'I thought you were supposed to stay in your office. Not be out and about like this.'

'You and Hank agreed to that. I never did.'

Maggie reached out and gently took her wrist. Sheila scowled as the doctor took her pulse, but didn't pull away. She had better sense than to do that. She would blithely cross a lot of people, but the chief of emergency medicine wasn't one of them. She couldn't help rolling her eyes again, though.

'I thought you weren't working today.'

'I'm not. I heard about the search though. And the patient. Do you think what he's saying is credible?'

Sheila paused. She'd been about to report on Culver's condition, but that wasn't what Maggie asked. 'Credible? Well, I don't think he's lying. I think he thinks he saw something. Whether that's actually a body, I don't know. He was pretty incoherent and shaky.'

She eyed Hank's wife. Usually, she had little interest in the law enforcement aspect of a patient's case. Why did she care about this one? Maggie registered the look and shrugged.

'I'm just curious. Hank called from somewhere out in the woods, but he didn't say much.' Her tone said that wasn't a surprise.

Sheila wondered, not for the first time lately, what was going on with those two. The fresh discovery that Maggie's mother had been murdered – not felled by a heart attack two years ago as everyone originally thought – had certainly caused the poor things a huge amount of stress. But that stress should've been aimed outward. Instead, they seemed to be directing it at each other. Which puzzled Sheila to no end. And led her to another thought.

'Where are the kids?'

'Ah. Yeah. Um. They're in the front lobby with the volunteers at the help desk.'

This next question was none of her business. 'Must be hard with your dad out of town. When does he get back?'

'Oh, sometime.'

That was not an answer. She started to ask another question, but Maggie pointed to the paper lying on the backpack. 'Do you even have an ID?'

'Yeah. Cindy found his driver's license. But we didn't have justification to dig through the rest of the pack. Until Sam found this.'

She showed Maggie the hatchet photo.

'God damn,' said the implacable doctor who seldom swore. 'I guess that does lend credence to his story.'

'I don't suppose you've gotten any patients recently with slash or cut injuries?'

Maggie scoffed. 'Nice wishful thinking, but no. I would've been notified about something like that. So you've either got a minor assault with insignificant cuts that just bled a lot. Or your hiker is right, and you've got a homicide.'

They looked at each other. Maggie suddenly looked more tired than Sheila felt. She said she needed to get the kids home and turned to leave. As she walked away, Sheila could've sworn she heard her muttering . . . *always ends up with a good excuse to miss something* . . .

Sheila watched Maggie go, sad for both her doctor friend and for Hank. Because she now had a feeling this investigation was going to tear at bonds more fragile than she'd realized.

'Why am I standing here without a squad car?'

The only thing on the side of the road was Sam's girlfriend's locked and empty hatchback. And a very irritated Hank.

'Because I took it.'

'Obviously.'

Sheila didn't dignify that with a response.

'You aren't supposed to be driving.'

'Oh, please. I wasn't going to sit there for hours on end. There's things need doing.'

'Yeah, and I thought you were doing them from the car.' He started to pace. 'Coordinating from the car.'

'Why would I do that when there's a suspect who needs interviewing?'

He stopped. 'Is he still at the hospital? Are you?'

'Yeah.' Sheila drew out the word. 'We're still at the hospital. He had a little asthma attack, so we might be here a while more.'

More pacing. Hank had a feeling he didn't want to know the answer to his next question. 'Did the asthma attack happen while you were interviewing him?'

Instead of answering, she launched into what she'd found in the backpack and learned about Mingo's apparent obsession with Alf Bolin. By the time she'd finished, Hank had worn a rut in the road's dirt shoulder and was cursing a man who'd been dead for a century and a half.

'I texted a photo of Culver's map to Sammy and Doug Gabler. Between the two of them today and the search dogs tomorrow, they've hopefully been able to narrow down the search area,' she said.

'They're getting ready to stop for the day. They'll start again first thing in the morning.'

'What about Alice? I haven't been able to get a hold of her.'

'She's on her way back to the station. She said she'd have the backpack contents processed by tomorrow morning.' It would mean overtime costs, but there was nothing he could do to avoid that until her evidence partner Kurt Gatz got back from vacation.

'I think you need to see all that paperwork in person,' Sheila said. 'I want to, too. I only got a quick look at it as I was taking pictures.'

They agreed to meet at the station early tomorrow and go over everything together. Then Sheila told him to go home.

'What about Culver? Is he in good enough condition to continue the interview?'

'They're not letting me near him. So my guess is, no. They might keep him overnight, but they're refusing to tell me anything about that, either. Damn HIPAA laws.'

Someone needed to keep an eye on him. Hank started to think through his duty roster. Sheila's voice stopped him.

'I'll handle it. You go home.'

'No, I think—'

'That wasn't a suggestion. Go. Home.' She hung up on him. It was one of her favorite ways to win an argument. She had others, but this was her quickest and most to the point. Today, he didn't mind. It'd be nice to get home before the kids went to bed. He looked around the deserted roadway.

Now he just needed to find a ride.

SEVEN

A spade and a non-bloody hatchet. Two empty water bottles. A fleece pullover. A rain poncho. Five granola bar wrappers. An excessive amount of crumbs. A dirty pair of socks. A dead iPhone. A wallet with ID, two credit cards, one debit card, a worn Petersburg Public Library card, twelve dollars cash, and ten business cards that said 'Mingo Culver. Everywhere.' A bundle of papers and a notebook. A clean pair of socks. A waterproof picnic blanket. A bird's nest worth of electronic cords. A Bluetooth speaker and a pair of headphones.

'No wonder the idiot ran out of charge on his phone,' Sheila said. 'Who needs to stream music out in the middle of the woods?'

Doug Gabler snorted in agreement. The deputy had been on his way to the search scene when Sheila diverted him to the hospital. She needed a witness to the search of Culver's backpack. They were spreading the contents on a gurney just at the end of the row of curtained alcoves where Culver still rested. The only way he could leave was to walk past them. And he wasn't going to be allowed to do that. But Sheila couldn't very well handcuff him to the bed, either. She didn't have enough cause. Yet.

'You're the expert,' she said to the experienced outdoorsman, 'but it seems to me that he did not pack appropriately for a multi-day camping trip.'

That had Gabler full-out chuckling. 'No, ma'am. He was barely carrying enough water for a decent hike. Certainly not enough for treasure hunting.'

She put down the wallet and stared at him. 'Say again?'

Doug waved a hand over the belongings. 'This all makes sense when you factor in where he was found.'

'In the middle of state park land?'

'Real close to Murder Rocks.'

Sheila would've gone white if she weren't such a nice shade of mahogany brown. 'Dammit. I didn't realize that. The guy came out near Highway G, not on Bushers Hollow Road.'

'Which does at least support his claim that he was back-assward lost,' Doug said. 'But I don't see any blood or anything that would connect him to the dead body.'

'The as-yet theoretical dead body,' Sheila corrected. 'But you're right. I don't see anything either. I'll want to know what Alice finds when she analyzes it.'

'Isn't she out at the scene? Where's Kurt Gatz?'

Sheila sighed. The department's other evidence technician was on vacation. 'Alice is all we've got for the next week.'

They photographed the paperwork and then carefully put the contents of Culver's pack in a white post office bin Nurse Cindy found in an administrator's office. Sheila ran evidence tape over the top and told Gabler to put it in the back of his squad car. 'Transfer it to Alice when you get out there.'

'Sure thing. You going to have another chat with him?' He gestured toward the curtains.

She smiled slowly. 'Oh, yeah. He and I are nowhere near done.'

She grabbed her cane from where it hung on the end of the gurney and hobbled back to Mingo's bedside. His eyes blinked open as she pulled aside the curtain.

'Let's go back a bit, Mr Culver,' she said as she gratefully settled herself in the comfy chair. 'Why did you decide to take a hike so far away from your home?'

He thought about that. 'To see the area. To see the Ozarks.'

'All right. And why did you choose that particular section of woods?'

He just looked at her. She folded her hands in her lap and waited. To anyone watching, she would seem to be patient. She often appeared that way, but never was. Just stubborn. Stubborn enough to out-stubborn anybody. Especially a soft, ill-prepared Gen Zer with sketchy motives who dared to saunter into her county and start causing problems. So she waited.

Five minutes passed before he finally gave in. 'There's a natural landmark I wanted to see.'

'And what's that?'

More silence.

'This is going to take an awfully long time if you don't start talking.'

He scowled and looked at the ceiling. 'I could just get up and leave, you know.'

Sheila waggled a hand back and forth. 'Really? Because you're still not looking very good. I would hate for you to get woozy again if you left the hospital too soon.'

'You're full of shit, you know that?'

She let out a genuine laugh. 'You're probably right. But not as full of it as you are. So why don't you cut the crap and tell me why you were out trespassing in those woods?'

He looked longingly down the hallway toward the exit. She nonchalantly buffed her nails on the side of her uniform slacks and straightened her name plate.

'Jeez . . . OK, fine. I wanted to see the rocks. They're called Murder Rocks. I thought it'd be cool. It turned out to be just a bunch of boulders. Not very exciting.'

'So why'd you take a shovel?'

His white-boy face turned pink. 'I dunno. It's just hiking equipment.'

'Really? It doesn't seem like it to me. You weren't going to camp. You didn't have a tent. You had no matches or other means to start a fire that you would need a shovel to help extinguish. You were just digging holes.' Her tone made it sound like what it was. Stupid. 'We've found quite a few of them out there so far.'

'"Quite a few?" How many?' he said before he could stop himself.

'Are you asking that because there might be more holes out there than the ones you dug?'

He clamped his lips shut.

'Did you find anything?' she said.

'No.'

That she believed. It would be in his pack if he had. 'But you were looking for something.'

He shrugged and stayed silent. She took out her phone and pulled up a photo she'd taken of a page in his notebook.

'You've made notes: 1861. Lone traveler. 1862. Wagon train. 1862. Union soldiers. Payroll. Unconfirmed. F fam. Confirmed.'

She looked up at him, his face blooming from baby pink to rose red. He started to slouch and wrapped his arms around his torso.

'You did go through my stuff.'

'I showed you the warrant.'

'I thought you were going to do it in front of me.'

She raised her eyebrows. 'Now why would I do that? You think I need your help unzipping a backpack?'

'I was going to . . .' He balled his hands into fists and glared at her.

'You were "going to" what?'

'Nothing.'

She acted like she didn't care and went back to the photos on her phone. 'Let's circle back to the 1860s, shall we? Now, I'm not originally from here, but I do know a little bit about ol' Alf Bolin and him ambushing folks on the Civil War road right there by Murder Rocks.'

Culver went from ruddy to pale in an instant. She started to worry about his blood pressure. Where was Cindy?

'You have to give that back to me. No one else can see it.'

'Why not?'

'Because I found it. I figured it out. It's my work product.'

She told him she had no plans to post it in the town square. He did not seem reassured by this, perhaps because she used air quotes around 'town square.' And called his paperwork an 'Ozark history report.' On the plus side, it did piss him off enough to bring a flush of red back to his face. So she felt medically safe enough to ask her next question. What treasure had he been hunting for and where did he think it was hidden?

'I'm not going to tell you that.'

'Oh, yes, you are. Because the odds that there is actually treasure, or loot, or Bolin booty, or *whatever* out there – those odds are basically zero. But the odds that the body you saw is near your X-marks-the-spot – those odds are pretty good.' She swiped through photos she'd taken of his paperwork until she got to the one of a topographical map. 'So you are going to explain this to me.'

He began to talk, but it came out as a wheeze. Then he made some congested snuffling sounds and his lips started to go blue. Sheila flinched. Then she leapt to her feet, dropping her phone and knocking her cane to the floor as she lunged for the nurse call button.

He apologized twice. Her expression didn't change. So they stared at each other from separate ends of the couch. He was about to try again when Benny ran out and threw himself down face first between them.

'I can't go to sleep,' he yelled into the couch cushion. 'I'm too excited.'

Hank wrapped an arm around his son's skinny torso and pulled him onto his lap. 'You have to, buddy. You need to be nice and rested for the first day of school.'

Benny eyed him skeptically. 'You can't just "go to sleep," you know.' He jabbed air quotes at his parents. Hank wondered where he'd learned that and wished that he hadn't. Maggie, on the other hand, burst out laughing. They both looked at her in surprise.

'You're going to just be off and running with school, aren't you?' She slid over and took Benny's face in her hands. 'So much new learning. You're just going to soak it up.'

She was thinking of things like math and reading. He was thinking of new kinds of behavior. Benny turned and gave Hank a mischievous grin that confirmed it. 'You can smile all you want, but you're going back to bed.'

He tucked the five-year-old in – again – and returned to find Maggie not nearly as impassive as before. He sat down in the same spot, each of them back in their respective corners.

'I'm not mad at you. I definitely don't expect you to blow off a possible homicide just to attend a marriage counseling appointment.' She gave a resigned shrug. 'What I'm mad at is circumstances, I guess. I'm mad at everything that keeps getting thrown at us. Why can't you have a stretch of simple burglaries, or budget paperwork? Why can't I find a qualified doctor to hire so I'm up to full staffing in my department? Why . . .' She trailed off, resting her elbows on her knees as she put her face in her hands. Hank knew what that final *why* asked. A lot of questions that counseling was supposed to help resolve.

He looked at her, as she tucked a strand of her long brown hair behind her ear and straightened with a deep breath, and decided the least he could do was broach a topic that would've undoubtedly come up in counseling – if he hadn't missed the appointment.

'How's your dad? Have you talked to him lately?' He also did genuinely want to know.

'Huh? Uh . . .' The question seemed to surprise her. 'He's OK. Fine. He and Aunt Fin are back from their road trip.'

'Oh. I didn't realize they did that. Where'd they go?'

'I don't even know. I just pray Dad did all the driving.'

'God, yes. If your Aunt Fin was behind the wheel, every motorist on the highway would need to be praying, too.'

They smiled at each other, almost in spite of themselves. He reached out a hand. She took it and kissed his scraped knuckles.

'Can we reschedule the appointment for next week?' he asked.

She nodded. 'I made it for next Thursday.' She gave him a look that was both wry and dead serious at the same time. 'That means you have a whole week to find that body and solve a murder.'

Great. As if a session of counseling weren't pressure enough.

EIGHT

Dear Brother,
I hope these lines find you well and in good health. I am sad to report that I am not likewise but rather have been wounded in a fight with raiders south of Ozark. My arm was shot by a bandit's rifle while defending the little wagon train I accompanied on the way north to Springfield. All of value was taken by the dirty thieves, including silver tableware and much jewelry belonging to the unfortunate ladies in our company whose households were fleeing Confederate forces farther south. Never have I seen people so terrified as when those guerrillas fired from atop a rocky outcropping and forced our hasty stop. I feel that we were lucky to be let on our way with only three wounded and none dead.

Upon reaching the safety of Springfield—God praise the Union forces here—I learned from friends that the whole road from here down into Arkansas has descended into the most awful realm of lawlessness. I heartily supported this notion when reporting our depredations to the Union authorities, who while sympathetic did not seem inclined to do anything about the problem.

I hope to make it to you and our father in Rolla before long. Until then I remain your steadfast brother,
James Johnson

'But this doesn't give a location,' Hank said. 'A "rocky outcropping" doesn't exactly narrow things down in this area. There're damn cliffs all over the place.'

They stared down at the spindly handwriting. Hank repeated his observation as he picked up the high-grade copy of what certainly looked like an original Civil War-era document. Alice had found no trace evidence on any of Mingo Culver's papers, so he and Sheila were free to handle them all they wanted. They'd barely paused to put on gloves before spreading everything out on the conference room table. Now it was covered with dozens of notes and maps and drawings in the pre-dawn quiet at sheriff's headquarters.

'Does something else here say anything about this wagon train's route? What made Culver decide it was connected to this specific area?' He still couldn't bring himself to use the term 'Murder Rocks.' It was painfully uncreative and sounded so jarring that it hit you over the head like, well, a boulder.

'It's going to take some time to read through all this stuff.' Sheila had settled into one of the room's rolling chairs, her cane leaning on the table nearby. He knew she was here for the duration – she'd brought the donut cushion she'd used on her office chair since coming back from disability leave. He pretended not to notice.

'Most of Culver's list of different Bolin robberies would've resulted in only minimal permanent reward. People with maybe a little bit of money,' Hank said. 'He could've gotten good perishables that made it worth it on his end, but food or horses or booze aren't going to last buried in the woods for a hundred and fifty years.'

She cocked an eyebrow. 'If we end up finding bottles of bourbon, I'm never going to let you forget it.'

'We're not going to end up finding anything. If jewelry and silverplate were buried in those woods, someone would've found it. Fackrell said people poke around pretty regularly, and nobody's ever found anything.'

'Nobody's ever *divulged* that they've found anything,' she said. 'Would you broadcast that you'd discovered something valuable, possibly on private land?'

'You're agreeing with people like this guy?' He waved a hand over the paperwork. 'Deluded treasure hunters using their history degrees for ill instead of good?'

Sheila chortled at that. 'No. I'm trying to play devil's advocate. This kid clearly thinks he's onto something. Which means if there is actually a body out there, that guy – when alive – was probably looking for the same thing.'

Hank nodded. 'And whoever swung that bloody hatchet – quite possibly Culver – is after it, too. Or, it was swung by someone who wants it all to stop.'

She grinned. 'If they do find a body out there today, I'd say a visit to old Mr Fackrell is first on our to-do list.'

Hank looked down at the document in his hand . . . *the most awful realm of lawlessness* . . . He certainly hoped not.

Sam had learned how to track from his dad and his grandfather. It was an art, they said. A skill and an art and something to be used with humble regard for nature and the animal being tracked. And he had, over the years, gotten pretty good at it. So he was quite annoyed with himself that he wasn't able to follow the trail of whoever left those footprints.

So far, there were no vultures today, either. He was also irritated about that. He still searched the sky, but that was basically because he had nothing to do this morning until search and rescue showed up and started a grid search. He heard Hank shout and his gaze dropped down to the Murder Rocks before he turned toward his boss.

'The dogs are here. Can you go meet them at the road?'

'Dogs? I thought we were only getting one.'

The non-profit organization from up near Kansas City had responded to Hank's request for a human-remains detection dog. But they were also, Hank said, sending a 'scent-specific trailing dog.'

'I wonder if it's going to be an actual bloodhound,' Hank said with a grin.

'How did you talk them into sending both?'

Hank got serious. 'I told them I have a deputy who's an excellent tracker and who verified that there's a suspect's trail leading away from a likely murder weapon. I said it was unlikely another human tracker would have better luck with it, and we needed some non-human help to follow it.'

Sam felt a little taller at that. And a lot happier. He was going to get to watch tracking dogs in action. He led Hank at a fast clip out the opposite side of the woods from where they parked. They were met on the roadway by a bunch of guys from Western County Fire District, milling around one another like a litter of puppies.

'They look awfully excited,' Hank muttered. He looked concerned about their antsy energy until Sam nudged him and pointed at the broad-shouldered man just emerging from around a large SUV. His handlebar mustache twitching upward was the only visible indication of a smile as he waved them over.

'Nice to see you, sir.' Sam shook Chief Bart Giacalone's hand and helped him spread the topographical map out on the SUV's hood as Hank nodded discreetly in the direction of the puppies.

'Yeah,' the chief said. 'They're newbie volunteers. I thought this would be good training. Work a grid, learn some procedure. It's perfect really. A real call, but not urgent. Nobody alive and in danger. Just dead and waiting to be found.'

'That does explain their eagerness,' Hank said. 'But you sure they won't need, you know, a grownup or two to go with them?'

The fire chief shook his head. 'Nope. The grownups are still on as light of duty as I can give 'em after that warehouse explosion. Some of them still aren't over it.'

Sam quickly turned his gaze to the map so no one would see the thought he knew was plain on his face. There was a man standing next to him who hadn't gotten over the explosion, either. Someone still wrestling with the agonizing aftereffects of hidden death and family life.

'So I'm still trying to give my regulars as much of a pass as I can.' Chief Giacalone chuckled. 'As for these kids, I didn't say they had no training. Just that this would be good practice for them. Plus, I heard a rumor you got dogs coming.'

'Two of them.' The words were out of Sam's mouth without thinking. He usually kept it shut when superiors were talking. But he was feeling a bit puppyish himself at the moment. *Please let it be a bloodhound.* 'I mean, hopefully two dogs. Sir.'

Hank smiled at him. 'Sam here's looking forward to seeing the only things that are better trackers than he is.'

Chief Giacalone's mustache twitched again. 'That so? Maybe I'll ask you to go hunting with me next time instead of my Lab. Can barely follow the scent of an open can of dog food.'

Hank laughed. The sound gladdened Sam's heart. 'You've never met my dog,' Hank said. 'He'd make yours look like "tracking dog of the year."'

Another mustache twitch. 'When you expecting the real trackers to get here?'

'They're coming separately,' Hank said. 'One is fairly close – the scent-specific dog. The human-remains detection dog is a ways out.'

'"Cadaver dog" not cool to use any more?' the chief said.

Hank shrugged. 'That's just what they called it when I asked for one. As long as they can smell a body, I'm happy to call them whatever they want.'

'Well, while we're waiting, let's get these fellas going on the body search.' The chief called over the group and divvied up grid areas on the map. Sam, watching their faces as Giacalone talked, thought of something.

'Hey, how many of you grew up around here?' All six raised their hands. 'And how many of you used to come to Murder Rocks to party?'

The rustling group noises quieted. Three guys stared at their shoes, two looked at the sky, and one picked lint off his shirt.

'So clearly, all of you,' Sam said. 'That's good.'

There was a collective sigh of relief. 'You know this area, then. Use that,' Sam said. 'Where do you think is easiest for a person to walk? Where would good shelter be? Don't go out of your grid assignment, but use what you know to search smart, OK?'

Hank clapped him on the shoulder as the Puppy Six disappeared into the woods. 'That was excellent, Sammy. Really nicely done.'

They worked with the map until the rumble of a diesel engine interrupted them. A GMC Sierra pulled up, its back window smudgy with nose prints. *Please be a bloodhound.* Instead, a bluetick coonhound leapt lightly out of the truck, followed by a man just as rangy and speckled with gray. The hound stretched into a spectacular downward dog. The handler just cracked his spine and groaned.

'Randy Kane,' he said, shaking hands all around after popping some more joints and donning a sun hat to cover his pale skin. 'Nice to see you all. We're looking forward to a little workout here, aren't we, girl?'

One graceful tail wave was the hound's only acknowledgment as she settled on her haunches and eyed them like the silly humans they were.

'So who's the one tracked it partways already?'

Hank pointed at Sam, who felt his face turning red. 'Um. Not very far. Just a little further on. We need to figure out where he exited the woods. And see if he left anything else behind as he went.'

'Starting where the object was at? A weapon?'

'Yes, sir.'

'It still there?'

'Yes, sir. With our deputy. But we haven't moved it.'

'Awright. Let me get Billy's lead and we'll get started.'

Sam left Giacalone with the vehicles and led the handler, the girl dog named Billy, and his directionally challenged boss through the trees to where Doug Gabler guarded the hatchet. Kane asked permission and then knelt by the bloody hatchet for a better look. Billy stayed standing, motionless but taut as a bowstring, sure that her work was about to start.

'When you said weapon, I guess I was expecting a gun or some such ordinary thing. Not this.' He shook his head. 'Damn. You Ozarkers don't mess around down here.'

NINE

Sam and his local knowledge returned to the command center to help redirect Bart's good ol' boys-in-training farther east, and Billy now had the run of the woods. The hound was laser focused and piecing together the trail Sam started yesterday. All Hank and Randy Kane had to do was keep up. One of them was doing a much better job than the other.

'So she stays on the lead the whole time?' Hank asked.

'Yeah.' Randy held a long bright orange tether as Billy roamed purposefully, steadily pulling them to the southwest. They were now far beyond where Sam had lost the trail. Billy vaulted a rotting log and the two men scrambled to follow. Hank let out a yell and threw himself to the left at the same time Kane swore and toppled over to the right. Kane ended up on his ass in the mud and Hank on his side in a pile of wet leaves. They both sat up and grinned at each other. There on the ground in between them was a perfect pair of footprints, so clear they could read the octagon logo.

'This was exactly what I was hoping for,' Hank said when they'd regained their feet. Billy had ignored the whole thing and was busy sweeping back and forth as far as her lead allowed. 'Not that we'll find the guy still in the woods, but that we can find evidence along his path. And hopefully figure out which road he ended up on when he left.'

He pulled out a GPS device he'd borrowed from Bart and noted the spot, then jabbed a stick into the mud and tied orange marking ribbon to it. He wanted to make it as easy for Alice to find as possible. Then they were off again, Billy hustling them along. The next big log they came to, she didn't jump. Instead she examined the entire thing, concentrating on one end.

'He probably stopped to rest here. The scent pool is stronger. Means he spent longer in this area.' Kane waved his arm in the same sweeping pattern his dog was doing. Hank planted another ribboned stick and they waited as she worked the area.

'How old is she?' he asked as the dog leapt on and off the fallen tree with a graceful agility no human could match.

'Four. Got her from a coonhound rescue organization. Best dog I've ever had.'

Kane had done this for fifteen years, crisscrossing the state to help find everything from escaped jail inmates to lost children. Billy was his third search and rescue dog. The other two, Boris and a very old Andre, were currently enjoying retirement in front of the fireplace at home in Moberly. He'd just gotten a puppy, too, but hadn't decided yet whether he was going to train her to track. Hank considered that as they started to move again, Billy tugging on her lead. He started to laugh.

'Billy isn't B-i-l-l-y, is it?' he said. 'It's B-i-l-l-i-e. Billie Jean.'

Kane lobbed him a wicked grin. 'Very good. That is her full name. Easy decision when the person with that name is one of my favorite tennis players.'

'And what'd you name the puppy? Steffi?'

Another sly grin. 'Serena.'

Of course.

'I'm not going to let you see him. Are you nuts?'

'C'mon, Maggie, he's a suspect,' Sheila said. 'I need to continue my interview.'

Maggie McCleary crossed her arms and frowned. 'Not a chance. You know better. Plus, a suspect in what? Littering? All you have is an abandoned ax or whatever it was, left in the woods.'

Now it was Sheila's turn to frown. 'That is low. You know there's more going on than that.'

A corner of Maggie's mouth turned upward. She looked like she was trying not to smirk. 'Maybe. Doesn't mean you get to see him.'

'Can't you ask him if he'll talk to me? If he voluntarily consents . . .'

Maggie walked around to the other side of the ER nurse station and accessed Mingo Culver's computer record. 'You can leave somebody here to make sure he doesn't go AMA, but otherwise, no dice. Not yet.'

Sheila smiled. Those were the key words. *Not yet* meant maybe later. As long as he didn't ignore doctor's orders and walk out 'against medical advice.' If he did that, they were screwed. Because they had no grounds to detain him. No body, no crime. Unless old Leo Fackrell wanted to press trespassing charges. She'd broach that with the old man if it came to that. But for the moment, she needed to sit down. She looked around.

'You're impossible,' Maggie said, but her tone was that of a friend, not an exasperated doctor. 'If you're going to stay, which of course you are, you can use one of these chairs.' She pointed at the ergonomic ones behind the nurses' counter, which were a damn sight better than the hard plastic ones in the waiting area. Sheila grinned at her and rolled one over to a corner where she was out of the way, but still monitoring Culver's only exit route. Then she nabbed a wheeled overbed tray and her makeshift workstation was complete. She pulled her laptop out of her bag, talked Nurse Cindy into giving up the staff Wi-Fi password, and got to work.

An hour later, she knew a lot more about Mingo Culver and liked none of it. He had a few misdemeanor arrests in Illinois and appeared to still be living in his parents' house in Petersburg, right in the shadow of a state maximum security prison. He was a prodigious tweeter with opinions on a wide range of topics, none of which he seemed to actually know anything about. Nothing seemed connected to him getting lost in the woods while searching for 'treasure' until a few recent tweets referred to his Instagram account. She switched to her phone and pulled up her own Instagram account, which her nieces had convinced her to open so she could like their posts. She poked at it for a bit until she found @mingogoldfinder. And look at that. A relatively new account, full of nature photos. Artful ones where you couldn't discern the locations. With captions just as vague.

Nothing here but getting close.

This time for sure. I can feel it.

Almost ready to share my findings.

You're not going to believe this one. I'm so good.

She paused at that one. Posted three days ago. When Mingo said he was lost in the Murder Rocks woods. She enlarged the photo of leaves piled against a rotting log, with a freshly dug hole a foot away. Like he'd found something. He was full of shit. Of course, most everybody on Instagram was also full of shit, so that didn't make him anything unique. But he was specifically full of it with this photo because she figured he'd been telling the truth when he said he didn't find anything. If he had found something, it would've been in his pack. Or he would've re-buried it in the woods, and currently be frantic that search and rescue personnel would find and take it.

And neither of those things was happening. Instead, the annoying

interloper was peacefully dozing down the hall and she was
beginning to think her chair wasn't really ergonomic after all. She
shifted and winced as her torso started to throb. She tried to ignore
it and went back to his oldest Instagram posts. The third one he
ever uploaded was actually a selfie. Kind of. It showed what had
to be his hands holding electronic equipment and a topographical
map. *I'm coming for you*, read the caption, and he'd tagged another
account: @hiddenhoards.

A rival treasure hunter? She clicked over to that account. And
realized she had a much bigger problem than that.

'You're wrangling those boys pretty good,' Chief Giacalone said.
'I grew up in Springfield, so I got no grounds to talk to them about
it being a teen hangout. It's always great to have local knowledge
during these kinds of operations.'

'Yeah, I am good for that.' Sam grinned. 'Born and raised here.
Definitely spent some evenings around a campfire at Murder Rocks.'

'I'm surprised we don't get calls out here, honestly,' the chief
said as he leaned comfortably against his fire district SUV. 'Spot
fires, that kind of thing.'

Sam shrugged. 'Most people camp and know how to put out a
fire.'

Giacalone raised an eyebrow. 'Even when they've been drinking?'

'Well,' Sam drew out the word, 'I guess when you look at it
now . . . when I look at it now – from an older perspective – there
does seem to be a lot of luck involved, too.'

Giacalone straightened and adjusted his ballcap. 'And that's why
you and me got jobs, son. For when the luck runs out.'

They both turned as the faint rumble of a car engine grew louder.
A Chevy Tahoe with streaky back windows pulled up and a short
woman climbed out. She was plump, with skin the color of hickory
wood and long black hair wrapped up in a bun.

'You must be Melanie Perez.' Sam extended a hand.

She smiled shyly and walked to the back of the vehicle. She
opened it and they heard the sound of a metal crate shifting. Then
four paws hit the ground. Not a single jowl or skin fold in sight.
Definitely no floppy ears. Sam sighed. The German shepherd stared
back at him like he knew what Sam was thinking. *Disappointed,
buddy? I'll show you.*

His name was Roscoe and he chose to ignore the two men as

Ms Perez put a GPS collar on him. She strapped on a backpack and asked who was coming with her.

'That'll be me, ma'am.' Sam grabbed his own pack, stocked with water, a first-aid kit, an evidence kit, hat, poncho, knife, some protein bars and one of Chief Giacalone's GPS device as a backup. She blushed and told him to call her Melanie. They stepped to the edge of the roadway. The energy came off Roscoe in waves, but he stayed calm. Then she gave the command and he was off.

Sam knew dogs with this skill worked off-lead, but Roscoe wasn't even within sight anymore. 'Um, how are we supposed to keep up with him?'

She smiled. 'He won't let us get too far behind. He knows we're slow. Plus, when he finds it, he'll sit. That's his signal. And he won't move until I release him.'

They hustled after the fleet-footed dog, who had immediately headed east. Like he could smell dead already, Sam thought. They walked for twenty minutes, with a bouncy Roscoe doubling back often to make sure his tag-alongs hadn't gotten themselves lost. Then he was off again, until he came to a small clearing. He circled and concentrated on one spot, nose close to the ground but tail still high in the air. Finally, he looked at Melanie.

'You'd better get your kit out,' she said. 'There's no body here now, but there was.'

Sam stared, stunned, and then snapped into action. He approached slowly, pulling on nitrile gloves. He walked a wider circle than Roscoe had, and froze three-quarters of the way around. Faint drag marks cut through his circumference, starting from near where Roscoe stood and lining straight into the trees. The carpet of leaves and weedy growth obscured it to the point where anyone would have walked by without seeing it if they hadn't been looking. Good thing they had something better than eyesight. He smiled at Roscoe and texted the GPS coordinates to Alice and Hank.

'Is he OK to wait? Can I take some pictures?'

'Yeah. That's fine. Do you want me to do anything? I could put up tape.'

He tossed her the roll of yellow crime scene tape and they worked in silence for a few minutes. 'I figure he must've been killed here then,' Sam finally said. 'And dragged into deeper cover. We'll need to go through all this ground cover. But . . .' He looked again at Roscoe, shifting back and forth with unfinished business. He nodded at Melanie, who barely got her hands together in a clap before the shepherd was off, zipping along the drag marks past where they disappeared from human view. Sam and Melanie broke into a jog. The terrain got rockier and less flat, with Roscoe confidently weaving around obstacles just as the person dragging the body must have done. He noticed a few drag marks here and there as they tried to keep up. They came to an outcropping that dropped down about eight feet. Roscoe stood on the edge, then darted to the right until he found an easier way to the bottom. By the time they reached the edge themselves and could see down, he had settled into a very satisfied sit.

'There we go,' Melanie said proudly, reaching for the treat bag on her belt. Sam scrambled down the same route Roscoe used and stopped next to the dog. The dead man had clearly been pushed off the outcropping and now lay covered in mud and leaves with an arm flung upward and one leg twisted underneath the other. Sam moved closer as Roscoe got his reward and vacated the space by the man's head. Sam pulled on fresh gloves and knelt down.

The man appeared to be in his twenties, white with dark blond hair in a longish cut. He was dressed for hiking – water-resistant cargo pants, Gore-Tex boots, loose, long-sleeve T-shirt. Sam wanted to brush off the mess to see the wounds, but knew he couldn't touch anything until Alice and the coroner's people got here. And Hank. Definitely Hank. He opened the camera app on his phone and carefully moved to the other side of the body to get a better look at the face. He knelt down again, angling his face as close to the ground as possible. In his peripheral vision, Roscoe was getting a celebratory pat-and-praise session.

'No. No, no, no.'

Both dog and handler looked at him in surprise. He sat back, still staring at the bullet hole in the man's chest. No slash or stab wounds anywhere. There was no way a witness would confuse a hacked-to-death body with one felled by a gunshot. He looked over at Roscoe. The dog's day might not be done.

TEN

Hank grabbed Randy Kane's arm, and the handler and Billie Jean jerked to a stop.

'What the hell do you mean, "the wrong body," Sam?' He switched his phone to speaker mode as Sam explained. Kane started to laugh until he saw the look on Hank's face.

'Sorry, man. I know that sucks for you, but damn. That is a doozy of a development.' He looked down at the coonhound, who was busy scratching behind her ear. 'Makes me wonder. Is that dead guy who we've been tracking? Is he the one who dropped the hatchet? Are we gonna end up at the same spot as Melanie, just coming at it from a different direction?'

Hank tried not to glare at him as he looked at Sam's GPS coordinates. 'No. We're not headed in that direction. Not at the moment, anyway.'

He put away his phone and took a deep breath. He agreed with Sam that Mingo Culver – even factoring in a certain amount of exaggeration and error – would not have described a gunshot victim as being hacked to death. So there were two. Unless the lost hiker was just making things up entirely. He wondered if Sheila had gotten the chance to talk to him this morning.

'So the guy who dropped the hatchet could be the one who got shot, or he could be the one who killed both of them?' Kane asked as they started tracking again.

'Well, in my experience, killers tend to stick with a method. Somebody armed with a gun isn't likely to reach for a hatchet.' Plus, hacking someone to death took an entirely different murderous emotion than pulling a cold and clinical trigger. It was unlikely a single person would be capable of both feelings in short order. It wouldn't be someone Hank wanted to meet.

They stumbled through a scattering of good-sized rocks as Billie Jean beelined to the south. There wasn't much down this way, certainly no access road, which worried Hank. Where had this person left the woods? Then the dog abruptly turned east and then north. Kane waved away his worried muttering. 'She knows what she's doing, trust me.'

They continued back north for another ten minutes, Hank trying to watch the GPS and keep an eye on the terrain at the same time. Texts kept coming from Sammy, who must've updated Sheila, because she started pinging him, too. He silenced his phone and focused on the hound, who dashed northeast through a tangle of broken brush. The two men fought through the undergrowth and saw Billie Jean concentrate on another scent pool and then turn east and start to pull.

Hank bent down to pull a sticker weed off his jeans. As he straightened, his eyes caught a flash of blue a few dozen yards off to the left. He hollered for Kane to stop. He got ten feet before he saw blood on the ground. It took another forty before even his human nose could smell what the huddle of blue was. He stopped two feet away, in the rotting leaves with the noontime autumn sun stunting shadows down to nothing and making the attendant flies lazy and slow. He heard Kane come up behind.

'Lord have mercy. That's worse than I imagined it would be.'

The body looked exactly as Mingo Culver had described. The man lay on his side, with a deep wound right at the curve where his shoulder met his neck. There was another on his left bicep, where the blade had sliced through the light windbreaker. Blood covered most of his top half. Hank motioned for Kane to stay put and walked around to the other side. The face was half buried in leaves, but Hank could tell that the man was Asian and probably in his fifties. There was a slicing gash on his cheek and multiple cuts on his left forearm, as if he'd raised it in self-defense. Whoever attacked the poor guy must've come at him straight on. He looked about six feet tall and fairly well-built. Whoever attacked him must've been either very big or very fast to gain the advantage.

Hank knelt and looked over the body at Kane, whose face was ashen under his sun hat. Billie Jean, unfazed, waited patiently, facing the direction her live scent had gone. Kane cleared his throat. 'What do you need me to do?'

'Keep at it with Billie. We need to know where that hatchet man went.'

Sam watched all the color drain out of Alice Randall's face. They both looked down at the gunshot victim and then at Sam's phone.

'No, there's no backpack,' Alice said. 'Just the body.'

'Shit.' Hank's muttered curse came through nice and clear. 'There isn't one here, either.'

Sam took Hank off speakerphone and stepped away as Alice got to work. 'I think you need to call Kurt in. She's not going to ask you to do it. She'd never want to ruin his vacation. But I don't know how one person is going to do this much work on their own.'

Hank agreed immediately.

'We also have a crime scene at the other GPS coordinates I sent you,' Sam said. 'We think that's where this guy was shot.'

Hank groaned. Sam wondered what was in the missing backpacks. If it wasn't something important, they would've been left with the bodies. And what would be important, out here by Murder Rocks? Alf Bolin and his infamous hidden treasure? He thought back to all those teenage campfire stories and rolled his eyes. And then froze. Some of the tales weren't tall at all. Some of them were true. He thought about the bloody hatchet.

'Hey, about your body – does it have a head?'

The other end of the line went dead silent. 'What?' Hank eventually managed to say.

Sam cleared his throat self-consciously. But now that he'd thought of this, he really, really needed to know the answer. 'Is there a head attached to the body?'

The open phone line seemed to vibrate. Hank finally spoke. 'Of course there is. Barely, but yes. There is.' There was another quiet pause. 'Now I have a question for you. What the hell?'

Sam sat down on a rock and thought about his local history lessons in school. About the many legends regarding Civil War-era bushwhackers, and the bits of proven facts scattered among them like the pebbles at his feet. He kicked at them and started to explain. Bolin was a Confederate sympathizer who would sometimes stop for a meal at a farmhouse owned by a woman who also supported the South. Until her Confederate soldier husband was captured by Union forces. Then she became a pawn in the chess match that Union officers had been playing with the outlaw Bolin for years. They offered her husband's freedom in exchange for her laying a trap on Bolin's next visit.

A Northern soldier, disguised as a weak and sick Confederate recruit, was sent to stay with her at the farmhouse south of Murder Rocks. When Bolin arrived, she said the man was recuperating in order to be strong enough to continue his journey south into Arkansas. Bolin eventually accepted the story and lowered his guard enough for the farm wife to serve the meal. Afterward, as Bolin bent to light his pipe, the Union man bludgeoned him to death with a heavy iron tool.

'And there was rejoicing throughout the land.' Or at least that was how his teachers put it. Bolin's body was taken north the twelve miles to Forsyth, maybe even near to where the sheriff's department headquarters now sat. And there, somebody cut off his head.

'Oh, God,' Hank said.

Sam ignored him. The body was buried, but the head – as proof-of-death – was transported farther north to the town of Ozark, where folks stuck it on a pole outside the courthouse and threw rocks at it.

'So . . . since there was a hatchet involved, it made me think of that.' Sam looked up at the rock outcropping and then down at the body. 'I'm glad yours still has its head.'

'OK, let's stop referring to this one as "mine," shall we?' Hank sounded testy. Maybe because he wasn't used to such history, growing up in California like he did. They hadn't fought a nation-splitting war out there like every Ozarker, civilian or soldier, had been forced to do here. They just fiddled around looking for gold and getting lost in snowy mountains.

Then Sam laughed in spite of himself. Looking for gold might be what this whole current mess was about, too. 'I just meant that if the guy didn't have his head, I'd think we had someone re-creating Bolin – instead of just looking for his loot. So that's a bright side.'

He heard Hank sigh. 'You haven't seen him. It's bad.'

Sam looked over at Alice, who was crawling around in the dirt and coaxing corpse-feeding bugs into a container. 'Well, there are different kinds of bad.'

And he really should be helping. He dug out a fresh pair of gloves as Hank kept talking.

'I'm going to send Kane and his dog on to keep tracking the live scent. See if they find anything. I'll wait here. And I'll call Kurt. Tell Alice it was my decision.'

'Oh, don't worry. I will.'

He hung up and took the container from Alice so she could start collecting trace evidence from the outcropping while they waited for the coroner's people to get there. The men were basically just transport flunkies. The real work was done by the forensic pathologist up in Springfield. But the coroner boys always had control of the body. He and Alice couldn't even go through his pockets until they gave permission. So he contented himself with a maggot round-up.

'You told Hank the Alf Bolin story?' She moved away and started
snapping photos of the blood-smeared rock embankment. 'Poor
guy's probably wondering how the hell he ended up in a place this
crazy. I know that's what I thought.'

'You knew about it already? You didn't grow up here?'

'Ha. No, but my kids did. My son came home from middle school
one day full of stories about war and soldiers and outlaws. And
heads on stakes. Well, one head at least. Of course, a twelve-year-old
boy thought it was the coolest, most disgusting thing. Me, I just
thought, "Dear God, what a way to contaminate evidence."' She
lowered the camera and looked around. 'Now, though . . . being
out here with nothing but rocks and trees reaching up like skeleton
fingers and a human being who was dragged along by a person
treating him like so much garbage . . . it's hard not to think the
crazy history isn't done yet.'

Sam looked at the backpack-less victim, and prayed she was
wrong.

Dear Sir,

*I write to you with update of the situation south of your garrison
in Springfield and the bushwhackers who continue to violate the
property and persons of those there. What men remain in the
area, the very old and very young, are run through or gunned
down, leaving the women defenseless and forced to give over
their food stores, livestock and whatever meager valuables they
have left. The bands of guerrillas make travel all but impossible
throughout and our units face ambush at every turn.*

*One of the worst of these is one recently named to us, a
Missourian called Alf Bolin who raids the countryside and also
will lie in wait for travelers along a much-traveled length of road
near the border with Arkansas. He and his followers make the
roads deadly by day and by night. He is claimed to have killed
a dozen men and surely wants for more. It is my firm belief that
he must be flushed from the rocks and brush that hide him and
taken into our custody or the welfare of our own troops might
begin to be at risk. In order to succeed, I will need more men.*

I await your orders.

Respectfully,

Capt. John Farmore

ELEVEN

Hank silenced her with a picture. If he was currently kneeling on the ground next to *that*, he wasn't going to care about *Hidden Hoards*. Yet. But he would, Sheila was sure of it. The Instagram account tagged by the irritating Mingo belonged to a podcast. *Hidden Hoards* was in its second season of treasure hunting, with each episode focusing on one particular tramp through the jungle/desert/forest in search of long-lost whatever. In theory, this was fine. Get a host and a travel budget and a talking-head historical expert, and there you go. Decent listening even when they didn't find anything.

But that wasn't what this podcast was doing. It threw out facts and rumors and some wild-ass supposition and then told its listeners to go search for themselves. The first season had been more aspirational – lots of pirate booty in the Caribbean and some ancient shipwrecks in the Mediterranean. Practically no one was going to go diving for doubloons who wasn't already inclined – and equipped – to do so. But this new season was trouble. The host was staying in the U.S., and touting all sorts of domestic 'treasure.' Loot within driving distance. Based on nothing but dubious legends, which Sheila bet had become concrete pains in the ass for local law enforcement agencies.

And Friday, the idiot set his sights on Branson County.

'Alf Bolin and the Finnegan Gold: Infamous Ozark Bushwhacker's Hidden Hoard Ten Times Greater Than Experts Say.'

Newly discovered letters have revealed a robbery that netted the legendary outlaw an entire fortune. The Finnegans, a prominent Carrollton, Arkansas, family of Union sympathizers, fled north in 1861 with their household goods and their gold, of which there was a 'considerable measure.' A cache of letters written in the 1890s by daughter Mary Louise Finnegan, and provided to this podcast, detail the extent of the riches transported by the family, as well as the terror Bolin inflicted on the travelers as they made their way through the foreboding Ozarks in search of safety. Listen now.

Sheila groaned and tossed her phone on the hospital tray. She did not want to 'listen now.' She wanted a stiff bourbon and a long walk. But she didn't currently have access to the first and wasn't yet capable of the second. So she dug out her AirPods with a sigh. And then put them away as she saw Mingo coming down the hospital hall.

'Where's my stuff?'

'In an evidence locker in Forsyth.'

'What the hell? You can't do that. That's government overreach.'

She shrugged.

'What am I supposed to do? That was all my money and ID and everything.'

She smiled and pulled a sealed evidence bag out of her tote. She showed him the chain of custody list and had him sign a release document. Then she handed over his wallet. 'There. Now you're not stranded. You're not getting everything else back, though, until we're through out at the scenes.'

'When will that be?' He glared at her as he stuffed his wallet in the pocket of his dirty cargo pants. 'Wait. You said yesterday you hadn't found anything.'

'Well, that's the difference that a day and two highly trained search dogs make. Proof that you were right.'

He took a nervous step back. 'About which part?'

'Not the treasure,' she said through gritted teeth. 'But we have found a body that matches the description you gave me yesterday.'

He started to go pale. She smacked her hands together. 'Don't you dare get woozy again. You're well enough to be released, which means you're well enough to come to the cafeteria with me and have a chat. I'll even buy you a cup of coffee.'

He looked down at her. 'You'll buy me lunch.'

Then he crossed his arms like a pouty five-year-old and waited for her to pack up her laptop. They walked slowly over to the cafeteria, and she found a table while he loaded a tray with food. Once they were settled and he'd started in on the potato salad, she mentioned the podcast. He'd listened to the first season, just because it was interesting. But this second season was hands-on. Participatory. And it lit a fire under him. The show was offering guest appearances to anyone who found something at a featured site. Plus, what you were finding was treasure.

'You roll your eyes, but there *is* treasure out there. All over the country. I drove to Louisville after episode three, when they had new information about that Kentucky Hoard of Civil War gold coins and the likelihood there's more out there.' He moved on to the ham-and-cheese sandwich. 'But I didn't know enough. There were hunters there who'd already researched everything. I didn't stand a chance.'

So he decided to get out in front of things. Anticipate. What was fairly close to where he lived and would likely be featured in an episode? He decided to bet on Bolin. If he could already have preliminary research done – be packed and ready to go – then when the episode aired and he knew the freshly released info, he could hit the road immediately. He'd beat the rush and have more knowledge for the hunt.

Sheila sipped her tea and eyed the dichotomy across from her. That was some very credible forethought from a guy who then didn't think ahead enough to bring extra water and a portable phone charger on a long hike through unfamiliar territory. She leaned forward. As interestingly ridiculous as new Alf Bolin information might be, it was the hike she wanted to talk about right now.

'Did you see or hear anything else, at any point, when you were in the woods? People, cars, noises, anything at all?'

Mingo shook his head. 'Just the dead guy.'

'Describe him for me again.'

He did, consistent with what he'd told her the day before.

He thought about it and started to look queasy, like he had the first time she'd talked to him. She pushed the slice of pecan pie at him and waited until he took a few bites to settle his stomach.

'Was there any kind of weapon around?'

He shook his head. 'There was just the guy and the blood.'

She took a drink of her now-cold tea. 'When you came out of the woods, you kept telling the deputy, "he found it." What did you mean?'

He looked at her like she was the world's biggest idiot. 'That he'd found the Finnegan gold. The hoard that Bolin took.'

'He had no backpack. How do you know he found anything?'

She waited patiently. He fidgeted, then finished off his pie. She didn't move.

'I assumed . . . I guess. Because why would somebody kill him if he hadn't found something.'

'If I find out that there was one and you did go through it and aren't telling me – you will be in a world of trouble. Do you understand?'

He nodded slowly and asked her permission to leave. She gave him a budget motel recommendation and watched him walk away with nothing but a set of filthy clothes, his wallet and a hospital-prescribed asthma inhaler. He didn't look it, and he certainly wasn't thinking it, but he'd been pretty damn lucky out there in the woods. He could've just as easily been shot or hacked to death out there, too. Unless he was the one doing the shooting and the hacking. Sheila might've bought him lunch, but that didn't mean she'd ruled him out as a killer.

[Orchestral music]
Mary Louise Finnegan was sixteen years old when she fled the Arkansas city of Carrollton with her parents, two older brothers, and as many belongings as they could carry.

It was a journey so traumatic that she couldn't discuss it until thirty years later, when she began to confide in a young relative. That series of letters reveals for the first time the extent of the violence – and the theft – perpetrated against her family.

We've been lucky to obtain these letters, boxed and forgotten in a dusty attic for more than a century. They've led us to a certain spot on the map and, as you've come to expect, loyal listeners, that spot is marked with an "X." I'm Victor Hardwick and this is *Hidden Hoards*.

[Banjo music]
Today, we're going back to the lawless borderland that was the Ozarks during the Civil War. Where brigands preyed on travelers and residents alike, and where they buried their takings in caves and hollows. The prosperous Finnegan family had no choice but to go through this area after they were forced off their farm by Confederate supporters who harassed them, and Confederate troops who took their crops and their livestock. They were headed for the safety of Springfield, Missouri, and its Union army forces.

They had two wagons full of foodstuffs, furniture, the household silver, and whatever other sundries would fit. They made it across the border into Missouri without incident. But ten miles from Forsyth, their luck ran out.

[Hoofbeats, clattering metal, faint screams]
Bushwhackers attacked the little group, firing pistols and running them off the road. One of the wagons overturned, spilling items everywhere, and throwing passengers onto the ground. Two men

cut the horses loose and made off with them. Others took aim at the young and strapping Finnegan sons, who took cover behind the damaged wagon and fired back in self-defense. In the ensuing gunfight, nineteen-year-old Tommy Finnegan was shot to death. His family barely made it out alive. They arrived at the relative safety of the town of Forsyth bedraggled and broken, with nothing more than the clothing on their backs.

[Mournful music]

At the time, Mary Louise never named the bushwhackers who attacked her traveling party. How would she know? – they certainly hadn't introduced themselves as they ambushed her. But in her letters all those years later, she believes – as do we – that it was none other than the murderous Alf Bolin.

The road was well done and flat but we were nervous all the same. We had heard tales of the men who roamed those woods and what they did to those on both sides of the war. So we hurried as well as we could and made excellent progress until we reached a stretch lined with boulders that loomed like evil giants. Behind them hid our undoing.

It was only later that I learned of one certain man who used those boulders so frequently and to such bad ends that they came to be called 'Murder Rocks.' That man, of course, was Alf Bolin. His name has been unwillingly burned in my mind ever since.

The Finnegan party limped from Forsyth to Springfield in September 1861. The parents, Ernest and Ruth, eventually bought a small plot of land near Rolla and eked out an existence until their deaths in the 1870s. By then, Mary Louise had married a shopkeeper and moved to St. Louis.

It broke my heart to leave Mama and Papa. I had no other recourse, however, if I was to marry Simon. They knew it and bade me go. Our misfortunes should not be yours, Papa said. You are the one of us who can recover from what happened. The one of us who can be happy.

This part of the Finnegan story has been known from the time historians started trying to compile lists of Bolin's victims. But what has not been known until today is this – Ernest Finnegan had in his

possession the deposits of Carrollton's bank at the behest of that
institution's manager. Much of that town was in the hands of home-
grown Confederate militias, and Union forces were closing in. Now,
it's unknown whether the manager's request was an officially
sanctioned bank action, or just the decision of a panicked employee.
Either way, the bank's entire remaining holdings made their way
north with the Finnegan family. It was enough gold and silver to
fill a wagon, and it never made it to Springfield.

[Swelling music]
*I have never before spoken of what happened when the
bushwhackers fell upon us. There didn't seem to be much point
of it – what is past cannot be changed – but you have asked and
I have committed to telling everything that you want to know. So
– the horses hitched to the second wagon bolted in fright at the
first gunshot. Billy always was the poorer horseman of my two
brothers and he could not keep them in control. The wagon rolled
over and all the sacks scattered. It turns out they were not full
of grain.*

*I still can hear the clinking and see the glittering metal as
everything fell apart.*
[Hoofbeats fading to silence]

But the poor Finnegans weren't the only victims of Bolin's
thievery. Other travelers also lost everything at the point of his gun.
We'll be right back after the commercial break . . .

TWELVE

'I've finally hit a road,' Randy Kane said. 'No idea where I am, but it's a nice little fire road, and where the trail ends.'

A satisfied woof came over the phone next. Hank wished he were there with the talented Billie Jean instead of still here at the blood-soaked body with Deputy Bill Ramsdell and a very unhappy evidence technician.

'Not only do you call me back from vacation,' Kurt Gatz said, 'but you give me the worse body.'

'I'm sorry. They found the other one first, and Alice was already there.'

Kurt harrumphed and muttered his way around the scene as Hank turned his attention back to Kane. 'Send me your coordinates. I'll get a deputy out to you to mark the spot.'

'Eh, the surface is pretty hard-packed. I don't see any tire tracks.'

Hank sighed.

'Sorry, man. I'll walk her up and down along it for a stretch, see if she picks anything up, but . . .'

'But you're just taking pity on me.'

'Well, you do sound somewhat pitiful at the moment. So yeah, we'll do a little walking down this way and . . .' He stopped talking, then started up again slowly. 'You know, I been doing this a long time. All kind of woods and fields and such. And this here feels like . . .' He paused again. 'I mean, I got no idea where I am. Of course, on the GPS I know exactly where I am. Satellite location whatever. But this road is not . . . there's nothing here. Just overhung trees and such. I don't even know if it'd be visible on Google Earth. So if this person entered or exited the woods here . . .'

'They would've had to know the area. Like a local.' Hank's voice was flat but his heart was racing.

'Yessir. I don't know that for a fact, but—'

'I think I know someone who would,' Hank interrupted. He thanked Kane, hung up, and quickly dialed Sam. He explained and sent the GPS coordinates. 'So is it a high school shortcut into the woods?'

'No way. Yeah, it's something only locals would know about, but no kids would dare use it. It's on Fackrell's land.'

Hank stepped back as Kurt grumpily shooed him out of the way. 'I thought you said kids do cut through his land to get to the rocks.'

'It's one thing to cut a corner of his property in the middle of the night. It's another to be parking a car in the middle of it and then traipsing a pretty long way through it to get to Murder Rocks. Kids wouldn't bother.'

'But somebody who didn't want their car to be seen?'

'Then it'd be the perfect spot. If you knew about it.'

A bank vault worth of gold. Even the possibility that it might be true made Sheila sick to her stomach. She looked around the hospital cafeteria. It was mid-afternoon and she was one of the only ones there. She needed to get to the office. She needed her white board and her pens and her stash of extra-caffeinated tea bags before she could handle listening to the rest of the podcast episode. She gathered her notes and stopped by the emergency department to thank Nurse Cindy before she headed out to the parking lot. She thought about swinging by the scene at Murder Rocks on the way to the office – it wasn't that far out of the way, really – but reconsidered as she walked to the squad car and her still-bruised internal organs told her in no uncertain terms they'd light a fire in her abdomen if she walked more than another ten feet. So no hike through the woods for her.

She gingerly maneuvered herself into the car and sat for a minute as her broken ribs joined the conversation. When she'd fought back the pain enough to be able to breathe properly again, she put on some Mavis Staples and headed for Forsyth. She kept the music going in her AirPods as she hobbled into the headquarters building and headed straight to the conference room. Her donut seat cushion was still there, thank God. She sank onto it and looked at the paperwork stacked on the table. She'd had copies made, so that Mingo's originals could be safely packed away in the evidence locker. It now made sense why he had so much research. Savvy guesswork and advance preparation. He'd gambled that Alf Bolin would warrant an episode, and he'd won. So to speak. She was pretty sure he didn't feel like a winner at the moment.

And the two men out in the woods definitely hadn't won. They had to be in that particular stretch of woods for the same reason as

Mingo. It was the only reason for anybody other than partying high schoolers to be out there at all. She wondered if those had done the same careful preparation as Mingo. She wouldn't know unless they found the damn missing backpacks. She checked her phone to see if anyone had. The last text from Hank was ten minutes prior. Suspicious access point. Local knowledge only. Fackrell land. She rolled her eyes and decided to decipher that later.

Then one came through from Sam. Body boys here pretty quick. No ID on victim.

She groaned. The other guy probably wouldn't have one, either. They were going to be very difficult to identify. They could be from anywhere. Because the damn show was available everywhere. She drummed her fingers on the table and thought about that. It was probable they'd come from within relatively near driving distance in order to have gotten to the area so quickly after the episode aired. It was also probable that they – and Mingo – were going to be the first of many. *Hidden Hoards* was one of the highest rated in the 'history' category of her podcast app. Yeah. It was history like diet shakes were nutrition.

She grabbed a dry erase marker and leveraged herself out of the chair. She needed to plan as if these three were going to be the start of a flood. Coming to town with their maps and shovels and poor regard for trespassing laws. She sketched a quick outline of the area, with roads to the north and east and a dotted line to mark the division between park land and Leo Fackrell's property. She left plenty of room for wherever the hell Hank's 'suspicious access point' was. A big black dot went just to the right of center. It was an appropriate color for that particular landmark, she thought. Then she grabbed orange and started marking where she was going to have deputies put up barriers. She'd do her best to keep folks out. But it was a lot of porous wilderness, and she had no illusion that she'd succeed.

As the body boys prepared to leave with the gunshot victim, Sam reminded them they had another crime scene and told them where to find Hank. They stared blankly.

'Dude, how are we supposed to find that? All these woods look the same.'

'Actually, we can show you.'

They all turned toward Melanie Perez, who'd been watching from a shady spot nearby. Roscoe sat quietly next to her, looking at them like they'd promised a walk to the park and quit halfway. 'He knows. That there's another one out there. It would be great to let him "find" it. He's not going to think his job's finished until he does.'

That would explain why she'd stuck around, Sam realized. 'I'm so sorry. I wish you'd said something. You could've done it already.'

She blushed and gestured at Alice, who was now photographing the ground where the body had lain. 'That's OK. I didn't want to interrupt your work.'

Sam quickly helped pack up the rest of the transport gear and the two coroner workers started for the command center and their van. Melanie and Roscoe rose to their feet as one. She gave him a pat and walked after them. He looked at her, looked at Sam, and stayed put. She turned around. He didn't move. She sighed.

'You don't want to go all the way back to the road first? That's what you're saying?'

He was poised to run, almost vibrating with delighted intensity.

'You can't say no to that face,' Sam said. 'I'll figure out another way to get those guys over to the other crime scene.'

'Are you sure? I don't want you to have to go out of your way.'

Sam looked at the woman who'd volunteered to spend countless hours raising and training a dog, then chosen to drive cross-state on her own time to slog through muddy woods with strangers. 'Um, I'd say you're the one who's gone out of your way for us. So I'd love if now he could do his job on his own timetable.'

They both looked at Roscoe. He raised hopeful eyebrows. Sam grinned at her, which triggered another blush. Then she gave the command and the dog torpedoed off through the trees. In the wrong direction.

Sam pointed toward Hank's scene and started to say something, but stopped when Melanie didn't bat an eye. If she had complete faith in her dog, who was he to say otherwise? He shut his mouth and followed behind her as she trailed after the bounding shepherd. He kept turning back to make sure he didn't lose them, clearly wanting their human feet to move more quickly. They hustled along, still headed away from the hatchet victim. Sam began to regret coming. He had work to do. Melanie could track on her own what would probably turn out to be nothing more than the scent of some woodland animal.

They crossed a rocky section, watching for cracks that could snap an ankle if they stepped the wrong way. The shepherd led them through fallen leaves and patches of mud left from the recent rains. They made it to the top of a slight rise and hit a little flat spot down below, dotted with trees and crisscrossed with fallen logs. Sam decided to say he was turning back. And Roscoe sat.

Hank crested the rise and looked at the trio. The little plump woman stood there with a stubborn tilt to her chin. Sam sat on a fallen tree, his elbows on his knees and a look on his face that was half-chastised, half-exasperated. The dog owned the spot in between them, regally waiting for someone to take action.

'You think he's found something?' Hank said.

'Not "think." Know,' the woman said. She pointed straight down at the ground. 'Human remains.'

Hank looked at Sam, who raised his hand and gave him a stop gesture. 'I wouldn't question anything, if I were you. Roscoe has signaled, and that means a definitive finding, and no one is going anywhere until we see that he's right.'

His deputy was clearly quoting the woman. She blushed a deep pink but didn't back down. 'Human remains.' She pointed again. Hank set down the shovel he'd borrowed from Kurt and stepped next to Roscoe, breaking the eye contact between the other two. Some tension left the air as he introduced himself to the dog handler. It seemed like it'd be necessary to do some digging in order to satisfy her. As long as it didn't take too much time. Sam needed to help Alice in the clearing where they believed the one victim had been shot, and he needed to check in with the volunteer search and rescue folks who were looking for the missing backpacks.

Sam picked up the shovel. 'Should I start digging right where he's sitting, Melanie?' She nodded and called Roscoe, who bounded to her for treats and ear rubs. That meant she thankfully didn't see the look he gave Hank. Hank nodded and mouthed 'five minutes.' He moved out of the way as Sam went at the wet ground, which looked like one of the only patches around that wasn't full of rocks. That thought started a tickling worry in the back of Hank's brain. He moved a fallen branch out of the way as Sam's hole got wider. Roscoe watched and wagged. Hank snuck a glance at his watch but let the digging continue. It started to take more effort as the deeper dirt hardened. Sam finally looked up at Hank.

'OK,' Hank said. 'We'll mark this, and come back out with better tools. I think that's all we can do with just a shovel.'

Melanie looked at Sam. 'That's fair. I know you guys have other crime scenes, too.'

'We'll take it seriously, I promise,' Sam said. He jabbed the shovel one last time to anchor it so he could hold onto the handle and step out of the hole.

'I think I just hit something.'

Both Hank and Melanie froze. Sam knelt down and rocked the shovel back and forth to loosen the soil. Hank got down with him and they moved dirt away with their hands. Melanie grabbed the shovel and used it to hold back what they were scooping out.

'It's either a tree root,' Sam muttered, 'and I'm going to look like an idiot, or it's—'

'Not a tree root. Shit.' Hank sat back. A yellowing knob of bone protruded from the ground. Without another word, they both resumed digging, and soon two long, thin bones that might be the tibia and fibula of a human leg came into view. He looked up at Roscoe and silently corrected himself. Not 'might be human.' Most definitely were human. And most definitely were, unlike the wondrous Roscoe, going to be a very unwelcome addition to his investigation.

THIRTEEN

Leo Fackrell was expecting them. It didn't do to show up unannounced this far off in the depths of the county. People tended to answer the door holding their shotguns. Or using what was loaded in them to run you off their land before you even got to the house. Hank wasn't keen on either of those options, so he called ahead. Now he and Sheila sat in his squad car in front of the big farmhouse as the early Friday sun rose over the peaked roof.

'This place is like a horror movie,' she said as she peered through the windshield.

'Oh. I think it looks kind of like a weathered *Field of Dreams* house.'

She shot him a look. 'You are such a white man sometimes.'

'I am not.'

'Well, you're certainly not doing your mama's Latino ancestors proud, thinking about sappy-ass white-ghost baseball movies. Anybody with any sense sees a place like this, they run.'

'Then how come you're getting out of the car?'

''Cause I got no sense. Clearly. Look at where I work. And live.'

She had a point. He waited as she grabbed her cane and slammed the car door. 'We telling him about the skeleton?'

'Oh, hell yes,' he said. 'It's on his land. So that and fresh bodies. Fun topics.'

She chuckled. 'Just another average conversation for us two, isn't it?'

He didn't bother to respond. They made their way up the porch steps and he rang the bell. A woman with a square jaw and a bodily frame the same shape answered the door. She had long gray hair and a mouth that didn't look like it smiled often. Hank introduced them both.

'I know who you are, Sheriff. Still can't believe you won the election.'

He couldn't tell whether she meant that as a good thing or a bad one. She let them in. 'I'm Darlene Fackrell. I thought we all could talk in the kitchen.'

She led them through to the back of the house, which Hank took as a good sign they weren't considering this a hostile interview. Kitchens were where friendly chats happened. He hoped there'd be coffee. They entered the big room to find someone tending a percolator on a butcher-block counter. When Sam had called him 'Old Man Fackrell,' he wasn't kidding. Leo looked about twenty years older than his wife, and she was at least in her late sixties. His build looked like it had once been as solid as hers, but was now softened with a paunchy middle and a bowed spine. But his grip was still firm as he shook hands and they all settled at the oak dining table.

'I'm glad you're here. I read in the paper about those two men you found dead, but it wasn't quite clear where exactly they were.'

Sheila reached for her bag, where Hank knew she had a map.

'I can see why you'd want to know that, sir,' Hank said. 'One was indeed on your property. The other was on park land.'

Darlene Fackrell groaned. 'What does that mean for us?'

'Well, ma'am, it does mean that we need continued access to your land. You've been very kind so far, and we're hoping we can keep coming and going as we investigate.'

Leo leaned forward. 'Speaking of access – you want to tell me why you got roadblocks up everywhere?'

'They haven't stopped you, have they?' Sheila said worriedly. She'd given her deputies strict instructions.

'Oh no, I get a smile and a wave.'

'As you should,' his wife muttered.

'They're guarding those roads because of why we think all this has happened in the first place,' Sheila said.

They both stared at her. 'Don't you dare say "treasure,"' Darlene said.

'I'm sorry, but yes.' She reached into the folder she'd pulled from her bag and slid a printout across the table. 'There's a new podcast out. It talks about Alf Bolin and purports to have newly discovered information about a large cache of banker's gold that he stole from travelers near Murder Rocks.'

Leo shrugged. 'They've always said there's stuff out there.'

Yes, they have, Hank thought as he pictured the skeleton being painstakingly unearthed nearby.

'Be that as it may,' Sheila said, 'this time it's had a broader reach. The podcast is available worldwide.'

'Meh. We can just handle folk like we usually do,' Leo said. Darlene shifted in her seat and Hank was pretty sure she was kicking him under the table. He bit back a smile and studied them both. The usual way wasn't what concerned him. What did was whether the Fackrells had reacted atypically to the current circumstances in a way that'd led to murder. But he'd get to that.

'We know that you're the experts on your land and its connection to Murder Rocks. And I got no quarrel with whatever your usual practice is.' So no need for more kicking. 'But this time is different. These treasure hunters are serious. Since we put the roadblocks up two days ago, we've already turned away fifteen people. And that's just ones naive enough to use established access points. We've also caught four more in the woods who hiked in cross-country.'

Darlene turned pale. Leo said nothing and got up to pour coffee. Once they all had cups, Sheila told the story of Mary Louise Finnegan's letters. When she finished, Leo shook his head.

'Bolin was a monster. But I don't think he was that good of a thief, or stuff would've been found by now,' Leo said. 'He just liked killing people.'

No one disagreed. The regulator clock on the wall ticked on as they sipped their drinks. Hank gave it a minute and set down his mug. Speaking of killing people . . .

'We do need to ask you some questions about the two murders. You know we brought in dogs, and one of them determined that the person who dropped a murder weapon either came or left at this spot.'

Sheila unfolded the map and pointed to the hand-drawn dot showing where Billie Jean had stopped on Wednesday. There was no indication on the map that a road was even there. Leo nodded. He said that was the only access into the back of his acreage – to get a vehicle in there to haul away wood or if he brought folks in to hunt.

'So how many people would you say know about it?' she asked.

Darlene scoffed. 'Lots. We let scout troops come in and collect firewood for fundraisers. We got friends who'll come get a deer in season. We got – hell, you want us to count them all?'

'I'm sorry. Let me ask that again,' Sheila said. 'You can't see it on Google satellite maps. Do you think people from outside the area would know about it?'

'Oh. Sorry. I didn't know that's what you were getting at.' Darlene had the grace to look a little sheepish. Her husband patted her hand.

'I don't think there's any way you'd know about it unless you was local. Or was told about it by a local,' he said.

Sheila moved her hand to the next dot on her map. 'One of the men we found was here. This is your land, correct?'

They both leaned forward, Leo tilting his head up to look through his bifocals properly. 'Oh yeah, that's us. That the stabbed one or the shot one?'

Hank silently cursed the *Branson Daily Herald*. How that reporter was always able to find this kind of stuff out was still a mystery to him, and it drove him nuts.

'The stabbed one,' Sheila said, not sharing that the cause of death wasn't quite correct.

'Do you know when he died?' Leo asked.

The medical examiner estimated that both men died on Sunday, Sheila said. 'Did either of you see or hear anything out of the ordinary that day?'

Hank leaned back, cradling his coffee mug and watching. They'd gone to church, of course, and then come home and worked in the vegetable garden, preparing it for winter. Darlene eyed them both straight on, daring them to question their story. Hank came at them sideways.

'When you went to church, did you notice any increased traffic? Any strange cars? We figure each man had to have been dropped off nearby, because we haven't found cars parked anywhere.'

Darlene said no. Leo stared at the ceiling. 'There was that sedan, little wind-up thing, parked on the side of the road.'

'When? I didn't see anything.'

'You were probably digging through your purse. It was right before the curve in road. 'Bout a quarter-mile from the driveway, I think.' It was blue, foreign, low-end, he told them. Out-of-state license plate. He couldn't remember which one, just that it wasn't Missouri. And it wasn't there when they came back home. And no, there wasn't anybody inside it when he drove by. 'I didn't think a thing of it.'

It sounded like a rental, Hank thought. It certainly wasn't Mingo Culver's car, an old Honda CRV they'd found parked on a road in the opposite direction.

'Well, I'm grateful you remember it. It could end up being very helpful,' Sheila said. She cleared her throat and switched the subject. 'About the other victim – he was shot, like the newspaper said. So I need to ask you, just to check. Are all your guns accounted for?'

'What?' Darlene spat the word and almost threw her coffee at Sheila.

'Darling.' Leo laid a hand on her arm. Sheila didn't flinch.

'Could something have gone missing without you noticing? That's all I'm saying.'

Because with a man this old, on this much-passed-down-the-generations family land, there was no telling how many firearms he'd accumulated.

'I don't think so.' Leo's tone said he damn well knew where all his guns were, but was too polite to shut them down outright.

'What do you own?'

He started ticking them off on his fingers. 'Five rifles in my locked cabinet, plus the one shotgun. My grandson's .22. The Walther P38 my daddy brought home from World War Two in my nightstand. Couple other handguns, all locked up in a box in the cabinet just in case, 'cause, you know, when the grandson was little. Oh, and there's the shotgun over the mantel in the living room. You want to count that one, too? Hasn't worked since the 1800s.'

'Could you check that they're all here?'

Leo sighed and pushed himself to his feet.

'And the handguns – we'd like to see them,' Sheila said, taking the bad cop role and letting Hank remain the one in better standing.

Darlene huffed indignantly the whole time it took Leo to shuffle out of the room. She moved to go with him, but Hank stopped her with questions about the house, the garden, the friends who came hunting. She spat out answers until her husband returned.

'Awright. Everything was where it was supposed to be.'

He laid three pistols on the table – one in a case, one in a homemade drawstring bag, and a naked Colt, worn and well cared for.

'Where's the Walther?' Sheila asked.

Darlene's huffing started to sound like a toy locomotive. Leo merely laughed. 'I don't want to go all the way upstairs. I'll tell you, no one goes in our bedroom, that's for sure.'

Hank had a feeling Leo was more annoyed than he looked. And it was going to get worse. 'We'd like to borrow all these handguns. Just to compare them with what shot the murder victim.'

'You don't have cause to do that,' Darlene said.

'You're very right. That's why this is a request. This will let us rule out all your firearms, and really help the investigation.'

'Why should we have to hand over our property just to help you?'

'It would be a favor,' Sheila said. 'And hopefully help us put all this to rest more quickly, so that we're off your land and all those trespassers aren't trying to get on it anymore, either.'

Leo looked at his guns. Darlene looked at Leo. Hank was pretty sure she also kicked him again. It didn't work. The old man sighed and pushed them across the table. Sheila slowly pulled an evidence bag out of her satchel, placed them inside, then sealed and initialed it, as Hank wrote them a receipt. Then she set the bag on the floor. Out of sight. Because the subject needed changing. She looked at Hank. That was fair. She'd done the heavy lifting with that topic. It was his turn. He leaned forward and put his elbows on the table.

'There is one other thing we need to mention.'

They both stared at him, clearly wishing he would just shut up and go away.

'One of the dogs found something else.'

Darlene rolled her eyes. 'You telling me there's an access point we don't know about?'

'No. I'm telling you there's a human skeleton on your property. What do you know about that?'

FOURTEEN

[Orchestral music]

Many elements brought terror to a certain swath of territory near the Missouri–Arkansas border during the Civil War. The law had largely left the area to Union and Confederate forces, and they largely left the region lawless. Depending on which way the war tide was turning, one side or the other would sweep through, 'foraging' crops, livestock and supplies from the area's residents. Partisan militias – often no more than bands of thieves – were next, stealing everything they could from the women, children and elderly who populated the home front while able-bodied men were at war. In fact, one historian calls the White River watershed area arguably the 'most guerrilla infested area of the entire Civil War.'

Bolin joined the pillaging in the early 1860s, when he was barely out of his teens. Born about thirty miles northwest of Forsyth, Bolin knew the land well and used that to his advantage. He knew every nook and cranny. And boulder. He and nameless cohorts eventually laid claim to not only Murder Rocks, but to the surrounding countryside as well.

In addition to stealing property, he also had no qualms about taking lives. And again, the only people left in the stony hills and shady hollows were those least likely to be a threat. He murdered an old man who was delivering food to neighborhood women and children. He shot and killed a twelve-year-old boy who was carrying corn to feed his horse. Other men also fell to his bullets, so many that the full count has never been known. He once bragged he murdered nineteen. Another account claims he killed forty.

Whether one of those is accurate or if instead the truth falls somewhere in between, Bolin was still an outlaw who engaged in a campaign of wanton killing and theft – one that continues to horrify and fascinate one hundred and sixty years later. We here at *Hidden Hoards* have pulled together every source we can find and come up with a list of what we think was stolen from innocent travelers, who were the ones most likely to own valuables. Residents of the area tended to have only consumable goods – horses, flour, clothing; items that wouldn't survive a century and a half in the woods. Travelers also were more likely to write to others about their misadventures.

[Chiming music]
I was relieved of my pocket watch as well as a golden locket I had been safekeeping for my sister. I was also beat about the head until they grew weary of their fun and let me go.

The guerrillas threw me against the huge boulders they had hidden behind before they ambushed us. Miss Katherine was knocked from the wagon and her skirts searched in the most abusing fashion. They found her jewelry sewn into a pocket there and her mama's jewelry sewn in another one. Why were we not warned beforehand that this road was infested with thieves?

My husband said that we were Southerners born and returning after being driven out of Springfield by neighbors who side with the Union. They said they did not care. Then they took the wagon and the horses and all the family silver. It took us fifteen days and the charity of many who share our allegiance to make it all the way on foot to our destination in Arkansas. Who could have known that of all those things, the horses would be the most valuable?

We were dirty and tired and not as alert as we should have been. They surprised us completely, so that we stood struck dumb as they surrounded us. The leader was tall and fierce and void of mercy. Stanton, who joined our party in Berryville, reached for his revolver and this thief who had his already drawn did fire at the good man and kill him. If we had been dumb before, we were a graveyard quiet now. They stripped us of every precious item and ran into the trees laughing. Poor Stanton lay dead at my feet.
[Chiming music]

The body count goes up. And the plunder does, too. More to come, Hidden Hoarders. We'll be right back.

*   *   *

'Well, it's not ours.'

They all stared at Darlene. They were talking about a skeleton, not litter left along a highway. The woman realized this, and her weathered white face turned very pink. Sheila tried not to laugh.

'What I meant was, we don't know anything about it.'

Sheila stayed quiet. She'd let Hank, with his confounding ability to remain patient in the face of obstinacy, take the lead. She slid her gaze over to Old Man Fackrell. Who looked more thoughtful than indignant.

'How old is it?' His raspy voice cut through Hank and Darlene's back-and-forth.

'We don't know yet,' Hank said. 'It's going to take some time to figure that out.'

If only it'd been on the park land. Then they could've waited to tell these people until they knew what the bones were – Civil War-old and not a pressing issue, or recent and an urgent problem. But the skeleton was on their property, so that forced her and Hank to divulge its existence so they could get permission to keep excavating. Leo asked for her map, and Sheila slid it across the table with a point at the last hand-drawn dot.

'As you can see, it's fairly close to Murder Rocks,' she said.

'Which is not on our property,' Darlene ground out through gritted teeth.

'But folks do cut through your land to get to the rocks,' Sheila said.

'Yes, they do.' Leo let go of the map and laid his hand over his wife's. Then he rose to his feet. 'And we appreciate you keeping this latest round of people away from the area. You'll let us know when you're done?'

Sheila thought she took the dismissal well. She only marginally exaggerated her limp on the way out and took the porch steps at the speed of a tortoise, when she could've taken them at the speed of molasses.

'You're incorrigible,' Hank said when they were back in the squad car.

'I don't like somebody else deciding when a conversation's over. You know that.'

'Yes, I do.'

They drove in silence for a while. 'I don't like that he didn't give us the World War Two Walther.'

Hank looked at her. 'Me, either. But if we'd pushed . . .'

'Yeah. He could've decided not to give us anything. Better to take what we could get and get the hell out.'

'And if on the slim chance ballistics finds that the bullet in our shooting victim came from something like that, then we'll have grounds for a warrant.'

Her gaze slid over him. 'Yeah. It'd be an easy sell, if we went to Judge Sedstone.'

He kept his eyes on the road and said nothing. But she could see his fingers tighten on the steering wheel. She decided to poke the bear. 'The new lady isn't bad, but she's pulling all the crap cases, and it's filling up her whole calendar. So she doesn't have enough time for me and I gotta wait. Longer than I'm used to.'

His knuckles were still white against the black wheel. 'It's good for her. To get trained by you.'

'Oh, I agree. And I'm happy to do it. Ain't nobody else going to do it right. But. That doesn't mean every time. There are occasions when speed and experience take precedence.'

'You're not asking, are you?'

'Nope. Just letting you know my intentions. Unless you got something to tell me that explains your thinking?'

She really did want to know. She wanted him to put it into words. Because maybe then he'd get over it. It'd been three months since his mother-in-law's natural death was reclassified as a murder, and as far as she could tell, things were still not healing in the Worth household. And the issue with Sedstone – whatever it was – was linked to that whole sorry business. If he put the judge work issue into words, maybe that progress would ripple into his other, more significant problems at home.

She looked over at him and waited. He calmly steered the cruiser toward Forsyth without saying a word. But his hand stayed tight on the wheel.

Hank closed the book and looked at his sleepy children. He had Sheila to thank for this. She'd insisted on writing up the Fackrell interview report, so Hank could get home in time to read the kids their bedtime story.

'I'm sad this is the last book,' Maribel said. They'd zipped through all the Percy Jackson novels on the strength of their begging for 'just one extra chapter' every night.

'Next we can do ones with the Roman gods,' Benny said. 'They have monsters, too.'

Hank looked at his five-year-old. 'How do you know about Roman gods?'

'There's Greek and there's Roman. Everybody knows that,' Maribel said.

That explained who told Benny, at least. Hank straightened from his slouch on the bed and slid the book back on the shelf. 'Actually, I've been thinking about it. And there are books that have gods from other places that I thought we could try.'

They both stared at him, unblinking. Finally, Maribel spoke. 'Why?'

'What do you mean, why? There's more to the world than the Mediterranean. Let's read something to do with your cultural heritage.'

Benny scoffed. 'There's no gods for Scotland.'

How had he fallen down on the job so badly? He tried to keep the irritation out of his voice. 'You do have another side of the family besides your McCleary grandfather.'

'You mean Gramps? He's from California. Are there gods there?'

Hank wasn't going to touch that one. Before he could deflect, Maribel did it for him.

'No, Benny, he means where Gramps's family came from. Like long ago,' Maribel said.

'Ooh, are they Vikings? There's lots of Viking gods.'

Hank pictured his balding, soft-spoken father, whose weapons had only ever been his wit and his garden tools. 'No, he's not a Viking.'

'Then where?' Benny said.

'I don't know. England, maybe? That's not what I'm getting at. I'm talking about Mexico.'

'Oh. Abuela?'

'Yes. Your abuela's family is from Mexico. Which has lots of ancient gods and myths.'

They both looked extremely skeptical. Hank levered himself off the low bed and stomped out of the room. He returned with his laptop and plopped down in between the two of them. 'Here's a world map. Look. Greece. Rome. Right next to each other. Practically the same. Now look over here.' He pointed at the Yucatán Peninsula. 'This had the Maya. And up here were the Aztecs. Nice and different from what we've just read. I looked it up. There's a whole series about it, just like the Percy Jackson books. It'll be exciting.'

They looked across his lap at each other.

'Nah. We'll go with the Romans,' Maribel said.

'Excuse me?'

'We vote for Romans,' Benny said.

'This is not a democracy.' He somehow sounded incredulous and weary at the same time.

Benny got in his stubborn cross-armed stance, and Maribel took on the expression her mother used when she was about to confront someone with the incontrovertible logic of a situation.

'It's our bedtime. We should get to pick the stories.'

Dammit. He snapped the laptop shut. 'We can talk about this later.'

He briskly tucked them both in and trudged out to the living room, where he found Maggie laughing.

'You were listening?'

'Si, señor. You got outvoted.'

He grumbled as he put the laptop on the coffee table and sat down.

'They're little. Familiar is good. Maybe when you're done with the Roman series, they'll be in the mood for the Latin American one.'

'I didn't say yes to the Romans.'

She looked at him like Maribel had. 'Honey, they actually agreed on something. You can't toss that aside.'

He grunted. 'We'll see.'

She took his hand. 'You know I'm not discounting your point. It's totally important that they know where your mom's family comes from. That they understand that part of themselves.' She thought for a moment. 'Maybe we could go up to that international street fair in Springfield next month. I think it'll have some Mexican businesses and culture organizations.'

He looked at her. She was trying. He was trying. The counseling was helping. The wounds left by Marian and her death might be starting to heal. He kissed the back of her hand. 'Gracias.'

FIFTEEN

The poor Bronco sat in the mechanic's garage, engine parts half-removed as the hood gaped open at Sam Karnes.

'What do you mean you don't know what's wrong?'

The guy stopped working the rag over his fingers and looked at him. 'It's a thirty-six-year-old car. It's not gonna go forever.'

'The last time it wouldn't start, you fixed it in three days.'

'The last time was the alternator, bro. Easy. This time, could be any bunch of things. And all of them would take a ton of cash to fix.' He clucked his tongue. 'Scratch that. Any of them would take a ton of cash. All of them – that'd cost you more than the price of a decent used car. Definitely cost you more than this thing is worth.'

Sam did not appreciate him referring to his Bronco as a 'thing.' Brenna sensed him tense and gave him a consoling pat on the arm. Or maybe it was a restraining pat. He was getting pretty irked. 'Those are awfully vague estimates. Can you give me some actual numbers?'

The guy sighed and stopped just short of rolling his eyes. He led them into the little office, which smelled even more strongly of motor oil than the main garage did, and jabbed at a laptop for a while. Then he gave Sam a number that ended with a smirk and too many zeros. Brenna barely got him out of there before he told the guy where he could stick it.

'How am I going to get it out of there?' he said once they were back in Brenna's Toyota. He stared through the windshield at it, all lonely and broken-looking. He'd already paid a second tow truck to bring it here from his house. He couldn't afford to have it taken anywhere else.

Brenna took a deep breath. 'I don't know if you're going to be able to, babe. The only way it's going to drive out of here is if it gets fixed. And that estimate was a lot of money. That much would almost cover a new car. Well, a newer used car, anyway.'

She was being so gentle about it that it was taking all the starch out of him. His shoulders started to slump and his fists uncurled. She reached over and held one of his chapped, sunburned hands.

'I know this isn't good timing. Like, at all. You worked all weekend out at that scene in the woods, and now this on a Monday morning. I get it. But we'll be OK. We can carpool and look around for a good deal on a used car. All right?'

He looked over at the garage again. Nobody was going to give him a loan to repair a circa 1980s Bronco. But they would give him a loan to buy a used car. Hopefully. He turned so he was looking straight at Brenna and couldn't see the Bronco anymore.

'I can come back later and get your stuff out of it,' she said.

He nodded. They pulled away and he couldn't help one last glance back. Then he faced forward and tried to focus on the future.

The forensic pathologist's report contained no surprises, thank the good Lord. Sheila scrolled through the PDF from Dr Ngozi Aguta, who the counties of southwestern Missouri kept managing to keep. She'd started three months ago on emergency assignment after the badly timed combination of a multi-fatality explosion and the death of the long-time medical examiner. She hadn't been – and still wasn't – quite finished with her education. No locals cared. She was already ten times more competent and twenty times better-liked than her deceased predecessor.

Some law enforcement heavyweights, including Hank, had started in on both the state medical regulatory agency and the University of Missouri, convincing both that she should be allowed to finish in an off-campus, on-the-job capacity. They pitched it like a fellowship. Just that instead of a sought-after one at a busy urban coroner's office, it'd be cobbled together at a semi-slow rural office that couldn't attract anyone else. Aguta, no fool and eager to run her own shop, said yes immediately. The agency and the university relented on a month-to-month basis, probably thinking the cops and prosecutors would get tired of the effort involved. Instead, the numbers had grown, and now every county sheriff in the region was on board. That, Sheila knew, was because once you got an Aguta report, you were ruined for any other doctor.

Her examination of the gunshot victim showed that he was white, twenty-five to thirty years old, seventy-one inches tall, approximately 170 pounds, and the owner – luckily – of several tattoos. He had a perimortem cut on his cheek and a bullet in his chest. The nine-millimeter caliber bullet had nicked the descending thoracic aorta and caused massive hemorrhaging. It and a shell casing recovered by Alice in the clearing where Roscoe the dog first stopped were now with the State Highway Patrol crime lab for ballistics testing. The hatchet had stayed here. Alice went over every inch of it, and then Kurt did it again. Neither found any fingerprints. It was a brand available at several major retailers. It was fifteen inches long, which was ridiculously excessive for the kind of minimum-level camping skill required on Fackrell's land. But if whoever packed it into those woods was anything like Mingo Culver, then it made perfect sense. Another newbie with more money than know-how, outfitting himself in the best gear. It weighed two and a half pounds, so could be handled by an adult of almost any size, at least in a short, frenzied burst.

Which led Sheila to Aguta's second report. It was a lot longer. Due to the frenzied burst. Seventeen wounds of varying depths, from shallow slices to the deep and fatal one on the neck. Many of the others were on the forearms – defensive wounds. There was a large one on the upper left arm. Was that the first blow? Before this unknown man had a chance to get his arms up in a futile effort to shield himself? He was an Asian male, between fifty and fifty-five years old, 220 pounds and seventy inches tall, with black hair and no tattoos.

Both men had died either Sunday or Monday. And neither man's fingerprints were in any database. Sheila sighed and shut the computer file. She hated that her main hope rested on rental car agencies lackadaisically checking whether they'd signed out a vehicle that fit Fackrell's vague sedan description. She checked her email. No responses. Next came her squishy stress ball, which she kneaded into a dense glob because not only were car agencies not replying, Victor Hardwick wasn't either.

She pulled up the *Hidden Hoards* web page. She'd already left three messages on the show contact form, asking to speak with 'world traveler, thrill seeker, and fortune hunter Vic Hardwick.' In response, she'd gotten auto-generated offers for a discount on show merchandise. Everything was slapped with the show logo, a silhouette of the tall, lean Hardwick with a shovel in one hand and a leg propped up on a treasure chest. She knew it was his outline because his tall and lean picture was plastered everywhere else on the website. Him, diving in the Mediterranean, hacking through a jungle in Central America, and holding doubloons in the Caribbean.

The website was her only avenue, because she wasn't getting

anywhere with a nationwide search that matched the specifics she needed. She'd found multiple Victor Hardwicks, but one was a child, two were elderly nursing home residents, and another was an insurance salesman in Omaha who swore he'd never left the state of Nebraska. She had messages out to the others, including a promising fifty-three-year-old in Phoenix and a forty-nine-year-old in Portland. Neither had a social media presence, so she couldn't see if either of their photos matched the podcast's Hardwick – with his chiseled, fifty-ish face, wavy hair just starting to go from pepper to salt, and ropey muscles that showed he knew a lot more about the outdoors than his doughy listeners. At least the one alive and two dead Sheila had encountered so far. She thought about that and then quickly dialed the phone.

'Mr Culver, I have a question for you.' She'd given Mingo permission to leave town on Thursday, once she had a signed statement and a promise to believe her warning that she'd come after him if he didn't go straight to his parents' house in Illinois and stay there. 'Do you have a minute?'

She heard him shut off what sounded like a video game. 'Yes, ma'am.'

'The electronics in your bag, that's recording equipment, correct?'

'Yeah. Why?'

'Why did you have it?'

'I was going to record finding the treasure.' He said it like the answer was obvious.

'Yes. I figured that. But then what were you going to do with the recording?'

'Oh. I see. I was going to try to get on the podcast.'

'On the Vic Hardwick podcast?'

'Yeah.'

'And how were you going to go about that?'

'I was going to offer it to him.'

This man-child was getting on her nerves again. 'How were you going to do that? Email him? Call him?'

There was a pause. She squeezed her stress ball and waited.

'I, um, was going to use the back door. It's an email address that goes straight to Vic.'

'Can I have that, please?'

'Um, well, it's private. I can't give it out.'

The stress ball hit the desk with a smack. 'How did you get it then?'

She could hear him moving around, agitated.

'There's a group. Kind of like a Subreddit. But private. Only by invitation. Because you don't want just anybody out looking for this kind of stuff.'

Wasn't that the truth. 'How did you get invited?'

'I got to know a guy named Charlie. We traded some intel on the Indiana pond treasure. That got me the invite.'

'How many people are in this group?'

He stopped moving. 'It's very exclusive.' She imagined him straightening with pride. 'There're only about a hundred.'

Sheila dropped her head in her hands. One hundred potential suspects. But, also, one hundred possible IDs for her two victims. That was a much smaller pool than small sedan car rentals. She raised her head. 'Do you have a list of these members?'

'I can't give you that.' He sounded offended and horrified at the same time.

Pulling out her own teeth would be easier than this conversation. She took a deep breath. Trying to get a warrant would take forever, because who knew what jurisdiction it'd be in or even what the group name was? She needed to play nice.

'OK. Then I need you to invite me to join.'

He snorted. 'You're not a treasure hunter.'

'I disagree. That's my whole job. I look for things that people have buried and want to keep hidden. That's what you do, right?'

Silence. She could practically hear the wheels turning.

'You are able to invite me to join, correct?'

More silence. Finally, 'It would be a betrayal.'

'Why? Is anyone doing anything illegal?'

The agitated moving started again.

'Look, I'm not interested in trespassing, or anything like that people might be talking about. I just need to find out who these two murder victims are. I'd just be a new member, observing the conversation.'

Eventually, Mingo's desire for Sheila to find other suspects and stop focusing on him outweighed his loyalty to people he'd never actually met. She kept him on the phone while he sent her the invitation. Only once she was approved did she say goodbye. Then she got to work.

SIXTEEN

Sheila stood in Hank's office doorway holding a stack of paper in each hand.

'Since you're the big boss, you get to pick. Car rentals or armchair treasure hunters.'

'Why do I get the feeling there's no right answer?'

'You would be correct. They're both grunt work. But that's where we're at.'

He thought carefully. He'd seen the mashed stress ball on her desk. 'I'll take the car rentals.'

That would leave her going after the podcast host, which he knew she was itching to do. Plus, with the car rentals, he could drive up to Springfield-Branson Airport and talk to folks in person. It was a good excuse to get out of the office.

She limped over and handed him the search warrant paperwork. Newbie Judge Havish had finally approved everything, so getting the information from the different rental companies shouldn't be a problem. He grabbed a notebook and headed out the door.

An hour drive and one drive-thru coffee later, he was arguing with a skinny, wispy bearded white kid who looked barely old enough to drive the cars he was renting out.

'Look, it says right here. On this official court-approved search warrant. The renter information and GPS tracking for any blue sedan with a non-Missouri license plate that was out on a rental between these dates.'

'What if they turned it back in on one of those dates?'

'I still want it.'

'What if they just picked it up that date?'

'I want that, too.'

'Well, what shade of blue?'

'All. The. Shades.'

'Oh.' He scratched his nose. 'That's probably a lot of information. I don't know how to do that.'

Hank had a feeling he'd been lied to. He sighed and waited for the dreaded words.

'You're going to have to talk to my manager.'

'You said you were the manager.'

'Uh, yeah. Just not for stuff that needs a password.'

That manager was at lunch. Hank gathered up his papers, gave the kid his best stone-faced cop look, and moved down to the next company.

'I don't like this.' The woman, whose name tag said Pauline, flipped her braids over her shoulder and crossed her arms over her ample chest.

'I'm sorry to take up your time.'

'I don't care about that. Ain't nothing else going on. What I don't like is you asking. It's people's privacy.'

'Yes, ma'am. Which is why we have a warrant. We're only asking for this very specific information. We're not just fishing around.'

Pauline raised her chin and eyed him skeptically. He pushed the warrant across the counter. He didn't want to press her. She was the only Black person he'd seen in the airport, and he was pretty sure her view of law enforcement probably wasn't positive. He thought for a minute.

'How about this? You look up everyone that meets these parameters. Then you look at the GPS data. If they never went near Branson, I don't need them, and you don't need to give them to me.'

She considered that and examined the warrant again. Then her fingers flew over her computer keyboard, and she let out a harrumph. 'We only got two as it is. A blue intermediate class Nissan Sentra, Wisconsin plates. And then a blue standard class. That one's a Volkswagen Jetta with Arkansas plates.'

'What do their GPS trackers say?'

More typing. The Sentra had gone west to Joplin. She swiveled her monitor around, with a hand over the name, so Hank could see. He nodded and confirmed he didn't need the renter's name. She turned it away again and called up the Jetta. She sucked at her teeth and pondered the search results. Hank tried to be patient. Finally, she turned the screen around.

The blue line headed straight south on Highway 65, directly to Branson. 'Can you Zoom in?'

She rolled her eyes and told him it was a multi-day rental. The data would be extensive and would need to be emailed to him. He whipped out a business card and slid it across the counter. 'Is the car still out? Or has it been returned?'

It wasn't due back until Wednesday, two days from now. She grudgingly handed over the renter's name and contact information. 'What you want him for, anyway?'

'I just need to know if he was in a particular area on that day. And whether he saw anything.'

'Fine. Don't tell me.'

He paused. 'It's a murder investigation. This driver might've been in a position to see something that will help us.' Or been in a location that incriminated him. Hank didn't say that, though. He watched as the woman entered his sheriff email address. He wasn't going to walk away until the GPS data landed in his inbox. Then he thanked her for putting up with him. That got him another harrumph.

By this point, every rental counter was aware of what he was doing. At the mention of the word 'homicide,' whispers started bubbling. One young woman darted into the back and emerged with an older man wearing a button-down shirt and tie instead of the standard-issue polo shirt. He headed there next, but they had no rentals that fit the parameters. Neither did any of the others, which led him back around to Wispy. The kid looked at him blankly until Hank asked for the manager – the one who knew the passwords.

'You got a warrant?' She was the same size as the Volkswagen lady, but so pale that the only color to her was the red polo shirt and a fresh barbecue sauce smudge on her cheek.

'Yes, ma'am.' He pulled out all the paperwork again.

She squinted at it. 'That's some kinda needle you're trying to thread.'

That was a very good way to put it. 'Can you help me out?'

She blew her white-blonde bangs out of her face. 'Sure. Let's see what I got.'

She had one. A blue Toyota Corolla with Michigan plates. It was rented the Saturday before last, the day after the podcast aired. It had been driven down to Branson and was returned Tuesday, the day before the bodies were found. It hadn't been checked out since. Hank told himself not to get his hopes up.

'I'm going to need to take a look.'

She tapped the papers. 'That is not covered in this warrant.'

He sighed. It had been worth a shot. 'Can you show it to me? I'm allowed to look at the outside.'

He was also allowed to impound it. Which was exactly what he did once he'd walked around it in the parking lot. He hadn't drilled into the street-level GPS data yet, but the dates matched too closely for him not to want to search it. He retrieved crime scene tape from his cruiser and sealed the Corolla. The manager stuck to his side the whole time.

'Is this the only airport you're looking at?'

'That depends. If we find what we need here, we won't need anything else. If we don't, we'll need these same warrants for Kansas City and St. Louis. Maybe even farther.'

She caught the unspoken *I hope not* in his comment and smiled. 'It'd be kind of cool if it was our car.' They started walking back to the terminal. 'Do you still want the GPS?'

'Yes, please. And all of the renter's information.' Then he could ask Havish for a warrant specifically for this particular vehicle.

'Then a judge will approve an actual search?' she asked.

'Yeah. We'll try to get everything done quickly so you can rent out the car again.'

'Oh, I don't care about that.' She blushed. 'I'm just interested in the process.'

He looked at her questioningly.

'I want to be a lawyer. I'm at Missouri State right now. Getting my undergrad in poli sci.'

Her name was Marcie and she was using her divorce settlement to go back to school. Pauline had talked her into it.

'Pauline from the next counter down?'

'Yep. She's a year ahead of me.'

Hank chuckled. The skeptical Pauline had the makings of a very good attorney. He thanked them both and went back out to his cruiser with printouts and emails and a pastry from the grab-and-go deli by the security checkpoint. He called up the emails on the car's laptop. The GPS data showed that both sedans had been in the vicinity of Fackrell's property. If you were an ordinary tourist, there was absolutely no reason for you to be that far south of Branson. If you were a treasure tourist, on the other hand, then it was exactly where you wanted to be. He went to the Jetta's rental agreement. Stanley Womack was a forty-two-year-old white male with a Colorado license. The photo showed a pudgy man with glasses and a goatee. Hank copied down the man's cell phone number from the rental form.

Then he pulled up the Corolla's paperwork. Philip Garvan was a twenty-seven-year-old white man with tousled dark blond hair.

Hank stared at the photo. This one would be easy to find. He was currently in Dr Aguta's morgue.

'Who returned the car?' He leaned on the counter and stared at a startled Marcie. She nervously called up the record on her terminal as everyone at the other car companies pretended not to watch.

'It was just dropped off. You can just drop and go. We give you a receipt and you're on your way.'

Nice. So not only was the poor man dead in the woods at the time of return, his credit card was still on the hook for the bill. 'So nobody signed anything?'

She shook her head.

'Which employee checked the car in?'

She sighed and jabbed a finger at Wispy, who was leaning against the back wall. 'Wendell.'

Wendell, it turned out, had no memory of anything longer ago than breakfast. He certainly didn't remember one short transaction six days ago. And neither of them remembered how many people were with Philip Garvan when he checked out the vehicle. Hank pushed away from the counter and regrouped.

'Where are the surveillance cameras?'

He heard a harrumph off to his left.

'I know I need another warrant, Pauline. I just want to get a sense of whether what I ask for is going to be any good.'

Employees from every counter pitched in, gesturing and explaining to the point where Hank had a pretty good idea of what angles he would see. There was more murmuring and whispering – how exciting to help catch a killer. That got an outright scoff from Pauline. 'He ain't asking because he figured out the dude was a killer in the last ten minutes from when he left to when he came running back in. Get real. He asking because he figured something else out that quick.' She went quiet, wielding the pause like a calligraphic flourish. 'Bet you the renter is the murder victim.'

Silence dropped like a blanket. Everyone stared at her except Hank, who acted busy counting cameras. She waved airily at nothing in particular. 'That's the only thing that'd have him back in here like his pants are on fire.'

They all looked at Hank. He looked at Pauline. There'd be no way he could keep the victim's identity under wraps now. Even if he refused to confirm it, they'd still all spread Garvan's name to every neighbor and news crew they met. She smiled back at him.

'I can't say for sure. We'll need to do some more investigating before we can confirm anything.'

She rolled her eyes. He grinned in spite of himself. 'Thank you for your help. And your pushback.'

She looked at him in surprise.

'You're going to make a good lawyer.'

Her harrumph was drowned out by Marcie's laughter as he left, hurrying out to his car. He needed to get the judge on the phone before she left work for the day.

SEVENTEEN

The third time Sheila's phone beeped, she swore and finally looked at it. Then swore again.

'I'm so sorry. I completely forgot we had an appointment.'

Prosecutor Malcolm Oberholz laughed. 'That's fine. It's not like you're on a porch swing drinking tea or something. I know you're back at work.'

'And we've got a homicide investigation. Well, actually two homicides. No, wait. Three.'

'What now? Just in the week since we last talked?'

'Yeah.' It came out sounding like a resigned sigh.

'I can't believe I haven't heard anything. Usually our TV news loves that kind of stuff.'

'Eh, none of them have really made the news yet, thank goodness. Just the local paper. And honestly, we don't even know if one of them is ours.' She told him about the skeleton. And then had to wait until he finished laughing.

'So it could be a hundred-and-fifty-year-old murder? Good luck with that.'

She didn't dignify that with a response.

'And it's honest-to-God called Murder Rocks?'

'Yes.'

'Huh. Your area becomes more and more interesting, the more I learn.'

'What do you mean by that?'

He laughed again, only this time it was sharp and rueful. 'I filed the change of venue motion. We already have a court date.'

Sheila was shocked. Court hearings were never scheduled that quickly. But things had come together, Oberholz said in a wry tone that said more about his skepticism than his words did. A judge had been found. Lanton Decker was from a county in the Bootheel, the region of the state that jutted out from the southeastern corner right up against the Mississippi River. It was as rural as Branson County, with its largest city no bigger than Branson itself, which meant the whole area probably had the same entrenched, inter-generational politics and favoritism that her county did. And this judge would be right at home with that kind of jury pool. Oberholz had hoped for an urban judge, who'd likely be more inclined to move the trial away from an insular community. The prosecutor desperately wanted a city jury. Twelve people living in the two-million-strong Kansas City metro area likely wouldn't give any deference to a defendant who was a county commissioner's son. Twelve people from a rural county sure would make note of it.

The hearing was scheduled for later in the week.

'No judge can clear his calendar that fast. What's going on?'

'He just retired. So he's not anciently old, but he is free, and clear, and quote "happy to come right on over," end quote.'

Sheila groaned.

'Oh, I'm not done,' he said. 'It seems that one of your county judges has volunteered his courtroom for as long as needed. Which would make it easy to have the trial here. Not that such things factor into judicial decisions or anything.' Again the wry, razor-sharp tone.

'Was it Marvin Sedstone?'

'Yeah. You know him?' He paused. 'Sorry, stupid question. You know everybody. That's half the reason why we're in this situation.'

She did know all the county judges. But Sedstone had become different. And she didn't know why. Ever since the Hank mother-in-law fiasco, he'd had Sheila handle all warrants and other court business and avoid Sedstone whenever possible. And it went the other direction, too. She'd heard through the grapevine that Sedstone was declining to take cases where Hank would need to testify. She wondered if Sedstone's courtroom offer meant that he was now extending whatever-this-feud-was to her by making it easy for this country judge to come to town. She hoped not. The hill was going to be steep enough without other powerful people joining the fight to keep her from climbing it.

'I'm not going to some sketchy car dealer out on Seventy-six.' Sam wished he'd ignored the knock on the door. Now he had Brenna's brother in his tiny living room, jocular and insistent and taking up all the space with his broad shoulders and floppy blond hair. Sam quickly stepped over to the coffee table and shut his laptop.

'No, no, bro. Don't be looking online. You got to go see stuff. Look a car in the eye.'

Corey Cassidy was three years older than Brenna and was the

family fix-it man. He knew everybody and had a guy for any situation. Including, apparently, a friend at one of the lots on Highway 76 east of Lake Taneycomo. He was at least easier to be with than Kyle, the reserved and studious oldest, who took his job as a big brother seriously. As in keep-a-close-and-skeptical-eye-on-little-sister's-boyfriend seriously.

'I was thinking that I'd go up to Springfield. They've got lots of used-car places. Bigger selection. Thanks, though.'

He looked at the front door, which was still open to the mild autumn day. Corey ignored the hint. Sam glanced at his laptop and wished Brenna wasn't at work. Or that he was at work. Either one. Because apparently wanting Corey to leave was not a wish that would be granted.

'So thanks for stopping by and—'

'OK. Then we'll hit the Springfield dealerships. We just gotta stop and get gas before we head up there.'

'Wait, what? Now?' He scrambled for an excuse. 'I've got other stuff to do, so—'

'Nah. What's more important than new wheels? Let's hit the road.'

The next thing Sam knew, he was folding his tall form into the passenger seat of Corey's Camero and speeding north on Highway 65 to Springfield with its used-car mega-stores and bona fide name-brand car dealerships. He spent the drive frantically doing calculations in his head, trying to figure out how much of a loan he could afford to take out. It was a careful analysis he'd just started thinking about when Corey showed up. He studied the guy out of the corner of his eye. He was the opposite of his lithe and willowy sister. He'd been on the wrestling team in high school and had the compact, muscular physique to prove it. It was a form that fit his personality. He barreled through life as a cheerful glad-hander. It wasn't a bad thing, just definitely not something Sam could easily relate to. He looked away and did some more addition. The sums didn't add up, no matter what he did. He was going to have to hope for more loan approval than he deserved.

They pulled into a pre-owned superstore and were surrounded before Corey even turned off the engine. Was the gentleman interested in selling? Did he want to discuss a trade-in? There were incredible deals to be found all over the lot. Corey winked at him and got out of the car. He did want to find out how much they might give him for the Camero. What kind of deals were they offering?

Sam sat there for a second before realizing that Corey was deliberately giving him an escape hatch. He took it, slipping away down a row of nondescript sedans. He headed over to the SUVs, looked at the sticker prices and turned right back around. A sedan it would be. Or maybe a little hatchback. Hah. He and Brenna could have matching cars. Corey would never let him live it down. He looked across the cars at the guy, who had two salespeople laughing and another one tapping away furiously on an iPad. He wandered through the cars and stopped with a sigh in front of a tan Toyota Camry, the woeful embodiment of what he was losing with the death of his Bronco. Individuality, style, headroom. And where would he put his hunting gear?

Suddenly Corey and a salesman were next to him and offering a test drive. A half-hour later, Sam handed back the keys and trudged back to the Camero. Corey gave him a slap on the shoulder. 'Let's try the next place, man.'

It was going to be a long day.

There appeared to be two kinds of weirdos. Armchair treasure hunters, and folks who were basically preppers. They'd be busy preparing for the apocalypse if they hadn't stumbled onto this obsession first. Sheila was sorting all the screen names into each type, with an obvious interest in the latter category. The number of them had exploded with this second season of *Hidden Hoards*. Why couldn't Victor Hardwick have stayed in the Mediterranean or the Caribbean or some other foreign body of crystal-blue water? Instead he was featuring domestic places inexpensively accessible by car or plane. And Americans like *LegendaryFinds02* were gleefully clambering right over those low barriers. *Only a ten-hour drive! This one might be worth looking into. Anybody know who owns the land?*

She cackled at the responses, all from armchairs.

There are such things as plat maps.

The history is as important as the objects. Read, study, then search. Or if your goal is to experience the Ozark backwoods in all their glory, then it sounds like you've achieved the proper level of preparation.

Way to do your homework. You do know you're going to need more than a shovel, right?

This was turning out to be much more entertaining than she'd expected. She scrolled down.

Heading to Branson tomorrow for the Bolin hoard. Supposed to be heavy woods. Taking all camping and survival gear – FoundIt72. That was posted on Tuesday, the day Mingo Culver walked out of the woods. Sheila swung her gaze over to her second computer monitor and pulled up a list of the deluded drivers stopped at the roadblocks that had been in place since Wednesday. The staff overtime was killing her budget, but there was no getting around it. The hunters wouldn't stop coming. She looked at the names from Wednesday and Thursday, and saw that a Cheryl Maclin from central Virginia, with a birth date in 1972, had been stopped at 07:52 on Thursday with a car visibly packed with equipment. Sheila jotted that down as a possible match of real name to screen alias and kept going.

As she read further and the divide between the two factions became even more apparent, she began to give Mingo more credit. The kid was a genuine combination of both the armchairs and the preppers, and that seemed like a rare thing. She wondered if there were any more like him. After a half-hour, she hadn't found any, but she had three more matches and a new name from Hank to concentrate on.

'You're kidding. You ID'd the hatchet victim?'

Hank explained what he'd found. Her email pinged as he forwarded her the rental agreements for both blue sedans.

'I got the search warrant for Philip Garvan's rental car,' said Hank, clearly still at the airport based on the jet engine roar she heard in the background. 'Now I'm just waiting for Kurt to get here with the evidence van.'

'Did you get a warrant for the surveillance video?'

'I've requested it with Judge Havish. But we still need ones for Garvan's phone records, credit cards, all of those things.'

Sheila was already jotting things down. 'So this other blue car – it's not the one Leo Fackrell saw.'

'I don't know. According to the rental company GPS, the Jetta was in that vicinity on Sunday. Not right where Leo said, but close.'

'And this Womack guy hasn't returned the car?'

'It's due back in two days. GPS says he's still in Branson. We need to get to him before he leaves. I've told the rental employees to call if he turns the car in, but there's no guarantee they will, or that he'll stay until we get there.'

Sheila looked at her current staffing levels, carefully marked on the white board hanging across from her desk. There was no one to spare. There never was. 'I'll figure it out.'

She reluctantly put aside her entertaining chat-room research and gathered the information she'd need. Then, since asking in person was always faster, she grabbed her cane and hobbled over to the courthouse. But the new judge, Delia Havish, was in the middle of a hearing with two elderly litigants warbling at her as their attorneys did paperwork. Sheila was not going to wait through that, no matter what Hank wanted. She backed out of the courtroom and walked down the hall.

'Ms Chief Deputy, how nice to see you.' Judge Marv Sedstone rose to his feet and came around his huge wood desk to shake her hand. He had the good sense not to pull out a chair for her, however. They both sat and she handed over her paperwork. Ten minutes later she stopped talking and Sedstone let out a low whistle. Then he mulled it over. He always did when she requested search warrants. She knew to be patient. She looked around his chambers as she waited. Most things were the same as they'd been for the eighteen years she'd been coming to see him – the antique fishing rods on the same wall as his ancient diplomas, the bookshelves crammed with legal reference material most people would just look up online, the George Brett autographed baseball bat shadow-boxed on its own special table opposite the window. His old leather desk chair had changed, though, replaced with a hulking ergonomic throne. And the family photos were different. There was a new one of his wife on his desk, and a recent one of the two of them on a beach somewhere.

He must be almost seventy by now. She wondered how much longer he'd keep working. And she wondered, again, why the hell Hank was suddenly steering well clear of him.

'All right, ma'am.' He leaned forward and peered at her from underneath his shaggy white eyebrows. 'I'll grant you all but this one. I don't see that you've got probable cause to access this Mr Womack's phone records. You haven't even talked to him yet.'

She'd figured that request was a long shot. But now the judge had the warrant, so if Womack became a solid suspect, she was a step ahead in getting the darn thing approved. Sedstone raised an eyebrow. 'I do know what you're up to. And I'll keep it right here for easy access when you bring me better information.'

She nodded graciously. She always did enjoy sparring with him.

He signed the documents with his usual flourish and wished her a successful investigation. She could tell it took all he had not to help her to her feet. Once she was standing, it occurred to her to take advantage of his discomfort.

'And thank you for loaning your courtroom to that out-of-town judge. Although it'll certainly be strange seeing someone else in your seat.'

He chuckled. She couldn't tell if it was forced, or if she was shading in meaning that wasn't there.

'Just trying to be helpful. You know, show a little Branson hospitality.'

She managed a smile and walked out of his chambers. Hospitality was certainly not a word she'd choose when talking about this place. She had a feeling Philip Garvan wouldn't have, either.

EIGHTEEN

[Orchestral music]

Welcome back to *Hidden Hoards*. In the early days of the Civil War, Alf Bolin and his gang were unstoppable. They owned the whole portion of the Missouri–Arkansas border area. As you've heard, possession of anything valuable put your life at risk. And resistance was met with fatal force. So why would people be foolish enough to resist? One reason was plain, old-fashioned communication. Or rather, the lack thereof. If you were fleeing the army of one side or the other, you might not have been lucky enough to hear about the villain who lay in wait on one of the roads from Springfield down into Arkansas. When you were stopped, you might think that his gang's guns were just for show. Or that you could easily get away by firing your own weapons, which was often true of other brigands. But Bolin was too experienced and too ruthless for that. And so people died.

Eventually, the region's makeshift authorities decided something needed to be done.

Brigadier General Lyon,

In my report dated the ninth of last month, I did describe our search for the bushwhacker Bolin. As of yesterday I have additional news to convey that I believe will sway you to grant me more men with which I may hunt down these guerrillas. We had ridden south from our garrison in Springfield and did come across a young boy digging graves. He related that the man he had just laid in the ground was his grandfather, shot by Bolin for the corn he was delivering to widows in the area. This boy could not have been more than ten years of age and was now the only male in the entire area of a dozen meager farms. Leaving these people with no protection and no hope will ultimately work against our cause, I believe.

While Bolin has shown no limits on which partisans he will attack, be it Northern or Southern, there are rumors he has

Confederate sympathies. I believe we can take advantage of that. If I may request a meeting when you arrive in Springfield next week, I will explain my thinking. Until then, respectfully yours,
    Capt. Jeremiah Waller

There was another reason authorities were worried. And another reason why travelers resisted. Because they had things worth protecting. Mary Louise Finnegan again:

Tommy hid behind the overturned wagon and started yelling in a most fearsome way. The horses were screaming in fright, as was Mother. Father had been knocked dumb and lay on his side in the dirt. Billy and I tried to unharness the horses, but they thrashed and kicked and we didn't succeed. The robbers leaped on the gold that was spilling from the sacks. Tommy fired a shot to warn them off. To this day, I wish he had not. The gold was not ours to begin with. It would not have been ours at the end of the journey either. To fight for it was foolish . . .

[Clattering metal, gunshots]
. . . I suppose it was also instinct. We were under attack, after all. And Tommy always was the one to stand fearless. He was that way even when we were young. He would catch copperhead snakes in the woods and fight the schoolboys who pulled my hair when I was little. He was the kind who would jump and then look, brave to the point of imprudence. Which made him charming and fun. Can you tell I adored him? I knew that he planned to join the Union Army once we reached Springfield. I was preparing myself for that and the horrible possibility of his injury or death. But to experience it that day in front of my own eyes, I still cannot find the words for it. What I thought might only happen much further in the future, and in a distant place, instead came true within a stone's throw of myself and for no good reason. And then my precious brother was gone. Shot in the heart and in the head. And the rest of us did also die just as surely that day, whether we lived on or not.

We'll be right back, after this message . . .

The pizza boxes were in the front seat and the kids were in the back. One set smelled great. The other did not.

'Did you guys have PE today?'

'I did,' Benny said. 'It's my favorite thing about kindergarten so far.'
Hank looked in the rearview mirror and saw Maribel roll her
eyes. The experienced first-grader. He hid a smile and asked about
the after-school playdate at Marc Thompson's house. Benny spent
the rest of the ride home extolling the virtues of Marc's toy closet
and his mom's fully stocked pantry. Maribel just hugged her
backpack and looked out the window.

They pulled up to their dark house and clattered from the garage
through the mud room and into the kitchen. The pizza went on
paper plates and he forced a few baby carrots on each of them.

'You know, Mommy at least gives us real dishes,' Maribel said.
'And Grandpop would actually cook us dinner.'

She didn't sound angry. Just sad. Which made Hank feel even
worse. He gave her a kiss on the head as he cleared the table and sent
them off to take showers. Then they all sat on Benny's bed for the
very last chapter of the last Percy Jackson book. Benny fell asleep
halfway through, which meant they'd have to read it again tomorrow.
Maribel sighed at that and trudged across the hall to her room. She
got into bed and curled up facing the wall. Hank sat down and smoothed
back her long, brown hair. 'How was Marc Thompson's house, really?'

'It sucked. Why couldn't I go to Vanessa's?'

'Because you both went to Vanessa's yesterday.' And he and
Maggie needed to spread out the imposition they placed on their
friends. Or find daycare. He shuddered. The expense would kill
them. He didn't know how people managed it. 'I'm sure you'll be
able to go to her house after school again next week.'

She sniffled. 'I miss Grandpop.'

'I know, my little bug.' He thought about what to say that would
be honest. His precious girl deserved at least that. 'It's really different
around here without him, isn't it?'

She nodded without turning. Another sniffle. 'Do you miss him,
too?'

And there it was. His hand was still on her head. He closed his
eyes and felt the warmth of her, both literally and figuratively. And
he couldn't take that away.

'Yeah, bug, I do.'

He kissed her good night and quietly left the room, not knowing
if it was true or not.

NINETEEN

Hank hadn't figured there would ever be anything complimentary to say about Wispy Wendell, but as he looked at the amount of evidence Kurt Gatz pulled from the rental Corolla, he got very pleased with the rental company employee.

'Geez, did this car even get cleaned at all?' Sam said.

Hank smiled and took a sip of his third cup of coffee of the morning. 'Not very well.'

He spread out the evidence list on the conference room table. Kurt had cataloged everything, from the Cheez-It crumbs to the half-melted lipstick tube under the passenger seat to the dried mud in the trunk. He'd cut out the trunk lining and was currently testing a suspicious stain that had Hank's hopes running high.

'It could be blood,' he said, pointing at a photo of the lining.

'You're always Mr Sunshine, aren't you?' Sheila stood in the doorway, cane in hand.

'He's got a reason to be,' Sam said. 'There're no fingerprints.'

She didn't bother with a response, just settled herself on her donut cushion and waited.

'The entire front was wiped clean. Steering wheel, center console, seatbelt clasps, everything,' Sam said. 'The only prints are from the rental car employee.'

She chuckled. 'Not how a normal, non-guilty car renter usually cleans before they turn it in, is it?'

'No, which makes me happy because whoever this person is, he's definitely a suspect,' Hank said. 'And now that we've got the car at the impound lot and there's no rush, Alice is going over all the nooks and crannies we're hoping this guy missed. Gas cap, trunk latch, things like that.'

Then Sheila asked about the surveillance video, the warrant for which Havish had approved last night after Hank's kids went to bed. That led to various laptops being retrieved and files downloaded. They each took a different camera and sat silently around the table, zipping through as fast as they could without missing anything. Sam was about to hit the pause button and get himself a cup of coffee when he caught something right at the edge of his screen. He had a grainy view of the rental car counters and a small slice of outside he could see through glass exit doors. And it was the slice he was interested in. He rewound frame by frame.

'Look it this.' The other two crowded in. Sheila squinted at his computer screen.

'A fat guy in a hoodie?'

Sam shook his head and went back another few frames, turning the man in a more profile direction in relation to the camera.

'OK, he's not fat, but I don't get . . .'

'Wait a second,' Hank interrupted. 'He's carrying two.'

'Exactly,' Sam said. 'Two large camping backpacks. One strapped to his front and one on his back. You can only see him in these couple of frames before he disappears off to the left.'

'I think I have the next camera angle,' Sheila said. 'What's the time stamp?'

Sam read it off as she fast forwarded her video file. Hank started to pace.

'Calm down, I'm getting there and – that son of a bitch. Or maybe it's just a bitch. You can't even tell.' The figure was visible head on, wearing a large sweatshirt with the hood up, baggy cargo pants, and big aviator sunglasses. The two large packs obscured everything else. Including the gender. Sheila stabbed at her keyboard. 'Well, that's even more consciousness of guilt right there. You don't wear those kinds of clothes on a balmy fall day, especially while carting around heavy packs like that.'

'Can we tell where they went?' Sam asked.

'Front of the airport. Do we have that camera?'

Sam pulled up the file while Hank went back to his own laptop. His camera overlooked the actual check-in section of the rental parking lot. He sped ahead to fifteen minutes before the time Sam saw the person through the glass doors and then slowly advanced. Five minutes of tape time later, the blue Corolla puttered into the parking lot and came to a stop. The driver got out with the sunglasses and hood already in place. The sweatshirt was too baggy to give any he/she clues as the person took the packs out of the trunk, gloved hands clearly visible. They exchanged a few words with Wispy and walked away.

'It looks like they got in an Uber,' Sam said. Hank came back

around and watched on the Pup's laptop as the packs went back
into a trunk and the Unabomber slid into the backseat of a newer
model Chevy Malibu. They were still wearing the gloves.

Sheila glanced over and then back at her own screen, which had
the only front view of the suspect. 'You know,' she said, drawing
out the words in a way that meant something had occurred to her.
Before she could continue, her phone buzzed.

'Sick? What? Fine.' She used the chair arms to push herself to
her feet. 'Somebody's called in sick at the jail. I got to go figure
out coverage.'

She limped out of the room lugging her laptop, cushion, and
cane. Both men knew better than to offer assistance. Hank turned
back to Sam's camera view. 'You track down that Uber driver. I've
got to contact Garvan's family.'

Sam cringed. 'Do they know yet?'

'I'm not sure. The local police in Cleveland were supposed to
do the notification. I don't know if they have yet.' He saw Sam's
sympathetic expression. 'Yeah, not something I'm looking forward
to.'

He looked at Sam. It was occasions like this that he wished he
were just a deputy – given the easier assignment and sent on his way.
Not that Sammy couldn't handle the tough ones. His young Pup was
developing into a top-notch investigator. And just as importantly, an
empathetic one. But the task of asking parents why someone would
want to shoot their son to death? That job fell to him.

Sheila was making an assumption. She knew what the adage said
about that, but after dipping into the *Hidden Hoards* chat room, she
was confident that the sort of people flocking here to treasure hunt
weren't actually going to sleep in the woods. They might have
'camping' equipment – shovels, tarps, ridiculously overpriced water
filtration bottles – but they weren't going to actually roll a sleeping
bag out on the ground. Especially when there were a dozen budget-
priced motels only a few miles away. And guess who already had
a group email list with contacts at every front desk in town?

She hit send and leaned back in her desk chair. Then she picked up
the phone. There was one hunter whose movements they now knew
exactly. Philip Garvan's missing Jetta had spent a good deal of time
parked at the Lazy Q motel. She hoped Violet Murcheson was working.

'Sheila, how are you?'

'I need your help, Vi. I think you had a guest last week, a guy named Philip Garvan. Can you give me the dates he stayed with you?'

Vi clacked at her computer keyboard. Garvan had checked in not this past Saturday but the one before. Stayed a week and a day. Like he'd taken a week off and had to be back for work on Monday.

'So he was supposed to check out on Sunday – two days ago,' Sheila said. The poor man had been well ensconced in the morgue by then.

'Supposed to?' Vi said.

'You don't necessarily have a check-out, right? You've already got their credit card. They can just leave.'

'Yeah, they can. I ask if they can return the key cards. We're not some big corporate chain. Those little expenses add up.'

'And did he return the key card?'

More typing. 'Nah. He didn't officially check out.'

Oh, yes, he did. Sheila bit back a laugh. *You are a terrible woman, Turley.* 'Were you there when he checked in? Do you remember him?'

'That day? Oh, Lord, I don't know. I remember we had a family with six kids. Had to be homeschoolers at this time of year. Probably Mormons. But he definitely wasn't part of that. He just had a single room. Is he a Black fella? We had one Black man come in that day.'

'No. He was white. I can send you a picture. Hang on.' She emailed Garvan's driver license photo. Vi let out an *ah-ha*.

'Yep. I do recognize him. He was . . . hyper. Excited.'

'How so?'

Vi thought for a minute. Sheila pictured the seventy-year-old behind her high laminate counter with the fake flower arrangement from Michael's off to the side and the painting of Table Rock Lake behind her. Sheila could hear the long, lacquered nails tapping and wondered if it was time for Vi's weekly wash-and-set down at the beauty shop on Main Street.

'Not hyper like a child. More like eager. Like he was in a hurry.'

'Did he say anything about why he was here? Was he meeting anybody? Going anywhere in particular?'

'Not that I recollect.'

'I suppose you've already cleaned his room?'

'Good Lord, of course we have. His reservation ended two days ago.'

Sheila sighed. 'Did he leave anything behind?'

She heard Vi muffle the phone and holler for someone named Rosita. When she came back, she asked the question Sheila knew she'd have to answer eventually. 'Why you so curious about this fella? He commit some kind of crime?'

'He did do some trespassing. We're hoping to find out as much as we can about why he was where he was.' That was a lot of words that said nothing, she thought as Rosita entered the conversation, her voice clear in the background. There was a thunk and an exclamation from Vi.

'This is a whole bag full of stuff. Why didn't you tell me?'

'You never say that. It goes in lost and found. Put label on. Put in lost and found.'

'You still should've told me, this is—'

'No. I do it right. I'm done.'

A door shut and Rosita was clearly gone. And also clearly not one to take any shit. Good for her.

'Vi, what's in the bag?'

'If stuff is left, they're supposed to bag it and label the guest name, date, and room number. Which I guess she did. But this . . . this is like he didn't check out at all. A shaving kit, a pair of tennis shoes, pajama bottoms, a little duffel bag, a big old fat envelope, a new-lookin'—'

'Wait – an envelope? With papers in it?'

'Yeah, it's got—'

'Don't touch it.' Sheila cleared her throat. 'Sorry, I didn't mean to yell. Please don't touch it. Leave it exactly where it is. All of it. I'll be there in half an hour.'

She moved her halting body as quickly as she could. When she walked into the Lazy Q lobby, the first thing she saw was a pair of beat-up sneakers and a cranky Vi.

'This ain't professional. I had to check somebody in with shoes on my counter.'

'I'm sorry. I do really appreciate it.'

Vi waved her around the counter, where the rest of Garvan's belongings were spread out on the lower desktop next to her computer monitor. Sheila snapped on gloves and reached for the big envelope. Vi raised a penciled eyebrow. 'If that's full of cash, I'm gonna really regret letting you know it was here.'

'It's not cash.' She undid the clasp. 'It's paperwork. The only question is whether it's the same stuff somebody else has or whether it's something new.'

She pulled out the papers. Many were in plastic protectors. Vi chortled.

'Those don't look new to me. They look so old they're about to fall apart.'

'Yes.' Sheila flipped through them carefully, stopping when she recognized words she'd heard read aloud just yesterday. 'They're letters. Originals.'

Written by Mary Louise Finnegan.

TWENTY

It turned out that Philip Garvan's parents were no longer alive. Just a sister named Candace who hadn't seen him since they argued about the sale of their late father's boat several years ago. She did not seem surprised he'd been out hunting for treasure.

'He was always looking for something. A new place to live, a new job, a new girlfriend. He switched colleges three times. He was never satisfied. To have actually found something that was a legitimate search, that's actually really funny. Or it would be, if he wasn't . . .'

She choked up. Hank waited, the phone line humming between them.

'Did he have a girlfriend right now?' Hank asked.

'No. He'd just moved to Cleveland. God knows why. We grew up in Memphis.'

The Cleveland police were currently going through Garvan's house, where he worked in a home office doing mundane call-center work for an IT firm. So far, officers hadn't turned up anything except a pile of mail next to the front-door letter slot and the remnants of several bird carcasses brought through the pet door by the man's self-sufficient cat.

'Do you know anybody who would know more about him and this podcast?'

Candace thought for a moment. He did have a group of friends in Memphis that he would get together with, to play poker or something. She called up her social media apps and poked around. Hank hoped there weren't too many degrees of separation between her friends and her brother's. 'Here we go. Try Tandeep Sidhu. He was in that group of them. Lives out by the Galleria. He's probably at least talked to Phil more recently than I have.'

The last word ended in a sob. Hank thanked her and hung up, trying not to think about family rifts that ended in tears. He easily tracked down Sidhu and, after telling him the bad news, quickly had him crying, too.

'What an idiot,' Sidhu sniffled. 'Man, I didn't think he'd ever follow through and actually go somewhere. I thought the podcast was just another one of his obsessions.'

'Tell me,' Hank said slowly, 'what you know about those obsessions.'

They were many and varied, Sidhu said. They'd met over their shared interest in board games. So their leisurely biweekly game nights lent themselves to talk about other things as well. Garvan had been infatuated with, at various times and in no particular order – pot-bellied pigs, Formula One car racing, photography, Delta blues music, genealogy, the Memphis City Council, and barbecue ribs.

'Yeah, it was when he got bored with the city council that he decided to move. Said he wanted a place with "more going on." Then he moved to Cleveland of all places.' Hank could hear the bewildered shrug in his voice. 'Those two things don't go together in my mind. But that was Phil. Things connected in his head that didn't in other people's.'

'So was it treasure hunting in general that he got obsessed with, or *Hidden Hoards* specifically?'

'I'd say the podcast. It's what started him on it. Before he moved, he talked about episodes with pirate gold and stuff like that.'

That would've been the show's first season. Garvan had moved to Cleveland right before the second season's episodes started to air. In all their conversations in the seven years they knew each other, Sidhu said he'd never mentioned the Civil War or the Ozarks.

'Was Phil ever interested in camping?'

'You mean outdoors?' Sidhu said when he got done laughing. 'Phil was an inside kind of guy. Definitely.'

That profile seemed to fit with many of the show's other listeners. The armchair detectives, as Sheila had taken to calling them. 'Do you know if he was a member of a *Hidden Hoards* online forum? It's an invitation-only thing.'

'He never said – but he did talk like he knew things. Things that other people didn't, I guess? And he liked it. Usually no one gave him the time of day, you know? Like the city council. Yeesh. He was obsessed with them, but you could tell he wasn't "in the know" or anything. But the treasure hunting. With that, he seemed to be . . . less haphazard. Like his obsession had some anchors to it. Which wasn't always the case with his other ones. So maybe he was getting inside information from people?'

'Did he ever say anything about old documents or letters? Did he know a lot about history?'

Sidhu had to think about that one. As far as he knew, Phil had never developed skills much beyond what was required for his call-center job. He certainly didn't have some history specialty or fancy library pass or anything. Although he was always researching his fixations, so he at least knew his way around the internet. Hank sighed. That assessment might explain how the young man found out more about Alf Bolin, but it didn't shed light on how a stack of 1880s letters ended up in his motel room.

'Can you think of any reason someone would want to kill him?'

Sidhu sniffled again. 'He was just an ordinary guy. Yeah, he acted like an excited little kid sometimes, but he wasn't a bad person. You might have wanted him to shut up during a board game, but kill him? That's just nuts, man. Especially out in the middle of nowhere. Who was he bothering?'

That was a very good question.

Sam tracked the hoodied Unabomber from the airport Uber ('Good question, bro. Kinda lumpy looking, never took the sunglasses off and didn't say a word. I got no idea whether it was a man or a woman') to the drop-off at a movie theater in the city of Ozark, where the same Uber driver, parked and eating his sack lunch, saw him get into another ride-share, an easily located pink Scion. ('I totally remember that guy. So weird to pick someone up at the movies with luggage. Or backpacks. Whatever he had. Although, yeah, I guess I'm assuming it was a he. Didn't say anything. Just hunched in the back with his hood pulled close to his face. Dropped him off at the Best Buy in Branson, right off Highway Sixty-five.')

Sam sent out a warrant for the name and credit card linked to the Uber account, which he knew would take a while. Same thing with his request for the parking lot surveillance video. It was a big retail area, with clothing stores and a Walmart next door, and a Target across the street. This person wasn't there to shop, though, that was for sure. Had they called another Uber? That question would be answered when the credit card info came back. He sighed and shoved aside the grainy screenshot from the airport camera. Then he pulled out the GPS data from the blue Volkswagen Jetta, which had wound its way around Branson over a weeklong period.

He knew Sheila was doing the same with the Corolla. She'd quickly pinpointed the driver's choice of lodging and was there right now. But Stanley Womack wasn't going to be so easy. The Jetta had started out last Saturday at a similar establishment – 'a luxury stay at a budget price' – but after spending time near the Murder Rocks woods Sunday and Monday, had not returned to the motel on Tuesday, the same day Mingo Culver wandered out of the woods. That night and the next two were spent at a Holiday Inn Express. Then the guy decided to upgrade. Friday through Sunday were at the four-star Ozark Hightop Lodge in Hollister. Womack might not still be there – Monday morning was the most recent data they had – but it was worth a shot. He picked up the phone. Ten minutes later he had a confused manager on the line.

'We've not had any guests with that license plate, sir.'

So he wasn't still there, Sam thought. 'Can you look and see when he checked out?'

Silence. 'What I'm saying is that someone with that license plate hasn't stayed here at all. And we make every guest fill out that information when they check in. I went back two weeks. No Jetta with Arkansas plates at all.'

Sam stared at the GPS data on his computer screen. It definitely showed the Jetta right there, not moving for the entire weekend. 'How often do you patrol your parking lot?'

'Excuse me?'

'How often do you have people go out and check those license plates? The reason you ask for the information is so that only registered guests park there, right?'

'Well, yes.' The manager started to stutter. 'I can't tell you exactly what the schedule is, but . . .'

'I'll be there in twenty minutes.'

He got to the lodge, a four-story hotel with assertive wood beams and copper flourishes, to find the plump little manager waiting under the porte-cochere and wringing his hands. Sam took a look at his worried face and chose a normal parking space in the second row instead of pulling up right in front and conspicuously declaring that the sheriff had interest in his establishment. The manager hustled over. And pointed.

'It is here. Third row. Next to that white minivan.'

They walked over. Sam peered in the windows. There was nothing visible. He'd need a warrant to do a true search. He turned to the manager.

'OK, Wayne,' he said, reading the man's shiny metal name tag.

'You just came out and looked for it, right? You still have no record of it?'

Wayne nodded.

'And no one named Stanley Womack is – or was – a registered guest?'

Wayne shook his head. 'No Womack at all.'

'Do you have any idea if this car has moved at all in the last few days?'

Another no.

'Do you have surveillance cameras?'

That brightened the look on Wayne's face. 'Yes, yes we do. I think I can show you. Let me just check.'

He pulled out his phone and started texting. Sam sighed and went back to his cruiser. By the time Wayne was finished, Sam had sealed all the rental car doors and the trunk with crime scene tape and taken pictures.

'I can show you anything you need. Mr Handler is happy to help.'

Thank goodness for locally owned businesses. A national chain would've told him to call the corporate lawyer, who would've told him to get a court order. Instead, within five minutes, he was given a cup of fresh coffee and a cushy chair in front of the security monitors.

'To be honest, this is mostly where the security guys work. They're not out checking cars against the license plate list. They're mostly watching out for car break-ins, that kind of thing. And they can see the back and front lot from here at the same time.'

They rewound the video to Friday evening, until they saw the Jetta arriving in the parking lot. It pulled in and tucked itself into a spot surrounded by other cars. A short and stocky man with glasses got out, opened the trunk, and pulled out a large hiking backpack. Sam groaned. So many damn backpacks. At least the man matched the description of Stanley Womack. He locked the car and, carrying the pack like a suitcase, marched straight into the hotel lobby. Sam swung around and stared at Wayne. The manager shrugged helplessly and called up the interior footage. Sam leaned closer to the screen. It was definitely Womack, nodding cheerfully at the front desk attendant and continuing through to the ground-floor hallway. Wayne quickly switched camera feeds. They watched as Womack, starting to strain with the weight of the pack, walked down the length of the hall. He bypassed twenty different rooms and only stopped in order to push through the exit-only door at the end.

Wayne looked relieved. Sam didn't. This guy was not acting like
an innocent tourist. He waited impatiently while the manager called
up the next set of cameras. Womack came out of the door at the
side of the building. He closed it carefully and tried to nonchalantly
sling the pack over one shoulder, but its bulk and the attached
sleeping pad had him struggling to balance it. He finally gave up
and used both straps to get it settled securely on his back. Then he
trudged off into the darkness.

'He's disappeared. Took his ridiculous hiking pack and walked out
of camera range and poof, disappeared. Hasn't returned to the car
since.'

Sheila frowned, trying to make out the background noises on
Sam's end of the line. 'So where are you now?'

'That undeveloped stretch of woods south of the hotel.'

'You think he's hiding out down there?'

'I don't know what to think.' He sounded frustrated. 'Except that
the guy is hiding something. Which makes me want to sit his ass
down and have a conversation.'

She chuckled. That was something she would say. To hear it
come from him was funny, and also a little concerning. Sammy was
nicer than she was. But he'd had a shorter fuse lately, and she hadn't
been able to figure out why. 'So what's your next step?'

'Kurt's going over the car now. I'm going to see if he found
anything. Then I guess I'll start checking motels within walking
distance. See if he checked in someplace.'

Sheila tapped her pen thoughtfully on the Lazy Q's breakfast bar,
Philip Garvan's half-bagged belongings spread out in front of her.
'Yeah. We should also check the walking route from where you are
out to Murder Rocks. See if he headed back there.'

'I don't know. It's like a seven-mile hike. He didn't look to be
in the best of shape. Plus, he's already seen the woods, either as a
treasure hunter or as our killer. And by now, he's got to know law
enforcement is all over those woods. I can't imagine him going
back, even if he thinks there's still treasure out there.'

She scoffed. 'You haven't seen the *Hidden Hoards* chat room. A
lot of these guys don't seem capable of logical lines of thought. They're
fixated on one thing to the exclusion of anything remotely sensible.'

'Are we still getting new folks trying to get into those woods?'
he asked.

'Yes.' Now she sounded as irritated as Sam did. 'Although at this point only half of them seem to care about the "treasure." The other half are interested in the murders.'

She hung up to the sound of Sam's disgusted muttering about the state of the world. It was bad, but as bad as the 1860s? She looked at Mary Louise's letters spread out in front of her and continued taking photos before carefully replacing them in the manila envelope Garvan used, then putting the whole thing in an evidence bag. How did the man have originals, if the stupid podcast was trumpeting its own recent discovery of these 'long-lost' letters? Was Garvan the podcast host's source? Sheila shook her head. If Garvan had discovered the letters first, he would have searched Murder Rocks before giving them to Hardwick. He certainly wouldn't have waited until the podcast aired and the whole world knew about the Finnegan family's supposed transport of a bank's worth of gold.

She chided herself. Standing here as if the whole thing were real. There was no hidden hoard out there to find. Unless the definition of a treasure hunt included searching for a killer. Then she was all in.

TWENTY-ONE

t had been weeks since all four of them had dinner together. They even sat down early, thanks to the beef stew Maggie had the forethought to put in the slow cooker that morning. Hank dished it up as she got the bread out of the oven.

'Please don't pick out the carrots, Benny.'

'I don't like them when they're squishy.'

'You'll barely even taste it.'

'Then why's it even in there?'

He looked at his son and gave up. If he came up with another rationale, Benny'd probably poke a hole in it, too. He'd rather just enjoy the meal and not think about his day, consoling the family of one murder victim and failing to identify the other. That decision got him a cheerful regaling of kindergarten recess and a stack of mushy carrots on the kitchen table. An excellent trade-off.

Maribel was just starting on her day when the doorbell rang. Hank looked at Maggie and the dark circles under her eyes from a long hospital shift. 'I'll get it.'

He walked out to the front foyer and swung open the door. And gasped. A man, old and beginning to stoop, stood on the front step. He had a bag in his hands and a look on his face that morphed from anxious to apprehensive when he saw Hank. They stared at each other. Hank could only imagine what his own expression looked like.

'Duncan. Hi.'

'Hank.'

He'd rung the doorbell. Even though he lived here. He hadn't technically moved out, although he'd been staying with his sister in Columbia for the last three months, an uncomfortable stasis none of them knew how to address. How much needed to be forgiven – on all sides – for things to return to normal? It was a three-pronged disaster, and every point was sharp with hurt and blame. Maggie resented that Hank had considered her dad a murder suspect. Duncan resented the same thing, with an added layer of shame due to the sorry state of his marriage to Marian and her affair with Judge

Sedstone, a fact he was desperate to keep secret from Maggie. Hank resented that they both refused to acknowledge the reality of homicide investigations, where the spouse was always a suspect – especially when the victim had been having an affair. Even more than that, Hank hated that the case – and by extension, Maggie's parents – had upended his marriage, through what he considered to be no fault of the two people actually in that relationship.

Which was why they were in marriage counseling. And why Duncan had exiled himself to Finella's house. Everyone in a tremulous limbo that showed no signs of changing. Except now Duncan stood on the doorstep. It seemed ridiculous to invite him in. His bedroom was downstairs. He took better care of the house than Hank did. He'd never once knocked in order to gain entry. He'd never needed to. But what was necessary now?

Hank stepped back, almost reflexively, and held the door open. This at least was required. Duncan stepped into the foyer. The minute his shuffling feet hit the tile floor, a six-year-old comet streaked out from the kitchen and threw herself in his arms. The five-year-old came flying close behind. Duncan dropped the tote bag and sank to his knees, hugging them both tightly. They stayed like that, none of them wanting to move. Hank stepped back to give them room. There was the clink of silverware from the kitchen and Maggie appeared. A fork slipped through her stunned fingers and landed on the carpet.

'Dad.'

Maribel turned, her face shining. 'Grandpop's home.'

'I'm sorry. I didn't think you'd be eating yet. I don't want to interrupt.'

'What? No – of course you're not.' Maggie scooped up the fork and moved forward. She stopped on the other side of the little hug cluster and looked over at Hank. All he could do was shrug.

'OK, let Grandpop up,' Maggie said. 'We'll get him some stew and you two can talk to him all you want.'

The kids reluctantly moved away. Duncan looked up at the other two adults. 'I shouldn't've gotten down here. I'm going to need some help.'

They each grabbed an elbow and hoisted him to his feet. He turned to Maggie, tears in his eyes, and put his hand on her cheek. 'It's good to see you, sweetie. Thank you for asking.'

Maribel grabbed his hand and pulled him into the kitchen. Hank looked at his wife. 'What did you ask?'

'I have no idea what he's talking about.'

'Did you know he was coming?'

'No. I hadn't heard from him since last week, and that was just a text saying he and Aunt Fin were back from their trip to Chicago.'

He raised a skeptical eyebrow.

'Don't you suddenly think I have control over what he does,' she said. 'You know better than that.'

It was true. The old goat always did exactly what he pleased. Since June, that had meant very little contact. Hank wondered what had changed. They followed the others into the kitchen, where Duncan teared up again at the sight of his chair in its normal spot at the table. The kids escorted him straight to it and enthroned him with the proper amount of pomp and grandeur the occasion warranted. They spent the rest of the meal telling their grandfather every bit of minutia that had accumulated since he left. Hank and Maggie watched silently, confused interlopers in their own home. Finally it was bedtime. No one but Grandpop was allowed to read the bedtime story, which Hank decided might be the most irritating thing about the man showing up unannounced. He was robbing Hank of the last chapter of the last Percy Jackson book.

'That is the pettiest thing I've ever heard.'

'I put a lot of time into those books.' He handed Maggie another bowl to put in the dishwasher.

'You could always read it on your own.'

'Where's the fun in that?' He carried the last dishes to the sink and turned to her. 'He really didn't say anything to you about coming back? Did Aunt Fin?'

'No. I wracked my brain all through dinner. I'm as surprised as you are. Although at least I don't look like I've been hit by a truck.'

'I know. I can't help it. I figured we'd have some forewarning, you know? Especially about what he's down here to do. Is he back for good? Is he back to be mad at me some more? Is he here to pack up because he's moving away permanently? How do we ask him those things now?' Awkward didn't begin to cover it.

She leaned against the counter and thought. She was still at it when Duncan and the dog came down the hallway. They both had a bounce in their step, although Guapo's looked much less arthritic.

'I can't believe you made it through those books so fast. Nice work.'

'They were really into them.' Hank felt he should return the compliment. 'It was a good choice on your part to start the first one back in the spring.' Back when everything was still normal.

'So.' Maggie pressed her palms against her thighs, which meant she was nervous. 'Can we help you get things out of your car, Dad?'

That was good. Neutral, but would still net them some information. They all walked out to his dependable Camry, where he'd packed a solidly uninformative amount of luggage. Not a lot, not a little. Not anything to lead them to a conclusion about whether he was back to stay. They carried it inside and Hank took it downstairs to Dunc's room in the basement. He came back up to find them in the middle of the conversational equivalent of skipping stones on a pond, chatting about Benny's art projects and the wilted houseplant in the corner.

'Well, I'm going to head to bed. That drive left me a little tired.' He turned and then stopped. 'That text. It was the best thing that's happened in months. I love you.'

He kissed Maggie's cheek and made his way down the stairs without looking at Hank. He scowled and shooed her into the kitchen, where they wouldn't be overheard. She spoke before he had the chance. 'A text about his trip to Chicago was the best thing in months? What is he talking about?' She held up her hand to stop him from responding as she walked toward the corner desk and her purse. 'I said hi, what've you been up to? He said that he and Aunt Fin just got back from Chicago, where she refused to go up in Sears Tower, and they ate too much pizza. Then I said I was glad he had a good time. And then after a while, he said "thank you so much." And that was it.'

Hank paused. 'That's what he said? That seems a little formal. He didn't just say "thanks"?'

She dug around in her purse until she found her phone. She scrolled through, and Hank watched her face flush. She handed him the phone.

Last Wednesday: I'm glad you guys had a good time.

Yesterday: When are you going to come back home? I miss you. I didn't know you wanted me to.

Yes. We miss you. You have to come home.

'I think we might have a phone hacker in the house,' Hank said.

'And it slipped right through. All I saw of the conversation was Dad's last "thank you so much" text,' she said.

'Shall we?'

They walked down the hall and slipped quietly into Maribel's room. She lay curled under the covers, pretending to be asleep. Hank sat down on the bed. Maggie sat cross-legged on the floor so she was directly at eye level. 'Sweetheart, we need to ask you something.'

Big brown eyes opened slowly, sliding from Maggie to Hank and back.

'Did you send Grandpop some texts?' Maggie said. 'On my phone?'

She nodded, her eyes wide and worried. 'I wanted him to come back.' She looked at each of them again. Her little body stiffened under the blanket. 'And you weren't doing anything. I kept waiting, but nobody did anything. He didn't say he was coming home. You guys didn't say when he was coming home. Everybody made it sound like a vacation, but nobody said when he was coming back. If it's a vacation, you know when you're coming back. So it wasn't a vacation.' The last bit was an accusation. An accurate one. Hank tried not to wince.

Maggie reached out and took their daughter's hand. He could tell she was picking through a verbal minefield to find her way to safe words. 'You're right. We weren't sure how long Grandpop was going to stay with Aunt Fin. Sometimes things are . . . open-ended. And that's OK.' She took a breath. 'But it's also OK to tell people how you feel. And you did that when you texted him. So we're not mad.'

Hank could feel her start to relax. He reached out and stroked the hair away from her face.

'Will he stay?' His girl still sounded worried. 'Or is he going to go away again?'

He saw the pain slice across Maggie's face. He stepped onto the minefield. 'I don't know, little bug. We didn't get a chance to talk about it tonight. But it's a very good question for you to want to know the answer to, isn't it?'

She nodded.

'Now you need to go to sleep,' Maggie said with a smile that Hank knew was fake. He hoped Maribel didn't. 'So you'll be well-rested to spend all kinds of time with Grandpop tomorrow.'

The wheels in Maribel's head were still turning. Before she could put them on the spot again, Hank kissed her forehead. Maggie did the same to her cheek and they tiptoed out of the room. They didn't speak until they were back in the kitchen.

'I guess I'm going to need to change my phone passcode,' Maggie said. 'That kid.'

'Yeah. She either paid close attention when you used it, or . . .' He paused. 'Or she just stuck the damn phone in your face while you were asleep and unlocked it with the facial recognition.'

Maggie groaned. 'I bet that's exactly what she did. She's certainly your daughter, a little detective figuring out how to get information any way she can.'

He cocked an eyebrow at his wife. 'Hold on. I don't know about that. Knowing what she wants and charting a straight course no matter the consequences? Sounds exactly like a McCleary to me.'

She rolled her eyes and started loading the dishwasher. There was more to say but they didn't, instead falling into the silence that had become habit and the distance that was now routine.

TWENTY-TWO

T he voice was unfortunately familiar. It had been in Sheila's ears for the past week, forcing its dulcet baritone into her head with tales of treasure and other bullshittery.

'You're a difficult man to get ahold of, Mr Hardwick.'

'I'm sorry about that, ma'am. I've been off preparing the next episode of the podcast and only just got the messages you left through the website. How can I help you?'

You can stop filling suggestible people's heads with ridiculous notions that lead unto major inconvenience, trespassing – and, in two cases, actual death.

'Have you heard what's happened here at the Murder Rocks site?'

'Season two, episode four? That had some really significant new information. We were quite excited to bring that to the public's attention.'

'Well, now the public is traipsing uninvited all over the southern section of my county, Mr Hardwick. You've sent ill-prepared treasure hunters down here and two of them have been murdered.'

Silence. Sheila rolled a dry erase marker back and forth on her desk and waited.

'I'm sorry, what?' he finally said. 'Murdered? How on earth is that possibly linked to my show?'

'There is absolutely no other reason for either of the two victims to be in those woods with that kind of gear, unless they were searching for gold you convinced them was there.'

'It is there.'

'This is not my point, Mr Hardwick.'

'Oh.' More silence. 'Your point is that people are dead.'

'Yes. And why would someone want to kill people who were looking for treasure?'

'Because they didn't want the competition?'

'Very good, Mr Hardwick. So I would like a list of your competitors. That means every listener who has subscribed to your podcast, and every screen name from that *Hidden Hoards* chat room.'

'I can't do that.' He sounded like she'd just asked him to hand over a federal witness protection list.

'Nonsense. None of that is proprietary information.' Plus, she'd already filed a warrant for it. But thanks to both the turtle-slow podcast app overlords and the chat-room company labyrinth, it was taking forever.

'We are looking for a killer.' Or killers, but she decided not to complicate things any further. 'A killer of two men who were out in my woods at *your* urging. You have a responsibility to help.'

There was rustling she felt sure was caused by nervous fidgeting. 'I . . . I'll see what I can do. I'm very busy at the moment. We're still in production.'

He hadn't asked about the victims at all. This guy was as self-absorbed as his promotional materials.

'Where are you now?'

'I'm not going to say. We need to keep these things under wraps until the episodes air.'

'How do you decide which stories to feature?' She asked it quickly, wanting to keep him off balance.

'Oh. Uh. Well, we have a list of possibilities, and when we can find new information about them, we'll do an episode. And now this season, since they're less exotic locations, people are starting to contact us with suggestions, too.'

'Did someone contact you about Murder Rocks?'

'No. That one was my idea.'

'Why?'

'Because it was the site of potential treasure.' The *duh*, while unspoken, was loud and clear.

'I'm sorry, I guess I need to simplify.' She knew her tone was brittle and she didn't care. 'Let's start at the beginning. How did you come to find out about it in the first place?'

'Oh. I see. I was looking into the Great Kentucky Hoard. You know – the one where the guy found Confederate gold coins on his own land. There're rumors of other Kentucky stashes from that time period. Then I thought, what about the other border states? So, across the Mississippi River and into Missouri. Did you know the Ozarks were basically a lawless mess in that time period?'

They're a lawless mess right now, thanks to you. 'Yes, I'm aware.'

'Ah. Anyway. Alf Bolin popped right up. Murderous bushwhacker with a hundred-and-fifty-years' worth of rumored treasure. That's right up my alley.'

'So how did you find the "new" Mary Louise Finnegan letters?'

'Why, you've listened to the show, Ms Turley. I'm delighted.'

'As part of my investigation, Mr Hardwick. Please answer the question.'

'Well, I'm afraid I can't divulge my sources. I can assure you that the letters are authentic.'

'And how do you know that?'

'What?'

'How do you know they're authentic?'

'We have experts who verify all of our findings.'

'Who verified these?'

'Why on earth is this important?'

'Answer the question.'

'We have a document expert. A lot of our cases have documents, so we have somebody who examines everything for authenticity.'

Sheila looked down at the neat copperplate script of Mary Louise, safely encased in plastic sleeves on her desk.

'And how did this person do that, in specific regard to the Finnegan letters?'

'They look at the paper and the ink.' Another *duh*.

'In person?'

Silence.

'What are you getting at?'

'How did your expert examine the letters? And where? And when?'

The sound of more fidgeting. 'I'd need to look at the paperwork for that episode. I'm out in the field and I don't know off the top of my head.'

He sounded smooth and assured, but she didn't buy it for a second. She had a feeling he was always capable of sounding that way, even when he wasn't. She pressed. 'Can't you call your staff and find out?'

'If that would help, Ms Turley. Then I'd be happy to.'

'As soon as possible, please. I am conducting a murder investigation.' *So think very carefully about how much you want to lie to me.* She told him she would call again tomorrow for that and the podcast subscriber list, and hung up the phone.

She placed her palm on the cool plastic protecting Mary Louise's painful history. She wanted to know how the authenticated documents got from Hardwick to Garvan. Or she wanted to get the podcaster on record lying about having possession of – and authenticating –

the letters at all. Which was why she hadn't told him she had what
looked to be the originals. Let him string himself up first.

The woods around the Ozark Hightop Lodge were empty. No Stanley
Womack, no anybody else. Sam really had thought he'd find the
guy out here camping. What else was he going to do after walking
off carrying a pack full of outdoor gear? Hide someplace else,
clearly. But there were no other hotels or motels nearby. The guy
must've walked to a road and gotten picked up. It was possible he'd
hiked farther than Sam had searched, but unlikely. He'd huffed and
puffed just walking through the lodge on the surveillance video.
Catching a ride was the only other plausible explanation.

Sam leaned against a tree and contemplated things. Despite the
lack of success, it had been a great morning. Wandering through
nature on an autumn day, when the light was that slanted orangey-
yellow that only happened in the fall, and the air was blissfully
free of humidity. He looked around. These were nice woods. They
felt good. They brought him back to center. The Murder Rocks
woods had knocked him off. There was something about them.
They were meaner. Unhappy. They felt full of hard edges, even
though the terrain was pretty much the same as where he was
standing. He'd never noticed it when he went out there as a high
schooler. But now – well, now he had a hell of a lot more familiarity
with hard edges, didn't he?

He wondered if Alice was out at Murder Rocks. He knew she
was going back out there again with the experts from some college
forensic anthropology department. He'd run into her at the station
first thing this morning. She told him they might be done today
and it couldn't come soon enough. 'They sure know their stuff, but
jeez. Is every old man with a PhD a conceited asshole? 'Cause I've
never met one who wasn't. The young ones – perfectly nice. But
old men? Think they're God's gift.' Sam figured it was generational.
Alice figured it was generational *and* sexist. At that point, Sam had
decided that nodding in agreement while walking away was the
wisest response.

He smiled at the memory and straightened, brushing tree bark
off his shirt. He headed back for his squad car and had just reached
the edge of the trees when his phone buzzed. Ten minutes later, he
was headed toward the PhDs and an Alice who sounded a lot more
amused than she had that morning.

'Hank's on his way, but he knew you'd be able to get here quicker, so he thought you could start to referee things until he got here.' They were standing about twenty yards away from the skeleton excavation. She put her hands on her hips. ''Cause I refuse to do it.'

'What am I refereeing? Wait, is that Old Man Fackrell?'

'Yes, indeed.' Alice grinned. 'And he wants to know all about what's going on. Asking every sort of question.'

'Why now? You all have been working out here for days.'

'I'm not sure, but he's driving the academics nuts. It's wonderful.'

'Then why do you want me out here to spoil it for you?'

'Not me. Dr Tweed Elbows over there is the one demanding that "the sanctity of his site be restored."'

Sam looked over at the man who actually owned the site. Mr Fackrell was leaning in as close as he could while being blocked by a younger man kneeling in front of the hole with his arms spread wide to keep the landowner away. Sam took a deep breath and walked over to introduce himself.

'Mr Fackrell, sir. Is there something the sheriff's department can help you with?'

'On my own land? No.'

Sam cringed. 'I apologize, sir. What I meant was that if there were any questions we could answer for you, in relation to this excavation—'

'And what exactly are you going to be able to tell him?'

Sam turned around. Tweed Elbows stood there on the other side of the hole, wispy gray hair waving in the breeze. He looked Sam's uniform up and down. 'Do you have experience in forensic anthropology?'

Alice stepped forward. 'Don't you start picking on him, too. He's trying to help your "site sanctity."'

The man didn't move, but at least did stop talking. Fackrell filled the gap.

'I want to know what's going on. Why's it taking so long? It looks like all the bones are gone. Why are you still here?'

The doctor glared at Sam. Sam gestured toward a tree off to the side and walked toward it, saying he'd be happy to explain. He prayed Mr Fackrell would follow. It took two painful minutes of Sam standing there by himself, but finally the old man did.

'Right now, they're making sure there aren't any small, or even microscopic, bits of evidence still left,' Sam said.

'What does it matter? That thing has been in the ground for hundreds of years. Well, since the Civil War, anyway.'

'We don't know that, actually, sir.' Each word was cautiously chosen.

'It's a skeleton. Not a body.'

'Yes, but it could be ten years old. Or twenty. Or fifty. They don't know.'

Fackrell started to flush an angry red. Sam fought the urge to take a step back.

'My family owned this land fifty years ago. Hell, my family owned this land a hundred years ago.'

'Yes, sir.' *Do not engage.* 'These experts just need all the available evidence in order to try to determine how long the bones have been here.'

Mr Fackrell was now a robust tomato color. 'First you slander me, then you say a whole lot of nothing.'

'Sir, that is not my intent. I'm only trying to give you the information you're out here looking for. I'm hoping—'

A flash of movement off to the right made them both turn. Hank came through the trees at a brisk pace. Sam gratefully took a step away, just before the old man jabbed a finger at the space where his chest had been.

'Your boy here is implying that my family's burying bodies on our land.'

What the hell? Sam shook his head. Hank gave a quick nod not to worry and let Mr Fackrell stomp back and forth, reciting his completely inaccurate version of the conversation. Then the old man beelined for the hole again, sending the poor young anthropologist scrambling back into protective position.

'I got to ask, Leo, if you're so fired up about this, why is this the first time you've been out here to see it?'

That stopped the old man in his tracks.

'They've been out here digging since you gave permission five days ago. Why did you wait until today?'

'I figured it would only take them a day or two. But since they're still here, I decided to come see why.'

Hank nodded in understanding and guided Mr Fackrell back over to Sam. He lowered his voice. 'I understand that reasoning, sir, but I don't think that's the full story. Why are you out here today specifically?'

Mr Fackrell's coloring shifted from red-angry to red-embarrassed. 'The wife's at her church ladies' lunch. Every Wednesday. So I could come down here without her knowing. Because she was telling me not to. That whatever it was, was none of our business. Old bones that had nothing to do with us.' He turned tired eyes to Hank. 'Lately it's just easier for me to go along with what she wants. I don't got the energy anymore to argue with her. But I do think it's my business. Especially since he's saying,' a hand waved wearily at Sam, 'that the damn bones could be only fifty years old. What's next – accusing my daddy of murder?'

'Sir, we don't know anything yet. We don't know how this person died, or when. It's going to take a lot of tests and analyzing to maybe answer those questions.'

'So you're telling me there could always be an unsolved shadow hanging over me and my land?'

Sam looked around the gloomy terrain and thought a crime would make little difference. It'd just be one more shadow cast over an area already dark with them.

'We'll do our best to make sure that doesn't happen.'

Dr Tweed punctuated that comment with an indignant snort. 'Our best is the best in the country and—'

Mr Fackrell spun toward him. The young anthropologist stepped from one old man to the other, then rolled his eyes and stayed where he was. Mr Fackrell ignored him and jabbed a finger toward Dr Tweed and then Hank. 'You make sure he tells me everything he finds out. That'd be just like these elitist assholes, to keep it all to himself.'

Sam could hear Alice chuckling softly as she bagged evidence at a workstation off to the side. He felt like doing the same. He stepped away as Hank steered Mr Fackrell away from the hole.

'Leo, you're welcome to stay, but—'

'What?' That came from both the anthropologists at the same time.

'No, he's not,' the old one said. 'I want him out of here.'

Hank ignored them and guided Mr Fackrell into the trees. They got about ten feet away and Sam thought of something. He rooted through Alice's supplies, found a roll of crime scene tape and went to work. By the time the landowner thought to look back around, he was on the outside of a ring of bright yellow. He stomped off as Sam finished the job. He handed the roll back to Alice as Hank joined them.

'I finished that off with the nice news that he doesn't get his guns back yet,' Hank said. 'He wasn't pleased with that, either.'

He gave them a wry smile and started helping Alice with the evidence bags. 'Have you heard from Kurt what the ballistics status is?'

The bullet recovered from the unidentified body was a nine-millimeter. Since they didn't have ballistics testing ability, Kurt sent Fackrell's two nine-millimeter pistols to the state highway patrol lab. He was trying to talk them into also firing the landowner's other two handguns – a newer forty-caliber Beretta PX4 and an old Colt Cobra revolver – just to have the results on record before they had to return the weapons to Fackrell.

'Kurt won the argument,' Alice said. 'Once he mentioned the skeleton and that we weren't done sifting through the dirt and might find a bullet at any time, they agreed to test everything.'

Hank smiled at that, but it didn't reach his eyes. He looked tired, weighed down again. Like he was at the beginning of the summer when all the Marian McCleary awfulness happened. Sam wondered why. Things had seemed to be improving. Not that he knew much. The family had closed off, retreating into a cocoon of silence and mourning that he and Sheila hadn't been able to penetrate. They'd decided the best way to help was to make Hank's job as easy as they could. And he felt they'd done a pretty good job of it. Until Murder Rocks came out of the history books.

TWENTY-THREE

[Orchestral music]

Welcome back to *Hidden Hoards*. After barely making it out alive, the Finnegans fled northeast to the relative safety of Rolla, Missouri, a city securely in Union hands. There, they avoided the brutal back-and-forth that characterized the borderland Ozarks and the Springfield area in the first years of the Civil War. Anywhere you turned, there were armed groups hell-bent on wringing all they could out of the local population.

My dearest Arthur,
They were not soldiers this last time, dear brother. They were a motley militia, I think with Confederate sympathies, although I am not certain. Why are these men not with an army? Did they desert? I asked them this when they demanded the contents of my larder. They asked me who I supported and I said, 'Peace.' I was assuredly not going to say I was the only Union partisan in the whole southern half of the county. I think they knew anyway. Because after they took all the food, they set fire to the barn. It still smolders as I write you this.
I pray the Army is treating you well and you are able to return home healthy and whole. Until you do, I shall persist.
Faithfully, Winifred

[Sound of crackling flames]
These militias, made up of firebrands, deserters, and occasionally straight-up bushwhackers, claimed to be protecting residents loyal to one side or the other. In reality, they did nothing but engage in fruitless skirmishes under color of dubious authority. And plunder the countryside. If that was all these poor people had to deal with, it would've been bad enough. But the actual armies – bursting with hungry, badly supplied, partisan men – were just as bad.

*   *   *

They are but locusts, an unthinking greedy pestilence running over us. I now shudder in fear at the sight of a blue uniform, for I know it means the end of whatever I have managed to accumulate since the last time. Flour, corn, chickens. The cow is long gone, and the last time, they stole the horse. Soon there will be no way to replenish anything. Everyone has nothing. I long for the time when I just taught school and helped my mother and brother work the farm. Now he is dead on a field in Georgia, and she is so distraught she cannot help with even the most basic tasks. I do not know what I am going to do.
    Diary of Amelia Bradshaw

[Sad piano music]
Dear Uncle,
The tide has shifted and the Confederates are headed toward Springfield. They pillage as they go. The last group took my fenceposts. For firewood, I suppose, although I did not bother asking. It is of no matter, however, as the cows were taken long ago. I told them that I – like many others – support the cause, but it made no difference. At this point, I think their only cause is themselves. And we are left in between, to fend for ourselves and starve in the process.

Please give my regards to Aunt Molly and watch for movement from the north. I do anticipate that the units marching through my territory will stir a Union response. Hide your allegiance and your valuables. The first will be used as reason to take the second. If our boys reach you first, you may share your allegiance, but hide your valuables all the same. I believe in our boys, but I do not trust them. I beg you to do the same.
    Your affectionate nephew, Ralph

But all of these groups at least pretended to be acting in service of the war. There was another contingent in the Ozark backwoods that didn't bother with such niceties. Yes, listeners, we're back to the true bushwhackers like Alf Bolin. Men with no real loyalties except to themselves, and no goals other than robbing and killing. If the other groups created despair, these created terror. No life, limb or coin was safe. Especially that fateful night in 1862, when the entirety of the Bank of Carrollton passed by Murder Rocks.
[Clinking coins]

Why did the bank move its gold? Why did it have so much of it? And where has it gone? More to come. Stay tuned.

Sheila had interviewed five trespassers over the past week, her deputies had talked to many more, and none knew anything pertinent. One had nothing on them but the podcast transcript. No supporting documentation, no other research, not even a bottle of water. And he was going to search a huge, unfamiliar area. They should've let him do it. By nightfall, the idiot would've given those novice search-and-rescue guys something to do.

The others had varying levels of competence. Nobody had anything that looked like original documents like Philip Garvan did. No one had dug into the history like Mingo Culver had. And no one knew either Garvan or Stanley Womack. But now, there was hope. Deputy Bill Ramsdell had gotten fed up with the repeated returns of one treasure hunter and arrested her. Sheila asked him to put her in an interview room after he booked her. She was waiting when he brought the woman in.

'Cheryl Maclin? Have a seat.'

She'd walked in radiating indignation. That evaporated as she saw the hard plastic chair bolted to the floor and the metal ring an interviewee could be ankle-cuffed to if necessary. She slowly sat.

'Deputy Ramsdell here tells me you've tried to get past my cordon five times. Why are you so determined, when nobody else has found anything in a hundred and fifty years?'

Maclin laced together long, thin fingers that matched the rest of her. Almost sixty, medium height and lean, she was one of those women who become nothing but muscle and sinew as they age. She was almost there.

'I have every right to be by those rocks.'

'But you don't have the right to go through private property to get there. Nor do you have the right to ignore a law enforcement roadblock.'

Maclin scowled. Sheila smiled. And flipped open her folder full of paperwork.

'So let's talk about what led you here. How did you find out about Alf Bolin's "treasure"?'

'The podcast. Like everybody else.' The last sentence was tinged with regret.

'It's not like Bolin was a secret,' Sheila said. 'If you're so interested, why didn't you know about it before?'

'My concentration is the Army of Northern Virginia. Particularly the impact that the battles in Virginia had on civilians, on the economy, things like that.'

'You're a scholar?'

'Yes. I teach history at a community college in the middle of the Commonwealth.'

'So what are you doing in the Ozarks?'

'This area is very interesting. There were multiple, intense hardships on civilians here, too. During the war.'

'Ah.' Sheila wondered if the woman's scholarship included the 'intense hardships' of another set of people involved in the conflict. Probably not. She told herself to concentrate on the murder instead of slavery. What an upbeat life she led. 'And you didn't know about this area? Until the podcast? But you're a Civil War historian.'

'My specialty is very focused. Currently. I'd like to broaden it.'

That was not the case with any expert Sheila'd ever seen. The more esoteric and specialized, the happier they all seemed. She put a look on her face that said as much. Maclin sighed.

'I'm not making any inroads. I can't get a job at a four-year. The field's too crowded. Everybody's an expert in Civil War Virginia. So I've been looking for somewhere that isn't so competitive.'

That brought a genuine smile to Sheila's face. Honesty, finally. 'And you figured the Ozarks aren't exactly teeming with scholars, is that it?'

'Pretty much.'

'So the treasure was what, an added perk?'

Maclin sighed and pushed a strand of brown hair behind her ear. 'The episode turned me on to this area. It was drivable, so I decided to come.'

Sheila shuffled papers for a minute, just to let the silence build. 'You're a little bit more than just a listener, though, aren't you?' She slid a screenshot printout across the table. Maclin's mouth sagged open as she stared down at the highlighted comments of *FoundIt72*. Sheila handed over another paper. And another.

'You seem to be very active in this community. And not just with this one particular treasure.'

'How did you . . .?'

'I'm also an expert in my field.' Sheila leaned forward. 'And I want to know, Professor – why have you tried so many times to get into those woods?'

She looked again at the *Hidden Hoards* chat-room printouts and her shoulders, bony under a Charlottesville Ale Trail T-shirt, slumped forward. 'I was supposed to meet someone. And we didn't have a backup location. So I wanted to see if they were there.'

'What about a cell phone number? This isn't the 1800s, ma'am.'

'They haven't been answering.'

Sheila thought back to the hours she'd spent reading that damn chat board. And the slightly more frequent interactions *FoundIt72* had with someone called *FortunesFave* than she did with anyone else. She leaned back and crossed her arms. 'Do you even have a name?'

Maclin sighed and shook her head. 'He – or she, I don't know – said they'd get in trouble if it came out that they were doing this. That's why they were all hush-hush.'

'What's the cell number?'

Maclin glared at her. 'That deputy who fingerprinted me took my phone.'

Sheila nodded and pulled out her own phone. She sent a quick text and tried not to break into a grin. An actual number. That they could trace. Please Lord let it lead to an ID.

'What's your friend's screen name?'

'*FortunesFave.*'

Sheila congratulated herself and rolled her hand in a 'keep going' motion. Maclin said they were supposed to meet at eight on Thursday morning. That was the earliest she could get there. And then, of course, she got stopped by the roadblock and couldn't make the rendezvous. It wasn't until the weekend that she heard about the two bodies found in the woods. Sheila frowned. So even if the unknown victim was *FortunesFave*, Maclin wouldn't be able to identify him. She flipped to the photo prints anyway.

'This is the murder victim we haven't been able to identify.'

Maclin turned very pale at the morgue photo and shook her head.

'This is another man we're looking for.' Sheila slid across Stanley Womack's driver's license photo. Maclin shook her head.

'What about this one?' Philip Garvan's license photo.

Maclin shrugged. 'Never seen him before, either.'

'He's the other man found murdered in the woods.'

She flinched.

'Which brings us back around,' Sheila said. 'Tell me, if you knew about the killings, why were you trying so hard to get into that area?'

Another shrug. Sheila leaned forward as far as her aching torso would allow. 'The minute I leave this room, I'm going to request a search warrant for your car, and everything in it. If I'm not satisfied with that, I'm going to get one for your residence in Virginia and I'm going to get your local police to send me everything they find. I'm going to go through it all, and I'm going to know what you know.'

Maclin sat very still, a deer caught in Sheila's headlights and unsure how to flee. Sheila calmly collected the pictures and put them back in her folder. 'Or . . . you can just tell me. Save both of us a lot of bother.' One last pause. She was curious. She honestly didn't know what the woman would do. Give in and talk, or choose to have her whole life laid bare?

From the look on her face, Maclin didn't know, either. She tugged at her T-shirt. Stared at her hands. Tried not to cry. And then shook her head. *No.* Sheila gave her one last look and was closing the folder when Bill Ramsdell walked in. He handed Sheila a Samsung Galaxy phone, shot Maclin an exasperated look and left. Sheila laid the phone in front of its owner.

'I'd like that phone number, please.'

Maclin didn't move. Sheila's voice turned hard. 'There are two issues here. One is whatever you're hiding and why. Fine. The other is *FortunesFave* and the fact that it could be him lying in the morgue right now. Figuring out his identity isn't a question you get to dick around with. You don't get to delay or obfuscate or hinder me in any way. It isn't about you. It's about his family being able to know where he is.'

She used a single finger and pushed the phone until it touched Maclin's now-trembling hand. It took her two tries to unlock it. She read out the number as Sheila copied it down on the front of the folder. Then Sheila stood up, took back the phone and walked out, leaving the woman in tears.

TWENTY-FOUR

H ank walked into the empty administration offices, curious as to where Sheila was. He made his way past her desk and into his own office, reflexively stepping over the lumps in the faded carpet on the way to his chair. He sagged into it and ignored the creaky seat springs as he looked at the stack of paperwork in front of him. A catalytic converter theft was on top. He pushed it aside and took out his phone. Maggie hadn't called. She wasn't scheduled to work today, so she was home with Duncan right now. Without the buffer of children, who were at school. He both wondered what they would talk about, and didn't want to know.

Was the old man back for good? Maybe Maggie could talk to Aunt Fin, see if she knew what Dunc was thinking. He'd stayed with her for three months; she must know something. Or not. Duncan was quite capable of keeping things hidden, that was for sure. They'd found that out when Marian's death came back to haunt them all. God, what would it be like if he stayed? Hank already felt like he was walking a tightrope with Maggie. Afraid any wrong word would upset the balance and send him plummeting. Would he now have to worry like that with Dunc, too? He didn't think he could take it. He dropped his head into his hands and tried not to think about it.

He sensed rather than heard Sheila arrive. She stood in the doorway eyeing him carefully.

'You've gotten pretty quiet moving with that cane.' He pushed himself back in his chair.

She held his gaze as she limped in and sat across the desk from him. 'Whatever happened out there with Old Man Fackrell can't have been that bad. What else is wrong?'

'It was fine. I just calmed him down. Also talked to Sammy about the search for Stanley Womack.'

Sheila raised an eyebrow. 'And?'

'And what?'

'And why are you sitting here like this? You look like your dog just died and you also have a migraine.' She tapped the floor with her cane. 'What's wrong?'

'Duncan's back.'

That left her speechless for the extraordinarily long time of fifteen seconds. 'I'll be damned. Huh. You weren't expecting him, were you?'

'No. Hell, no. He just showed up. Rang the doorbell. Trunk full of just enough luggage to be unclear either way – is he back for good? Just a visit? Who knows?'

'And he didn't give you an explanation?'

'Yeah . . . that's the entertaining part. We did figure out why he's here at this particular point in time.' He explained about Maribel sending texts on Maggie's phone, then waited wearily for Sheila to stop laughing.

'So it's a six-year-old who's kicked you all in the ass,' she said. 'I'm so proud of that girl.'

'Please don't tell her that. I'd like to not encourage any more phone hacking.'

Sheila waved dismissively. 'Somebody had to jump-start things. You adults are too close, with too much at stake, to keep flitting around each other like mute shadows. It's affecting more than just the three of you. Clearly.'

He looked at her, the full misery of it all clear in his expression. He could almost feel his face sagging under the weight of it.

'OK, fine,' she said. 'It is horrible. I don't mean to be discounting that. My point is that you all got to get back on track. For your own sanity and for your kids' happiness.' She looked at him with sympathy and a liberal dose of pity. 'Don't worry. I know that they're all of your highest priority. Let me know if you need me and Tyrone to take them for a day. We'd love to see them again, take them to the movies or something. Give you all space to talk.'

Hank cringed at the thought. A day of talking. He couldn't think of anything worse. And that included the three dead bodies on his case list. He ran a hand over his face. 'You're carrying paperwork. Does that mean you have news?'

'Maybe.' She pulled out the *FortunesFave* phone number and explained.

'Did you call it?'

'Not yet.'

'Ah. Sidetracked by a mopey colleague's family problems, were you?'

She laughed, which made him glad. At least she wasn't looking at him with pity anymore. She pulled out her phone, dialed and put it on speaker. It went to voicemail – an automated recording that just recited the number. She left a message.

'So do we think we'll get a call back? Or do we think the owner of that number is in the morgue?'

'Is it terrible to say I hope he's in the morgue? At least then we'll have an ID on the body.'

'And what's your plan for this Maclin lady? You going to let Ramsdell keep her in custody?'

She chuckled. 'He was so damn irritated, he would've thrown her in the lake if he'd thought of it. But yeah, we hold her at least until we search her car and get the phone number info back. I'm not trusting that she was entirely truthful with me. She wanted into those woods so badly for more than just rumored treasure. She's not leaving until I find out what it is.'

Rain swept in and stopped all work on the skeleton. They scrambled to cover everything and then the anthropologists fled the scene. Sam, after such a lovely morning, got to spend a soggy afternoon under an extra tarp as he watched over the dig site.

Sheila was not going to be happy that the scientists didn't finish today. That meant another overnight deputy earning overtime pay the department couldn't afford. Sam called it in and looked around for a better spot to stand guard. He found one on a flat rock about a dozen yards away, where he could better huddle underneath the tarp as the rain beat down. He wiped dripping water off his nose and pulled out his phone. And things suddenly got a lot better.

The warrant request was back for the credit card information on the series of Ubers taken from the Springfield Airport to Branson. Sam clicked on the email. It was a Visa card in the name of Jordan F. Markham. It had been used for every ride through to the pink Scion that dropped the hoodie-wearer at the Best Buy. After that, the only charge was $9.42 at an Arby's fast-food restaurant in the same shopping center. Otherwise, nothing. No further transactions at all, either before or after that day. It appeared to be a brand-new card. He requested another warrant for Markham's bank information as the rain intensified. That could take another several days, if he was lucky.

He sighed and looked around. The cover over the skeleton dig was thankfully still in place. The downpour was steady, but at least it wasn't windy. He unlocked his phone again and pulled up a saved webpage. Everything cost so much. He quickly swiped it closed and opened another one. That prompted a rueful laugh. These were just as bad. The only thing he could afford out-of-pocket was a 2002 Ford Escort. He loved Ford and all – clearly, look at his Bronco – but the Escort was not their finest hour. He kept scrolling. If he could get a loan, that would expand his potential selection significantly. But how much was he willing to apply for? He didn't want to be in a lot of debt. He'd had it all plotted out down to the penny, every expense. Everything was on track. And then the Bronco died.

He couldn't let that derail him. He punched numbers into the calculator app, checked his savings account balance, the rates on a car loan, and did even more math. That got him to the outside possibility of a car made in the 2010s. He would be more than satisfied with that. Hell, a 2009 pickup would be fantastic if he could find one in good shape. Soon. Because he certainly couldn't keep borrowing Brenna's car. One, she needed it. And two, he looked ridiculous in it. Some cars were just girl cars and that was all there was to it.

That thought led to him picturing her behind the wheel, bopping around town with her sunglasses on and her music playing too loud. His chest got tight and it took a minute for him to be able to swallow. He would figure this out. He had to.

TWENTY-FIVE

While Cheryl Maclin cooled her bony little heels in a jail cell, Sheila enjoyed a cup of tea and read through more of the *Hidden Hoards* chat room – specifically the postings of *FortunesFave*. He or she was one of the more fanatical members. An opinion on every episode, knowledgeable about every treasure, certain of every location. If he wasn't the murder victim, Sheila might want to kill him herself.

But why would someone who seemed to be nothing but a blowhard suddenly come out into the field? What made Murder Rocks special? And why bother to team up with Maclin?

There's more here than even Hardwick knows. The rocks hold secrets.

She scoffed. No kidding the rocks held secrets. This was the Ozarks. Every rock and tree and creek bed hid something dangerous.

I've seen documents he doesn't have. You'll have to wait & see what I find.

She made a note to ask Maclin about that. The pair's texts hadn't been particularly informative – just logistics for meeting up at the site. Which means they had to have spoken directly about the documents or whatever else this guy had. Because there had to be a reason the intense college professor was deigning to cooperate with some armchair windbag.

All you people who just think this is entertainment. You'll see. Everyone will realize this is the big one. The Civil War left ruins everywhere & treasure if you're smart enough to know how to look.

The question was whether he had indeed come and looked. Had he emerged from behind his computer screen and come to town? She would love to put him on her suspect list. She stopped scrolling and was reaching for another tea bag when the phone number ID came through. A man named Alan Takama with a billing address in Fort Worth. Sheila looked at the surname and her fingertips started to tingle. She quickly went to work. It took ten minutes until she was staring at a Texas driver's license photo. She picked up the phone.

'I'm sending you the photo of a fifty-one-year-old Asian man
with a chubby face and a bad haircut.'

'I have one of those here in person,' said Ngozi Aguta. 'Does
yours have a name?'

Sheila read off the specifics as she emailed the photo. She could
hear the medical examiner moving around the morgue.

'Well. Hello, Mr Takama. It's nice to give you a name.' Sheila
could picture Aguta laying a gentle hand on the body as she spoke.
She wasn't the kind of doctor who believed patient courtesy ended
when life did. They both fell silent.

'But me comparing a photo isn't exactly a positive ID,' Aguta
finally said. 'Please tell me Texas fingerprints you when you apply
for a driver's license.'

'They do. I've got his thumbprint right here. I'll send it and the
print you took from the victim for matching right now. I just wanted
you to tell me if it was worth doing first.'

'Great. I'll be glad to send him home. You'll contact next of kin
first, though, right?'

'Yes. I need to find out if they know anything about this whole
mess,' Sheila said.

'Speaking of the "whole mess," what about the skeleton?'

Sheila groaned. 'They're going to take it, right? Those
anthropologists? They don't even know how long it's been in the
ground. They say when it's nothing but bones, it's "extremely difficult"
to date. Well, they're the ones with the PhDs. Figure it out.'

'Well, I can tell you it's a male who was at least six feet tall.'

That did not make Sheila feel better. 'Right now, I don't care
who. I care when. If it's from the Civil War, I need to know. Because
if that's the case, it's not going on my books. I'm not going to have
my homicide clearance rate ruined by some bushwhacking
highwayman asshole.'

That had Aguta laughing as she hung up the phone. Easy for her
to do. She didn't have three simultaneous investigations, too many
deputies on overtime, roadblocks, idiot out-of-towners, and a
spooked local constituency screaming for answers. Sheila looked
again at the picture of Alan Takama and had a bad feeling that
knowing his identity wouldn't lead to answers, but only more
questions. She sighed and got up to make a fresh cup of tea.

*   *   *

The rain kept getting worse and the wind was picking up. Sam shifted under the blue polyethylene tarp and comforted himself by thinking that at least he wasn't having to do a death notification. Sheila had called to tell him they'd ID'd the gunshot victim. It was great news, but she hadn't sounded like it was. She'd also said there was no one to relieve him for several more hours. By then, he'd have combed through the inventory on every used-car website in the state. He'd already done all the lots in St. Louis and was starting on the Kansas City area. There were a few possibilities, but hell, they'd probably be gone before he even got out of these woods.

He hunkered down in the descending darkness and pulled up the ESPN college football page, thankful Alice had lent him her portable phone charger. He was in the middle of the SEC football standings when a gust of wind almost took his tarp. He kept hold of it, but the one covering the hole had no such anchor. It peeled off, exposing the gaping wound in the ground. Sam stuffed the phone in his windbreaker pocket and bolted after it. Too heavy to get caught and lifted by the wind, it instead bunched up and tumbled down to the right. He shifted toward it, slipping onto one knee and then sliding in the mud before he was able to catch himself. He scrambled toward the tarp, which took another gust and whipped farther away.

He turned to look back at the hole. The edges were already dissolving. Those PhDs were going to lose their minds. He gauged the distances and then struggled back up the hill to his tarp, which he'd earlier anchored to the rock he was sitting on. He made it the last few feet on his hands and knees and freed the slick covering, then worked his way back down. He half crawled around the hole's perimeter, using the same rocks the professors had to weigh down the covering. This time he did a better job, grinding them into the mud in the hope that would keep them from shifting and setting the tarp loose.

He finished, with only one side of the hole bad enough to be officially labeled 'collapsed.' The others might hold if the damn rain would only lighten up. He struggled to his feet and tried to wipe water out of his eyes. That just got mud in them. He swore and looked around. The hole's original tarp was wrapped around a tree twenty yards away. He could put it on the hillside above the hole, maybe divert water away from the damn thing. No point using it to put over himself. He was already as wet as a person could get. What he needed was a change of clothes and a waterproof tent. He scoffed at himself as he trudged toward the tarp. It wasn't like he could call for help. *Yeah, hi. The rain is kicking my ass. I need reinforcements.*

He weaved through the shortleaf pines, eyes pinned on the one that caught the tarp. He finally got there and wrestled it away. It was bigger than the one he'd been using, so he rolled it in as much of a ball as he could and wrapped his arms around it to drag-carry it back. That made the terrain even harder to navigate. He concentrated on where he was putting his feet, not wanting to slip and take another mud bath. He side-stepped around the last tree in his way and looked up.

A man stood next to the hole. Barely visible through the downpour. Nobody should be out here. Not only was it private property, it was a closed crime scene. Sam blinked rapidly and risked using a hand to wipe at his eyes. The man was still there, bending toward the covering.

Sam rushed forward, yelling for the person to freeze. The figure whipped around, noticed the soaked deputy, and turned to flee. Sam dropped the tarp and sprang after him. The man headed in the direction of the easiest route out to Bushers Hollow Road. Sam knew it and angled to cut him off. The man doubled back, now heading uphill and away from Sam and the road access. Sam scrambled up, passing the hole and gaining on him. He had nothing to lose, no nerve that wasn't frayed, no part of him left to keep clean. He stopped yelling and instead used his breath to fuel a last lunge at the figure, who'd stumbled on a jutting rock just below where Sam had been sitting.

He caught him around the knees. The man screamed and fell flat, Sam landing heavily on his legs. He tried to jerk away, but Sam slithered up until he had a knee in the man's back. The man started to thrash around and his bulk made Sam lose his balance on the incline. Sam managed to fall in the uphill direction, one arm still wrapped around the trespasser. Then the ground gave way. They slid sideways down the hill on a sled of mud, the man bucking and screaming and Sam trying not to lose his grip. Everything crashed into the hole – rocks, humans, mud. Sam landed on top of the intruder. Hard. Only then did the guy stop screaming.

Sam covered his own head against the sluicing mud and grunted in pain as one of the rocks landed on his leg. They huddled like they were in it together as the mud kept coming. It felt like hours passed before it stopped. When it did, it covered almost their entire bodies. Sam felt himself start to shake. He felt buried in a nice coffin-shaped hole in the creepy forest. No, that wouldn't give him nightmares.

He told himself to calm down. Even though he was on his stomach, his head and shoulders remained free. The trespasser wasn't as lucky. His lower body was encased in several feet of mud and everything from the waist up was pinned under Sam. He could only still breathe because of the air cavity created by Sam curled on top of him. Sam needed to move fast.

He pushed himself up on his hands and knees, using the trespasser as a floor of sorts. That shed a lot of the mud off his back. He yanked his arms free and started frantically hand-shoveling muck away from the man's face. He worked until he was sure nothing would tumble back onto his head, then started on the rest of their bodies. It was dirty, sloppy, slow work, and the continuing rain made it exponentially worse.

The man just lay there whimpering, even after Sam cleared his arms. 'You have to help,' he yelled. More of the hill could come down any minute and Sam did not want a re-burial. He kept digging and wiggling and finally freed his own legs. He stood up, looming over the trespasser. Whatever hell he looked like finally jolted the man into action. He grunted and huffed and tried to wipe the coat of mud off his face. Sam yelled some more. They had to get out of the hole – now. The man started scooping, and Sam helped, until they were able to yank one leg out. Then he started to moan.

'No. There's something wrong. It's twisted.'

Sam thought he was lying until he uncovered it, honestly bent at a very bad angle. Great. Now the guy, already clearly not the self-reliant type, couldn't walk. How was he supposed to get him out of the woods?

He manhandled the guy over to the trees, where they were at least out of the path of the mudslide. Then he wiped his hands on the least dirty patch of his windbreaker lining, unzipped its pocket and pulled out his phone. The man leaned against a tree and tried to wipe off the gunk still stuck all over his face. Sam ignored him and dialed Sheila. She didn't answer. He clicked on Hank's number. It rang just as the trespasser cleaned off enough mud for Sam to start to see the pudgy cheeks and close-clipped goatee.

He'd found Stanley Womack.

TWENTY-SIX

Hank found them limping through the woods looking like sasquatches. They'd made it halfway to the road from the dig site. He had a feeling Sammy was getting more irritated with every step. Hank then didn't help matters by making the kid sit in the cruiser's plastic backseat with Womack.

'I got to put you somewhere that can be hosed out.'

'I know. It's fine.'

But Sam's silence spoke louder than Womack's whimpers on the way to the hospital. Once they sent him and his wrenched knee off to Maggie, Hank hurried to get Sam a cup of coffee. He returned from the cafeteria to find him standing in the middle of the waiting room, trying not to touch anything.

'The chairs are plastic. I think it's OK for you to sit down.'

A passing nurse stopped. 'Oh, honey. You poor thing. Let me get you a towel.'

'Can I sit down?' Sam asked.

She raised a cautious eyebrow. 'Is it just mud?'

'What? Oh. Ew. Yes, it's just mud. I promise.'

'Then you go right ahead. I'll be back.'

Sam sank into a chair and gulped at his coffee.

'I can get someone to drive you home.'

'No way. I've got questions for that whiny little . . .' He stopped himself.

That was hard to argue with. Hank would want some answers, too, if he'd been the one mud-wrestling with the guy. He was about to say that when the nurse returned with a package of baby wipes and several paper drape sheets. Sam sighed and trudged off to the bathroom. He was still there when Maggie came out from the exam rooms.

'I can't tell you his condition.'

He eyed his wife. 'Is he awake?'

'Yes.'

'Then we're going to talk to him.'

'Hank. You know better.'

'This one is under arrest, honey. Full-on in custody, lucky-he's-not-in-handcuffs under arrest. If he invokes, then he invokes. But until then, we're asking him some questions.'

She set her jaw. 'So you probably also want to take him straight to jail?'

'Yes, please.'

She glowered at him and said she'd write up the prescription. 'But you're not getting him until he has everything he needs.' Then her face softened. 'And you need a towel. You're soaked. How did you avoid the mud?'

'I missed that fun.' He turned as Sam's wet shoes came squeaking unevenly down the hallway linoleum. 'He's the one who got caught in it.'

Now Sam's face and hands were clean, stark white against the dark mud on the rest of him. He'd also scrubbed at his hair, but that had only turned it into a frothy mud mess. He looked away before Sam caught him trying not to laugh. Maggie, on the other hand, took one look at the young man's limping form and hauled him back to an empty exam room. Hank waited ten minutes and then followed.

'It's just a bruise. Not a big deal.' Sam stood next to an exam table smeared with mud.

Maggie gave them both a cutting look. 'He should go easy for a day or two. Not much walking.'

Both men readily agreed and she rolled her eyes at the lie. Then she took them to Womack as she said she wouldn't release him until he was fitted for a leg brace. They walked in to find a pudgy white man with a mud-crusted goatee and scrapes down the side of his face. He was in a paper gown that made him immediately cleaner than Sam, although he still had brown smears all over his arms and filthy ankles and calves where his socks and pants had gone in opposite directions. He looked like he could barely find a hole in the ground, let alone dig one.

Hank gestured for Sam to take the one chair in the room. He stayed at the foot of the bed, pulled out his phone and started recording. 'What were you looking for, Mr Womack?'

The man picked at a dirty thumbnail. 'I was just out for a walk. There was a hole. It was natural to look in it.'

'Out for a walk? In the rain? Miles from nowhere? On private property?'

'I, uh, wasn't aware it was private property.'

'And how did you know there was a hole there?' They'd managed to keep the skeleton's existence out of the news. The only members of the public who knew about it were the Fackrells. And Hank had a feeling that if they chose to leak it, it wouldn't be to a treasure hunter.

'I . . . I didn't. I randomly came upon it.'

'That's not true.' Sam was on his feet. 'You were totally searching, and you snuck up on it like you were hiding. And then you ran. What does that say?'

Womack flinched. Hank gestured at Sam out of the man's sightline and his deputy slowly sank back into his seat.

'So you were prepared, it sounds like,' Hank said. 'And you brought all that with you when you came. When you flew into Springfield and rented a Volkswagen Jetta. When you stayed at the Come Again Motel, and then the Holiday Inn Express. And when you parked – yet did not stay – at the Ozark Hightop Lodge.'

Womack's slight coloring drained away as Hank spoke.

'Have you been camping since you left the car?'

Womack nodded, almost in spite of himself. Hank's recitation of his movements seemed to have the same dazing effect as a blow to the head.

'And it took you this long to walk from the lodge to where Deputy Karnes found you?'

Another nod.

'Why'd you come to Branson in the first place?'

Womack started on his thumbnail again. 'To see the shows?'

Sam started to stand again. Hank waved him back down, not bothering to hide the gesture this time. 'We might traffic in folksy Ozark hokum here, but we have yet to stage an outdoor show in hard-to-access woods in the dark during a rainstorm. So let's try again. Why are you in Branson?'

He looked from Hank to Sam and sighed. 'The podcast. To see what I could find. To hunt for treasure.'

Hank crossed his arms. 'Yeah, but here's the thing. The podcast only mentioned Murder Rocks. That's the only location anyone had. So why were you off looking somewhere else?'

Womack gave a tired shrug and wiped at his face with a sniffle. 'I'm really tired. And I can't see. I lost my glasses when he . . .' He trailed off and pointed at Sam.

'When you disobeyed a law enforcement order to stop?' Sam
retorted.

'When you tackled me.'

'Don't forget the part where I arrested you.'

'OK, OK,' Hank said. 'Mr Womack, do you participate in any
chat rooms associated with the *Hidden Hoards* podcast?'

He said no, then said he didn't know any of the people Hank
listed off – the two murder victims, fellow treasure hunters Cheryl
Maclin and Mingo Culver, Uber credit card holder Jordan Markham.
He was just a listener who thought it would be fun to come try his
hand at treasure hunting since the location wasn't too far away from
his home in Colorado. He'd never done it before, and hand to God,
he'd never do it again.

'That's not really what I'm worried about right now, Mr Womack,'
Hank said. 'I'm concerned that you're not telling us the whole truth
and that you might try to go back out there. So we're going to book
you on charges of trespassing and resisting arrest.' That would hold
him while they asked Marvin Sedstone again for his phone records
– the one request the judge denied Sheila earlier in the week. Also,
Hank wanted the man in an interrogation room where he could show
him photos. Specifically, the ones of his treasure-hunting competition
and what had happened to them. See if that shook anything loose.

It was midnight before Sam got home. Hank dropped him off in
the driveway and told him to take tomorrow off. Actually, he ordered
him to sleep in, watch some Netflix, order take-out from the Roark
Diner and tell Clem to put it on the Worths' tab. Sam managed half
a smile in response and limped away. He got to the house and looked
around. It might be late, but that didn't mean his neighbors weren't
up. He trudged past Brenna's car and around to the backyard before
he stripped down to his underwear, leaving everything but his duty
belt on the back step. He quietly let himself in the back door and
stood in his blissfully dry, silent kitchen.

He took several deep breaths. He felt like he hadn't gotten a
complete one into his lungs since the first tarp blew off the hole.
That damn hole. What did it really hold? Problems, that was for
sure. Almost certainly not treasure. He'd lived here his entire life
and nobody had ever found anything out there. Not from his
generation or any of the ones before. All that ever happened out
there was stupidity. And violence.

He laid his belt on the kitchen table and squished across the linoleum down the hall to the bathroom. He didn't turn a light on – he didn't want to wake Brenna. He hadn't expected her to be here, but she knew he'd gotten stuck with guard duty out at the site. She must've come after he told her he expected to get off at nine o'clock, when they could've still had an evening together. Now he could see her asleep in bed through the slightly open door. He stood there for a moment, bruised and clammy, damp and filthy, and thought about how lucky he was.

He stepped away and tiptoed into the bathroom, waiting to turn on the light until he shut the door. He got a fresh towel from under the sink and as he straightened, he caught himself in the mirror. Dear God, why hadn't Hank said something about the mess he'd made of his hair? Instead of washing clean in the damn hospital restroom, it had lathered and was now in the process of hardening. And the line where his shirt collar had met the mud was comically demarcated. He looked like some kind of mud clown. It was enough to briefly distract from the livid welt running down his right cheek all the way to his jaw and the left eye starting to blacken.

But the worst was his leg. His left thigh had started to hurt the minute the rock landed on it, and was steadily getting worse, radiating pain through to the bone. It was starting to swell and had that first blush of purple that meant a deep bruise was coming. Dr McCleary had wanted to take his pants off – now there was a phrase he'd never imagined using – but he hadn't let her. They were so dirty and stiff, he knew he'd never get them back on and he'd be forced to walk out of the hospital in a pair of paper shorts. They should've told him his dignity was already gone and leaving half-naked wouldn't make a difference. Instead she took an X-ray to confirm it wasn't broken, then told him to ice it and stay off the leg for a day or two. And he planned to, as soon as he was clean.

He got in the shower and started at the top. He'd just finished his second shampoo when the shower curtain tugged open and a naked Brenna stepped in. She didn't say a word, just took the bar of soap and started on his back. Then his chest. Then the soap dropped into the tub. And Sam forgot about his leg and took the only thing worth remembering into his arms.

TWENTY-SEVEN

'You don't have to be here.' Malcolm Oberholz knelt next to Sheila's seat in the back row of the courtroom. The tone of his whisper clearly implied that he wished she wasn't. She understood his viewpoint. But.

'Look. I can't attend the trial since I'll be testifying and not allowed to hear what other witnesses are saying. Wouldn't want to taint my testimony.' She gestured toward Judge Sedstone's unoccupied bench. 'So these hearings are the only chance I'll get to see things.'

He sighed. He did not, however, argue with her. Which reinforced her decision to like him. He rose to his feet just as Lanton Decker entered, black robes billowing behind him. The judge was white, of medium height and a little stooped, with no hair except a steel gray bristle around the back of his head. He waved down Fizzel's attorney, Dolores Jacobsen, who'd also stood up.

'I don't hold with that "all rise" nonsense. Not 'til trial anyway. I just want you punctual and prepared. Even if it is this early in the morning.' He settled himself with a great flapping of black sleeves and smiled from under a mustache just as bristly and gray as the hair. 'Mr Oberholz, it's your motion today for change of venue. I've read your and Ms Jacobsen's submissions. Did you have anything you wanted to add?'

'Before we're heard on this matter, Your Honor, if I may?' The still-standing Jacobsen spoke crisply but deferentially. Sheila supposed she knew just as much about this judge as she and Oberholz did, which was next to nothing. The man in question raised an eyebrow at her.

'We object to the deputy being in the courtroom.' Jacobsen placed a hand on Eddie Fizzel Junior's shoulder. Decker's other eyebrow raised to join its mate. He made a show of looking over the gallery and its only two occupants.

'I'm guessing that the young lady in the uniform is who you're referring to?'

Sheila scoffed softly. In the back row across the aisle, the newspaper kid tried to stifle a snicker.

'Is anything going to be argued today that she shouldn't hear?'

'Well, sir, witnesses shouldn't be privy to—'

'Your Honor, there is nothing that the *chief* deputy should be prevented from hearing in regard to this particular issue,' Oberholz said.

'I can't think of anything either. So she can stay.'

Jacobsen, whose posture seemed to be aided by a steel rod stuck up somewhere uncomfortable, sat. Eddie Jr leaned over and muttered something in her ear. Sheila scolded herself for not sitting directly behind them. She could stomach being that close if it meant hearing what they said, or even kept them from communicating at all. Next time.

Oberholz remained standing. 'Back to your question, Your Honor. I'd like to add this morning's *Branson Daily Herald* article to my court exhibit of media coverage.' He pulled out a Xeroxed copy and looked back at the reporter kid. '"Hearing Will Determine If Fizzel Jr Trial Is Moved: Bootheel Judge to Decide If Local Jury Pool Is Tainted," by Jadhur Banerjee.'

'Well, now.' The judge held out his hand and Oberholz approached to hand over the article. 'That is a loaded word, now isn't it? Tainted?'

Sheila heard the faintest groan from across the aisle.

'I don't believe Mr Banerjee himself writes the headlines. I'm not sayin' that,' Oberholz said. 'My point is that news coverage continues, and will only increase as pretrial proceedings get more frequent. Potential jurors will know extensive details about the case, in addition to likely personally being acquainted with one or more of the people involved. They will have already formed opinions, which as we all know is—'

'This is a non-issue, Your Honor,' Jacobsen cut in. 'Nobody reads the paper anyway.'

That generated an indignant huff from the other back row.

'Based upon coverage when the assault – and the stalkin' and the property destruction and the resistin' arrest – occurred, there'll be plenty of TV news coverage as well when jury selection starts.' Oberholz slid his hands loosely into his pants pockets and turned his head to look at defense counsel, keeping the rest of his body facing the judge. It showed he didn't think his opposition was important enough to warrant a full facing. Sheila was enjoying herself immensely.

'This is not the little county it once was, Your Honor,' Jacobsen said. 'There are plenty of people who don't know my client, or the "chief" deputy.'

Her air quote inflection had Oberholz cocking an annoyed eyebrow. 'But they do know of his daddy.' He plucked a paper from his binder and waved it around. The photo of an angry little man with hedgehog hair appeared to be from a TV news website. 'Edrick Fizzel Sr has served on the county commission for almost fifteen years. Even if people don't know him personally, they know of him or have had dealings with his office. And he's a well-known critic of the sheriff's department. Which is – to be fair – a reason you'd think the defense would want the trial moved. Havin' jurors who know that fact certainly won't help the defendant.'

Oh, he was a wily son of a bitch. Sheila almost applauded.

'So now Mr Oberholz has joined the defense bar? He thinks he can strategize this case better than I can?' Jacobsen said it with amused derision.

Oberholz shrugged. 'All I'm sayin' is that having a jury pool who's unaware of the personal and political animosity Fizzel Senior has for the victim and the victim's boss . . .' he paused. 'Well, that certainly isn't detrimental to your client.'

'Thank you, but I'll stay with my position that a change of venue would be costly, unnecessarily burdensome and just flat-out unnecessary all together. Any problems with individual prospective juror opinions can be dealt with easily in voir dire.'

That started a spirited discussion about what juror questions could successfully weed out biased candidates. Sheila thought about that. While many people were indeed idiots, they weren't stupid. And they weren't honest. So what good was questioning them about who they knew and what they believed? Plenty of good, if you were the defense and the trial stayed here. Lie, lie again, and get put on the jury. Let the silly Fizzel boy off the hook.

Or maybe they'd lie in her favor. She chuckled. That was as likely as a meteorite landing in the parking lot.

'That's enough on voir dire,' Decker eventually said. 'No point in hashing it all out until we know what kind of jury pool we're working with. I'll issue my ruling within the next week.'

He and his robes swept out of the courtroom. Oberholz walked back and gave a quote to Jadhur as Sheila wrestled herself out of her seat. After the reporter left, they ducked into a small workroom and closed the door.

'So what do you think of our chances?' she asked.

'I don't know. I like him, though. He seems sharp.' He stuffed all his papers into his bag.

'So do you think a change of venue would actually benefit them, too?'

'Yeah. I do. Prospective jurors who aren't aware of all the times Daddy Fizzel attacked Sheriff Worth in the press. Or that he backed someone else for sheriff who then sued you and Worth for wrongful termination. The list goes on. All kinds of motivation that could plausibly have rubbed off on Junior.'

'So would it be a balanced assist for both sides if Decker agrees to move it?'

Oberholz leaned against the wall and smiled. 'Oh, no, ma'am. Because we'd get clean jurors who haven't accepted favors or gone fishing or attended church or whatever with the Fizzels. They'll get jurors who start out not knowing those nasty motivations – but that's only until I find a way to get it all into evidence.'

She didn't even try to stifle her laugh. 'You are a crafty bastard.'

He shrugged. 'Eh. Not especially. She knows what my plan is. That's why she's fighting so hard to keep it here. But I'll take the compliment. Thanks.'

She tapped her cane on the floor. 'You have a safe trip back up north. See if you can find all those g's you dropped when you were talkin' in there.'

His surprised laugh echoed down the hall as she opened the door and walked out. 'Noticed that, did you?'

'Like I said. Crafty bastard.'

The pudgy little man made a show of arranging himself in the chair, which was bolted to the floor of the interrogation room. He finally settled on sticking his full-length leg brace out to the side and moaning under his breath. Hank ignored him. Instead, he slowly opened the thick folder in front of him and pulled out a stack of photos. First he slid across Cheryl Maclin's mug shot. Womack denied knowing her. Hank put it to the side. Next came the driver's license photos for both Alan Takama and Philip Garvan. Womack shook his head. Hank left them on the table.

'You said last night, Mr Womack, that you were aware there've been two murders out near Murder Rocks. These are the two men who were killed.' He pushed the photos closer to Womack. 'Feel free to pick them up if you need a closer look. I know you lost your glasses.'

Womack ignored the pictures. 'Yeah, my glasses. And my stuff. Am I going to get my pack back? All of my stuff is in there.'

Hank stared at him. The guy wasn't being investigatively informative, but he certainly was saying a lot about himself. 'What's so important about your stuff?'

Womack bristled. 'Well, I can't fucking see, for one thing. And the rest, it's . . . there's . . . all my camping equipment. My wallet, you know, stuff like that.'

Hank pretended to mull that over. 'To be frank, it doesn't speak very well of you that you're more concerned with your property than the brutal deaths of two human beings.'

Womack slapped his hand down on the photos and slid them back across the table to Hank. 'I didn't know them!'

Hank left them where they were and put down two new ones. Crime scene ones. 'But did you *see* them?'

Womack sucked in so much air, he started to cough. Hank didn't even pause. 'He was killed near Murder Rocks.' He tapped the photo of Garvan as Womack wheezed. 'And then his body was dragged through the woods and shoved down a rocky hill.' He moved his finger to the other photo. 'This man, he was left where he was killed. Hacked to death, farther away from Murder Rocks, but not by that much.'

Womack put his hand over the photo of Takama, blotting it out but not touching it. His normally deep voice came out a shade higher as he struggled for breath. 'I don't . . . please . . . that's awful.'

'Yeah, it is.' Hank's own voice raised, in volume if not in pitch. 'That's why I need you to be honest with me. You were near those woods last week. We know you were. We have your rental car movements. So I want to know if, while you were walking around in those woods – did you see either of these men? Alive or dead?'

Womack looked down in his lap. Silently. Hank left the photos where they were and waited, leaning back in his chair like he had all day. And in a way, he did. The man in front of him was the best lead they had at the moment, so nothing else was as high a priority. And that's what he planned to tell Sheila when she finally showed up. He knew she'd want to kill him for starting the interview without

her. But he couldn't find her. She wasn't in her office and her phone
was turned off. Those were good arguments in his favor. She was
still going to kill him, though.

'I . . . I didn't see them. Either of them. I only found the rocks.'
He didn't look up.

'When was this?'

'I got here two days after the podcast aired.'

'Tell me what you did.'

'I rented a car, drove down to the woods and hiked in to the
rocks.'

'That's very succinct. Let's elaborate a little. Where did you park
your car?'

He didn't really know.

'How long did it take you to find the rocks?'

A few hours. He had a compass but wasn't very good with it.

'What did you do when you got there?'

Looked around. Tried to see where the Finnegan wagons would
have overturned. Based on the Mary Louise letters read on the
podcast. Found a few possible spots.

'What'd you do then?'

Dug some holes.

'How many?'

He wasn't sure. Some. A few.

'You don't know how many holes you dug? I think that means
you dug a lot of them.'

Well, maybe. Maybe not. He couldn't remember.

'I'm looking right here at a crime scene report that listed fourteen
separate holes in the vicinity of Murder Rocks. That sound about
right?'

He couldn't really say. He hadn't counted. He was just trying,
poking around like. He'd never done this sort of thing before. He
was always just a listener. Of the podcast.

'Where did you go once you were done digging holes?'

He just left. Straight out back the way he came. Minding his own
business.

Now Hank leaned forward. 'Your entire trip was about *not*
minding your own business.'

Silence. Womack carefully studied his hands, which hadn't moved
from his lap. Hank waited. He wanted to let him stew for a bit
before starting the next subject, which was why Womack had left

his car in the lodge parking lot and walked all those miles back to the rocks. He was about to start talking when one soft rap came from the other side of the two-way mirror. He got up and walked out into the hallway. Sheila emerged from the observation room at the same time. She had her cane in one hand, a to-go cup of coffee in the other and a smirk on her face.

'That's quite the interrogation you got going. Both of you sitting there silent.'

'Where've you been?'

'Court hearing on my assault case. It just ended.'

'If I'd know that's where you were, I would've waited,' he said.

She harrumphed. He gave her a quick rundown, and they both walked into the room together. Womack looked up in surprise at another person joining them. Hank took his seat. Sheila put her coffee on the table and went to pull the extra chair out of the corner.

'Stanley and I were just going to start talking about why he made the curious choice to abandon his rental car in a hotel parking lot and walk all that way back to those woods.'

Womack looked from Hank to this new woman, who despite the limp did not look at all like a pushover. He cleared his throat. 'It seemed like a good idea. And I needed the exercise.'

Sheila's cane clattered to the floor. She spun toward Womack so fast, the table jostled and her coffee tipped. Hank shoved back before he got soaked and Womack froze.

She smacked her palms down on the table and leaned toward him. 'I didn't introduce myself. I'm Chief Deputy Sheila Turley. It's nice to finally meet you, Mr Hardwick.'

TWENTY-EIGHT

[Orchestral music]

Welcome back, listeners. Imagine you are a local bank before the Civil War. You're well known in your region and you print your own banknotes, as there was no national paper currency. This worked for banks all over the country, because their notes were redeemable at their specific institutions for gold or silver. All value was anchored to the precious metals, and a certain amount of consumer confidence was in place.

[Sound of cannon fire]

Then war breaks out and two things happen. Ordinary people get very worried and start exchanging all those banknotes for the security of actual gold. And the U.S. government, fighting an expensive war, runs out of money. It doesn't have the gold and silver it needs to finance the war effort. So it creates its own money, abandoning the gold standard. The Legal Tender Act of 1862 makes paper notes issued by the federal government just that – legal tender. These 'greenbacks' aren't linked to gold at all. They're money only because the government says so.

Suddenly, banks aren't obligated to give out their gold or silver when depositors come to them with paper tender. Now, many of these institutions already had greatly diminished holdings from the bank runs by consumers earlier in the war. But some had been able to hang onto at least some of their original stores of gold. The Bank of Carrollton was one of them. But this banking triumph turned into a dangerous problem as the Confederate Army gained strength in the area.

The farms ringing the south side of town have been stripped of all livestock and goods. They advance like the cicada hordes, devouring everything possible. And heaven help if they suspect Union sympathies. Those poor souls wish that theft and looting were their only tribulations. Their homesteads are also put to the torch. They are lucky to be able to flee with only what they have about their persons. Some have staggered into town, where people are fearful of helping. No one wants to do so and thereby mark themselves as well. I am shamed to say I am one of them. I know God will judge me, but better Him than the Confederate Army.

That's just one example of a worried resident in this bustling – and mostly Southern-leaning – town in the middle of Arkansas. The most terrified of the whole population, though, had to have been Mr Bartholomew Handelsman – manager of the First Bank of Carrollton and, not to put too fine a point on it, keeper of the keys to the vault.

[Keys jingling, coins clinking]
That day I did so wish to forfeit the position. I had aspired to it for so long and had grown quite comfortable in it. Then the war came and I was consumed with worry. Then the Army came and I was consumed with fear. I begged the help of a friend who was heading north that very night. I did not know what else could be done.

This was written years after the war, but it illuminates his mindset at the time. And when taken with the newly discovered information in Mary Louise Finnegan's letters, what scholars guessed was Handelsman's talking about sending his frail wife to safety becomes something very different. Instead, he's enlisting Ernest Finnegan to carry a king's ransom in gold across the state border into Missouri. And the last sentence of his 1888 letter to a brother now makes sense.

If only I had not asked. I would dig a hole in the ground and say I'm sorry.

The only sound was the drip, drip of coffee onto the linoleum. Sheila didn't move. Womack didn't move. Hank tried not to look confused.
'You crafty little fucker.' She looked him up and down. A short, dumpy, dweeb of a man with scrapes all over his arms and an *oh, shit* look on his face. She finished arranging her chair without taking her eyes off him and sat down. Her cane stayed on the floor, the coffee pooled on the table, and Hank started to relax and enjoy the show.

'I'm beginning to think that *Hidden Hoards* has some truth-in-advertising problems.' She sighed. 'So disappointing.'

He started to fidget but couldn't seem to look away from her. Good. 'You told Sheriff Worth here that this is the first time you've gone to one of the "treasure" locations. Is that true?'

'Yes.' The voice was small and hesitant, but still had the same mellifluous bass tone familiar to any of his podcast listeners. A group that apparently didn't include Hank. She resisted glaring at him.

'So you're not a globe-trotting adventurer, either? Along with not being a six-foot-two, attractively weathered dreamboat with a full head of hair.' She waved dismissively. 'So disappointing.'

'That's why it's a podcast,' he snapped.

Ah, she'd found a nerve. 'So why bother being Hardwick at all?'

'People were not going to want to listen to some guy with my stupid name talking about fabulous pirate treasure.'

She raised an eyebrow. 'But an alias wasn't all you did. You took it to the next level with your sexy fake Hardwick. Where'd you find him? An "active-adult" vitamin commercial?'

He finally tore his gaze away from Sheila's.

'It's AI.'

'You're kidding.'

Hank started laughing. 'You used artificial intelligence? You made *everything* up out of whole cloth?'

'No. Just the persona.' He looked desperate for them to understand. 'It's good content. And nobody would've paid any attention to it without Victor Hardwick out front.'

'So why are you here?' Hank was no longer laughing. 'Why did you choose to leave your little recording studio in Colorado and come to our location? You've done twelve other episodes. Why come out for this one?'

'It's the closest.' He clasped his hands in his lap and hunkered into a slouch. He knew what was coming. Sheila obliged him.

'Bullshit,' she said. 'There's a real reason, and we want to know it. Because people are dead.'

The room fell silent. Hank slid the crime scene photo of Garvan out of the coffee puddle and closer to Womack. He flinched.

'This man also had, in his motel room, several letters. Written by Mary Louise Finnegan,' Hank said. 'Now, we had somebody take a look at them. They're the originals. Our expert couldn't

confirm they were actually written by Mary Louise, of course, her
not being a historical figure with other verified writings. But they
were definitely written in the 1880s. So if Mr Garvan had them,
why did you say on your podcast that you did?'

He started shaking his head. 'No, no. I said that a cache of her
letters had recently been found.'

Hank flipped open his only slightly coffee-stained folder and
pulled out a printout. 'No, you didn't. You said "recently obtained,"
according to your own show transcript.' He tapped the paper and
leaned forward. 'You're clearly quite the . . . fabricator. But I don't
think you'd lie about the research. You seem to be a stickler for
that.'

He paused. Sheila let it go on, even though she wanted to pounce.
Instead, she quietly pushed the photo of a hatcheted Takama at him.
That knocked him back enough to start talking in spite of himself.
He'd gotten the letters from a retired St. Louis couple who'd found
them in their attic. He was always keeping an eye out for things
like that online, and happily bought them for a thousand bucks after
seeing them for sale.

'How did Garvan end up with them?' Hank asked.

'He heard the promo for the episode. I hadn't used the Finnegan
name, but I said enough that he figured out it was his family. His
mother's great-great-whatever. And he wanted the letters.'

They both looked skeptical.

'Exactly.' He threw his arms wide. 'I made a legitimate purchase.
I owned them. He had no grounds. But he threatened to start trolling
me. Normal social media, and that damn chat room. And those are
my best listeners. They're the ones who really talk up the show.
They up my metrics, get me new followers. If he started trashing
me there . . .'

'That make you mad?' Sheila said.

He glared at her. 'Mad enough to go hunting him through the
Ozark woods? No. I was pissed off, sure. But the episode was done,
I'd already used what I needed, and I kept copies. So I sent him
what he wanted. That was less costly than what he could do to me
if I didn't.'

He sent Garvan the letters by FedEx the day before the podcast
aired. That would've been a Thursday, Sheila thought. Garvan got
them Friday and hopped on a plane Saturday. And was dead by
Sunday. She sighed.

'See here's the thing,' said Hank, who was calculating distances, not days. 'The podcast only mentioned Murder Rocks. That was the only location anyone had. So last night, why were you off to the west at our hole in the ground?'

'I was just looking for treasure.' He shrugged helplessly. 'I wanted to give it a shot.'

'But why there?'

He sat and twisted his fingers together. 'I saw people there earlier. Digging. Of course I was going to want to come back and see.'

Hank folded his arms across his chest. 'That doesn't explain why you were so far east.'

He flushed, red blooming from his jail scrubs collar up into his thinning brown hair. 'I got lost, OK? Really damn lost.' He was shouting now. He flung out an arm. 'I didn't know where I was. Then I saw all the people. I waited and they left, but then it started raining and was getting dark. So I said forget it and left. But I couldn't find a goddamn road. All I could do was retrace to that hole. So what the hell? Let's take a look in it. But then that . . . that kid attacked me. Buried me in mud. Fucked up my leg. And now I'm here.'

'That's all on you, pal. And you shouldn't even feel special. You're not the only one who walked out of those woods all messed up,' Sheila said, thinking of Mingo Culver. 'Let's go back to your super-listeners for a minute. You told people in that chat room they could be on the podcast if they found treasure from any of the episodes?'

His expression brightened before he quickly forced himself back to solemnity. 'Yes. It was very well received. Everyone became a lot more excited and there were some great discussions. I just really wanted to, you know, foster a sense of community.'

Sheila tapped on the table. 'Never mind that between season one and season two, your advertising revenue increased ten-fold. And two episodes into this season, you hit the big time and landed commercials for a major restaurant chain.'

'That's merely a . . . by-product of good work. And good community.'

She just stared at him. 'Has anybody ever found anything and gotten to be on your podcast?'

'Not yet. I'm enthusiastic, though.'

She scoffed, wishing she had her own case file as she looked over at Hank's. He had leaned back in his chair in that loose-limbed way of his and was pondering the little man.

'In the podcasts you've done so far, which ones would you say realistically had no chance of having actual treasure?' he asked.

The anti-Hardwick shrugged his rounded little shoulders and looked to the side. Then he crossed his arms, still staring at the tiled wall. They both waited. Finally, Sheila cleared her throat.

'Maybe sixty percent.'

Hank let out a whistle. 'That's even bigger false advertising than good-looking Victor Hardwick is.'

'No.' It came out as a whine. 'My listeners know there're no guarantees.'

Hank leaned forward. Womack instinctively tried to scoot back, but the bolted chair wouldn't let him. 'So why weren't you out there with them, being honest and above-board about wanting to search? Why were you sneaking around, motel-hopping, ditching your car? You were already incognito. Why do all these other things?'

'For exactly that reason.' He was both highly irritated and begging them to understand. 'The minute I run into somebody and start talking, they'll know who I am. And then my whole persona is blown. And there goes the show.' He shot Sheila a dirty look. '*And* all my new advertising revenue.'

'Then why risk it?' she asked. She had a few questions to get to where she wanted him. 'Why come here at all?'

All three of them sat there and thought it – because he honestly believed there was gold out there. She and Hank waited. Finally, he let out an exasperated puff of air and admitted it. Sheila smiled. 'So explain to me – why didn't you come search before the damn episode aired? Why did you create a horde of competitors? You could've had those woods all to yourself.'

He glared at her for such a stupid observation. 'I wouldn't have had much of an episode then, right? If treasure had already been found?'

'Seems to me treasure would be more valuable than good content.'

An emotion flitted across his face, too quickly for Sheila to identify. 'Not to me.' He paused and then sighed. 'I didn't expect to have to give up the letters. I didn't know if there was something in them I'd missed, that Garvan would figure out. I guess I panicked. And got on a plane.'

'Then you arrive here and suddenly Garvan's dead.' Sheila crossed her arms and immediately regretted it as her injured insides shifted. She'd been sitting too long.

'I didn't kill him. I never saw him. I couldn't even tell you what he looked like. Or the other guy.' His voice rose in pitch with every word. 'I'd never kill anybody.'

'They were getting close,' Hank said. 'To your treasure. Your bank gold.'

'You don't even think there's anything out there. So screw you for sitting here and accusing me of killing to protect something you don't even believe in.'

'It's not what I believe that matters. It's what all those people out in the woods believed and what got them killed.' Hank pointed straight at the little man. 'And that's on you.'

TWENTY-NINE

H ank went too far. Which was surprising, because Sheila had fully expected she'd be the one to push too hard and cause Womack to stop talking.

'I don't believe it – that he thinks Philip Garvan might've found something he missed,' Hank said. He paced around Sheila's office as she settled her aching body into her desk chair. 'He might not have any confidence in his physical abilities, but his mental ones are top notch. He didn't miss anything.'

She took a sip of tea and looked around for her stress ball. So she could throw it at him. 'Speaking of missing things – how many times did you talk to him? And not know that he was Hardwick? How did Sam not know? Did none of you idiots listen to the podcast?'

'I read the transcript. It was faster.' He stopped prowling the perimeter of the room. 'Which now does seem like the wrong choice.'

She dunked her tea bag. 'Apology accepted.'

He glared at her and went back to pacing. She found her ball, but by then the moment had unfortunately passed. She rolled it between her palms and watched him go back and forth.

'Let's say our pretend Hardwick did miss something. What would Garvan know that he didn't?'

Hank disappeared into his own office and returned with a sheaf of notes. 'His friend did say that one of his many obsessions was genealogy. So it tracks that he told Womack he was a Finnegan descendant. Whether that's accurate or not, who knows?'

'There wasn't anything genealogical in the paperwork Garvan left in his motel room. It was only the Mary Louise letters.' Sheila paused. 'Where's Womack's stuff? In evidence?'

Hank shook his head and wandered over to the window. She envied him his mobility. 'It's still out there. He and Sammy were barely able to carry themselves out of the woods last night. Hauling a big camping pack was beyond either of their capabilities.'

'So we don't know what might be in there.'

'Don't sound optimistic,' Hank said, stepping all over her thin ray of hope. 'It's not like there's going to be a gun in the side pocket.

Where would he have gotten one? He couldn't have taken one on the plane flight from Colorado. And there's no indication either he or Garvan acquired one once they got to Springfield. The only people who potentially could've brought one are the ones who drove.'

'Takama drove up from Texas. He could've been carrying one and had it taken by whoever hacked him to death.'

Hank pressed his hand against the glass, like he was trapped here in the office. 'And there's your college professor lady – she drove. And that Mingo kid from where? Illinois?'

'Yeah. I don't really like Mingo for either killing, though.' After experiencing all these other loony treasure hunters, she'd started to actually appreciate Mingo Culver and his relatively sensible – and moderate – approach to things. 'I definitely don't think he has it in him to hack someone to death. I guess he could've shot Garvan, but then why bother to move the body? He wouldn't have known where that ravine was.'

Hank turned from the window as her words sunk in for them both.

'Yeah. He didn't know those woods,' he said. 'I think it's time to have another talk with people who do.'

'You keep coming out here, Sheriff. I'm a little sick of seeing you.'

'It's always a pleasure, Mrs Fackrell. Is your husband here?'

Leo was out in the barn feeding the goats, who weren't getting their daily graze due to the continuing downpour.

'I'm hoping to talk to you both,' Hank said. Darlene pursed her lips and sighed. And they stood there. Her on one side of the threshold and him on the other. She had on a long green cardigan over a paint-splattered T-shirt, faded jeans, and slippers that were apparently nailed to the floor. Because she wasn't moving.

'May I come in?'

She frowned, then leaned around him and eyed his squad car. 'No secretary with you this time?'

He silently counted to ten. 'She's actually second in command of the entire department. She outranks everybody.' Even him, most days.

'Huh. She's the boss of all those patrol boys you see everywhere?'

'Yes, ma'am.'

'That'd be a kick to see. Good for her.'

Hank nodded, shifting from foot to foot as the rain dripped off the porch roof. Finally she let him inside with an eye roll and a point toward the coat rack and then the living room. No cozy kitchen coffee this time. She waved him into a stiff wingback chair that backed to flowered wallpaper.

'I hear you wouldn't let Leo near that skeleton.'

Hank tried to get comfortable. 'We needed to keep everybody away. It's a potential crime scene.' At least it had been before the rain. Now it was nothing but primordial ooze.

She walked to the window and stood looking out, her arms crossed over her chest.

'How do you feel about the treasure hunters?'

She didn't turn. 'How do you think? They're a pain in the ass. It's one thing for local kids to cut through. Who cares. But these greedy idiots. Bah.'

'Before this time, when did you last have problems?'

She thought. 'Maybe three or four years ago. Got a batch of them all at once. Since then, it's just been lone people that we catch.'

She eyed him over her shoulder. Practically daring him to ask why they hadn't reported those trespassers. He didn't take the bait.

'Have you and Leo ever searched for treasure?'

'The rocks aren't on our land.'

'Some of the old wagon trail is.'

She let out a theatrical sigh that fogged the glass and turned back toward him. 'I'm new here. The second wife, you know. We've only been married thirty-four years. Fackrells owned this land three times that long. So yeah, I'd imagine someone sometime had a poke around. Obviously didn't find anything. I'd be living in a lot nicer house if they had.'

He nodded slightly, conceding that point but not letting her off the hook. 'But you – have you ever searched?'

'No. There's enough past around here. I don't need to go trying to dig up more.'

She pulled her cardigan tighter and resumed watching the rain. Hank tried to keep his wet feet off the rug and waited, wondering how many goats they owned. By the time the back door finally slammed, he'd decided the answer must be quite a few.

Leo padded slowly into the room in his stocking feet, sniffling into a tissue and asking if the pompous professors were finally gone.

'That's one reason why I'm here,' Hank said. 'The skeleton site has had an intruder.'

Leo glared at him over the Kleenex. 'You mean besides all those people out there yesterday?'

'Yes. An actual trespasser, not somebody associated with the investigation team.' He paused. 'And there's been some damage.'

He explained about the late-night mudslide and the need to re-excavate. Which meant the professors would be back.

'Are you kidding me? Why? They have all of the skeleton. Why do they need to come back?'

'They weren't done sifting through all the dirt.'

Darlene stepped away from the window. 'Well, seems to me that a mudslide is a pretty sure sign from the Good Lord saying that they are done. So we're going to go with that. No more digging.'

They had no say in the matter. But Hank didn't want to get heavy-handed.

'What they have left to do could be really beneficial. There might be other artifacts. It could be what tells us how old the bones are.'

Leo sank onto the sofa. 'So you still don't know.'

'No. It's extremely hard to tell the age of bones unless they're really recent or very, very old.'

The old man slumped back into the striped upholstery. 'So more digging is the only way to prove it's a Civil War body?' He waved the tissue in surrender and consented to another dig. 'And where's the trespasser now?'

'In custody.'

That improved the couple's mood considerably. Hank pulled Sheila's map out of his pocket and spoke quickly, before it could turn angry again. 'How often do you both walk your property?'

They kept a close eye on the pasture acreage, but the woods were more random. Just whenever one of them felt like taking a walk. Or when they saw cars parked in certain access spots along the roads. Hank asked about the section where Garvan had been shot.

'That little clearing?' Leo shrugged. 'That's always been there.'

'And it seems like it's relatively easy to get to?' Hank kept talking rapidly as Darlene started to bristle. He didn't want to tick them off by insinuating Leo was a suspect. Yet. 'Like, is it a shortcut to anywhere that other people might be aware of?'

'Oh. I see. It's not on the way to Murder Rocks, if that's what you mean,' Leo said. 'But it's along a stretch that's an easier walk than if you went more to the west. So I guess if you're following the lay of the land, you'd hit it.' He looked over at his wife for agreement, but she refused to give up her stone-faced expression.

'And what about here?' Hank tapped the little ravine where Garvan had ultimately come to rest.

'Well, that's the opposite. That's some hard walking to get there.'

'Which you already know,' Darlene said. 'So why are you asking again?'

'Because why would someone move the body?' Leo said as he looked at the map. 'Right? From here to here is hard terrain.' His thick finger tapped the clearing and then the ravine. 'Why bother? I can tell you, I don't know. Yeah, the clearing is easier to get to, but it's still out in the middle of the woods. Not like it's a city street corner and you gotta quick hide evidence of a crime.'

Hank watched him as he spoke. The man was measured in the way that came with many years of living. But the murder of Garvan was measured in its own way, too. The shooting *and* the moving.

'Have you ever found trespassers in either of those areas?'

'Probably,' Leo said. 'It's hard to say all the places we've found them.'

'And what do you do when you find them?'

'We tell 'em to leave,' Leo said.

'Do you, ah, reinforce your request in any way?'

'You mean, like repeating it?'

'No,' said his wife. 'He means like having a gun when you say it.'

'Oh.'

Hank waited. Darlene leaned easily against the wall, a woman secure in both her Second Amendment and property rights, and said nothing. Leo fiddled with the tissue.

'Sometimes I go out with one, sometimes I don't. Haven't needed to during this ruckus, what with you all out here all over the place.'

Except for the three days between the podcast premiere and when a parched Mingo Culver stumbled out of the woods. The sheriff's department had been in blissful ignorance then. But had the Fackrells? Or had they known, and taken matters into their own hands with an expeditiousness born of long practice? Hank made a mental note to find out why the ballistics results from the bullet in Garvan's body were taking so long. And speaking of. He pulled two photos out of the front pocket of his button-down shirt.

'These the dead men?'

'Yes. Their driver's license photos. Philip Garvan and Alan Takama. Do you recognize either one of them?'

Leo took and studied them for a moment before shaking his

head. He turned and handed them back to his wife as she stepped closer.

'No. Sorry.' She handed them back to Hank. 'But you know for sure they were out here because of that podcast?'

'Darlene, we are not suing.'

'Why the hell not? Nobody would be out here if they hadn't said these things. Spread all those rumors. That podcast should be liable for damages.'

Hank stayed quiet. Darlene seemed like the kind of person hostile to most everything, but on this, she had a point. Between damage to their property and plain old inconvenience and harassment, *Hidden Hoards* had caused them quite a shitstorm.

He wondered why Leo didn't feel the same way. He waited to see how it played out, but Darlene got impatient and raised an eyebrow, waiting for an answer.

'Yes. They were in town because of the podcast,' he said. 'Both men were listeners and only came here after the episode aired.' Sheila had tracked down a co-worker at Takama's computer programming job, who'd confirmed his friend left in a rush that Saturday morning. He was dead by evening the next day.

'I told you,' she said to her husband.

He ignored her, instead smiling wearily at Hank. The old guy was probably ready for a nap after his morning of labor. Hank rose to his feet. Leo did, too, and walked him to the door. Once he was back out on the soggy porch, he stopped. 'I'm curious, sir. Why don't you want to sue?'

Leo chuckled.

'Couple reasons, I guess. Mostly, it'd put her in a state of permanent agitation, I think. I'm used to sometimes agitated. I don't want to take it to the next level.' He smirked at Hank and then turned serious. 'And a lawsuit would keep the whole thing in the public eye. I just want it to go away. I want for people to forget about Murder Rocks and Bolin's treasure and especially about this new talk of bank gold. The first is in the past, the second is a fairy tale, and the third is just crap. For there to be not one piece from a whole bank wagonload found in a hundred and fifty years? Nothing stays that well-hidden. Which means it's crap.'

Hank shook his hand and walked through the rain to his car, thinking about futile hopes of treasure. The gold might be the stuff of fools, but that didn't mean it wasn't a motive for murder.

THIRTY

B renna left just as Sam's mom drove up the street. They both came to a stop in the middle of the road and exchanged a few words before Brenna drove off to work and Leslie Karnes parked in front of the house. She ran quickly through the rain to the house and was met by a scowling son.

'What were you talking about?'

'You just stop. All I did was ask her how your leg is doing.'

'How do you even know about it?'

'Margery from church knows Wanda.'

Wanda, the sheriff's department records clerk, broadcast juicy gossip much faster than she transmitted actual records.

'How the hell did Wanda find out?'

'Samuel.'

He sighed. 'How the *heck* did Wanda find out?' Her church grapevine would be the death of him yet.

'Margery said that Wanda knows someone named Dean who was in a position to know what happened last night.' She shrugged. 'I figured even if it wasn't true, it's still a good excuse to come say hi. And bring you this.'

She put down a reusable grocery sack. He caught a whiff of raisin bread and his frown started to fade despite his best efforts.

'Fine.' He tried not to limp as he turned toward the kitchen. She told him not to be silly, the bruise was so big she could practically see it from the street, for goodness' sake; there was no use pretending with her. He made some noncommittal mumbling noises and tried to take the bread. She swept by him and into the kitchen, where he heard the rattle of melamine plates. She reappeared with a slice and a napkin, and made him sit on the couch before she deigned to hand it over.

'Has Brenna gotten you to start eating breakfast?'

He thought about what they'd done instead of breakfast that morning and quickly shifted so she couldn't see his face. 'Maybe.'

Mom leaned back in the easy chair that had once been Dad's and gave him a soft smile. 'You know I know that means yes. Good.'

He gave her what he considered to be his best side-eye.

'I mean it,' she said. 'That's wonderful that you're listening to her. She's good for you. And I like her, too, so that's about as good as you can get.'

She gave him a broad wink. He rolled his eyes without even thinking about it. 'I mean it,' she said. 'You can't just sit back and enjoy yourself with a girl who's that much of a catch.'

This conversation was not worth the raisin bread. If he gave it back, would she leave?

'Um, so I shouldn't be enjoying having her as my girlfriend?'

'That's not what I mean. What I mean is . . . well . . . just keep your ears open, sweetie. And your heart. To what you . . . just remember I love you.'

'Yeah? OK?' He really had no idea how to respond to that. He took a big bite of bread. 'Don't you have to go to work?'

'Dr Nguyen is on vacation. So since there are no patients, I thought I'd take a day or two off, too.'

She managed the local rheumatologist's practice, which meant she knew a lot about fibromyalgia and nothing about bones. He told her that when she started asking if he needed an MRI. An X-ray had showed nothing broken. That didn't dissuade her. Finally, he threw out Dr McCleary's name. That calmed her down.

'Then how did you get home from the hospital? Bren—'

'No.' He cut short the smile forming on her face. 'Mom, enough. Hank was there, too, and he dropped me off. Standard, normal way of getting home. Especially since I don't have a car.'

'Your father's been searching the internet for you. I told him nothing more than ten years old.'

'That's not helpful, Mom. I can't afford anything that new.'

'Well, don't worry, he never listens to me anyway.' That was both true and not. Patrick Karnes never listened to anything his wife had to say about cars. Or hunting. Or making Christmas cookies. Otherwise, Leslie Karnes ran the show. 'Has he sent you any good listings?'

Sam shook his head. It was because his parameters were so woefully low-budget. There weren't any cars out there that came in at his price range and also met the requirement that they actually be operational. He pulled out his phone to prove his point, scrolling through a used-car superstore website at a speed impossible to read.

'What about Craigslist?'

'There hasn't been much of anything for sale, let alone something I can afford.'

She eyed him in the way she had, which laid him bare better than any X-ray ever could. He tried not to fidget.

'You've never had money problems before.'

He knew she was estimating his household budget and theorizing about where things had gone wrong. Which meant it was time for her to go. He hustled her out the door as best he could, considering his bum leg and her protests. They made it outside just in time to see someone even less pliable pull into the driveway. Corey Cassidy hopped out of his Camero and sauntered up the walk, raindrops bouncing off his Missouri State Bears ballcap.

'Hey, man. You found a car?'

Sam shook his head and introduced Brenna's brother to the owner of the sensible Chevy Malibu sedan. His mom couldn't have been more delighted. She pumped him for information about his family, and Corey easily matched her with his own boisterous questions. They had a rollicking conversation until Sam couldn't stand it anymore. He put his arm around her shoulders and marched her down the walkway to her car. Corey gave her a cheery goodbye wave and then turned his high wattage on Sam.

'Phew. I was a little worried when I drove up, 'cause that was a definite mom car. Not what we're looking for, right?'

He was just trying to help. Sam knew that. His mom was, too. And Hank and Dr McCleary and everyone else. He knew he should be grateful, but all he felt was overwhelmed. He stood there in his little front yard and tried not to show it. Corey considered him for a minute. Sam wondered what he saw.

'Soooo,' Corey said, breaking the silence. 'I think I found you one. My friend at the place out on Highway Seventy-six says he just had a Subaru Forester come in. He hasn't put it out on the lot yet. Let's get over there.'

Every excuse that pinged through Sam's head was ridiculous. He'd be a fool to pass up a look at a feasible car just because he wanted to lie on his couch and mope all day. He grabbed his wallet and locked the house.

'It's lucky you suddenly had the day off. I wish I had a job like that.' Corey strode toward the Camero but stopped when Sam didn't keep pace. 'What's with the limp?'

Sam refused to explain as they made their way out to Briscoe's

76 Cars. They took the Subaru for a test drive. It worked. That was Sam's verdict. The silver color wasn't bad, the engine ran, and it was water-tight, based on the fact that the interior was still dry in the middle of this deluge. Two hours of paperwork later, the lot had closed and he was waiting for the salesman to finish the last printouts when he saw movement out the window. And not browsing-the-lot's-inventory type of movement, either. He left the office without a word and wove through the cars. He could hear Corey behind him but didn't want to make noise by telling him to go back inside. He gritted his teeth against the leg pain and hustled to the edge of the lot. He squatted next to an old pickup and then whacked the side panel with his palm.

'Sheriff's department. Come out slowly so I can see your hands.'

Nothing. Sam bit back a groan and reached down to grab at an ankle sticking out from underneath the truck. The guy tried to wiggle away but was stopped by a much meatier hand attaching to his other leg. Corey looked over with a wicked grin.

'Can we pull him out?'

Sam nodded.

They dragged out a squirrely little guy and a bag of tools. Corey marched him over to the building while Sam called for a squad car to transport him to jail. While they waited, Sam finished signing documents and Corey stood too close to the suspect, ominously cracking his knuckles. Finally an on-duty patrol deputy arrived.

'Good grief, let me get him in the car. You stay inside.'

'But this is fun.' Corey took a reluctant step back.

Sam tried not to think about it. He shouldn't have let Corey participate at all. But he was unarmed with a bad leg. He never would've caught the guy if he'd bolted. Corey had made his job a lot easier. He grabbed the suspect's arm and steered him outside. When he came back in, Corey was pantomiming the under-car grab for the salesman.

'That was just righteous, bro. How did you even know what he was up to?'

'Legit buyers don't crouch down as they run between rows of cars.'

'Good point. You could be a detective.'

'I kind of am.'

Corey slapped him on the back. 'I believe in you. You can go all the way. Maybe once you get rid of that limp.'

* * *

With Sam injured and off duty, Sheila decided to take over his tracking down of the Uber passenger with the big backpacks. He'd already done the hardest part – getting a name out of the credit card company. Jordan Markham was a twenty-four-year-old white kid who lived about an hour north of Kansas City in the city of St. Joseph. She stared at the totally average-looking face in the driver's license photo. He could easily be the person in the Unabomber hoodie and sunglasses. Or just as easily not be.

He had no criminal record. His LinkedIn profile said he worked for a construction company, and when she called, his boss said he'd never missed a day of work. But he had variable stretches of time off, so there were plenty of days when he could've driven the four hours to Branson without anyone knowing. And he'd reported his credit card lost forty-eight hours after Garvan's rental car was returned to the airport and the two-backpack mystery man Uber-hopped from there to Branson. Which meant someone stole it, or he was a liar. With her faith in human nature being what it was, Sheila was betting on the latter.

She picked up the phone to call the number he'd given the credit card company, but put it back down again without dialing. She couldn't stop looking at his driver's license. Her eyes went from the name to the address and to the photo again. She called his construction boss back. 'The paperwork you have for him – does it list a middle name? All I have is an initial.'

The man put her on hold and came back with an answer. Then she called Jean Utley over at the Branson library and gave her a specific date. Jean, who loved a good research project, was delighted and said she'd start right away. A half-hour later she called back, sounding disappointed it hadn't been a more difficult assignment. Sheila, however, was thrilled. It was confirmation that Jordan Fackrell Markham of Steele Construction Company in St. Joseph was born twenty-four years ago to a woman named Sara Fackrell Markham, who in turn had been born to Leonard Fackrell and SaraJane Simpson Fackrell, who had died of cancer a decade after her daughter was born.

Sheila thanked Jean and the old-time local newspapers that cared enough to print birth announcements and obituaries. Then she called the St. Joe police and asked them to monitor young Jordan's movements until she got there. This was way past a phone call now.

THIRTY-ONE

The therapist sat there and nodded thoughtfully. Just like she did when they talked about how in tune with each other's feelings they needed to be. But this was different, Hank wanted to scream. Duncan had showed up with no warning and no indication how long he would stay. Or was he back permanently? Who knew? Not him and Maggie, because the old man had been back for two days and all three of them had spent the entire time tiptoeing around in awkward silence.

'I know it feels like it could be a difficult conversation.' Lila Hernandez leaned forward, hands clasped on top of her notepad. Hank and Maggie could hear the rain spit against her office window as she paused. 'But I don't think it has to be.'

She'd never met Duncan.

'You just need to know what you want. Each of you, and then both of you together.'

That was difficult *before* Duncan came back into the picture. It was going to be agony now.

'Let's both of you write down what you'd like to happen now that he's back.'

They both scribbled on their own sheets of paper and handed them over. She read them. More nodding.

'So. Hank, let's start with you.'

Shit.

'Sure.'

'You write that you'd like to know what his plans are. Is he back for good? If he is, then you'd like to start talking about how to get him involved with the kids again.'

Maggie's right eyebrow slowly climbed toward her hairline. To her credit, Hernandez didn't nod this time. 'You have a feeling about that, Maggie?'

She sighed. 'It's reasonable. Really. I want to know too, whether he's back for good. But it also sounds like we think he's the hired help.'

Wait a minute. He'd written that with the skill of a U.N.

ambassador. He turned to his wife. 'I'm trying to be diplomatic. If he's only back for a visit, then he plays with the kids and everyone has fun and then he goes back to his sister in Columbia. If he is back here permanently, then . . . we can go back to normal?'

Now she looked at him like he was a fool. 'Normal? Back to normal? After all that?'

'Go ahead, say it. After I considered your dad a suspect in your mom's death.'

He saw the muscles in her jaw tighten.

'It wasn't unreasonable.' He ground out the words as he looked over at her.

'Let's go back to this for a minute.' Dr Hernandez was now the only one in the room without clenched fists. 'Maggie, you've talked about how hard it's been for you to see different sides of this. And you've acknowledged that your dad wasn't any more of a suspect than anyone else.'

Maggie didn't respond. They both waited. Finally she loosened her jaw enough to speak. 'But he isn't just anybody.'

Lord, was that the truth. Duncan was a cantankerous old goat whose idea of a good time was ribbing his son-in-law while enjoying a nice glass of whisky from the Scottish homeland as Johnny Cash played on aforementioned son-in-law's nice sound system. Granted, he also was a devoted grandfather with a sharp sense of humor who drove the school carpool, did the laundry, and taught himself to cook so he could be even more of a help to their combined household. And not a single one of these things had any bearing on what they were talking about.

'You know him,' Maggie was saying. 'That's what I can't get over, I guess. You know him. And you thought it anyway – that he could be a killer.'

'Anybody can be a killer.' The words came out before he could stop them. Which he should have, judging by the looks on both women's faces. He leaned back in his chair and spread out his hands. *This is how it is. Human nature.* Now that he'd said it, he was sticking with it. It was a professional assessment he was more than qualified to make.

Maggie turned toward him. 'I hate that you look at people that way. That you have to think the worst. All the time.'

He blinked in surprise. He thought that, on the whole, his outlook was pretty damn sunny – considering what he'd been subjected to since becoming sheriff of this damn county.

'I don't mean,' she said, 'that you walk around thinking horrible things. I just mean that I hate that you have to carry this burden. For all these people. When we lived in Kansas City, it didn't feel that way. You'd go to work and then you'd leave whatever happened there when you came home. That's not how it is here.'

He thought about that. She was right. Maybe it was because he now had a lot fewer co-workers to lean on. Maybe it was because he was in charge. Maybe it was because this place seemed to be an epicenter of greed and rage and corruption. He allowed himself a silent chuckle. There was no 'maybe' on that last one. It *was* a cluster of all of those things, his own personal funhouse.

This all zipped through part of his brain, while the rest of it figured out how to respond. Maggie didn't make him.

'None of that is your fault. I know that. And you do a good job of hiding it.' She paused. 'I guess that's why this hurt so much. Because it came directly into our home. Because it made me hurt like you hurt. And it made me realize how that hurt feels. Where I didn't before, not exactly.'

He started to speak, to say that he knew she saw horrible things, too, in the emergency room. Accidents and addiction and violence and a whole lot of death. She held up her hand before he could talk.

'I'm one of the lucky ones. I know what happened. I know who killed my mom. So many people out there aren't that lucky. That's what I keep telling myself.'

But she didn't know everything. Even today, she didn't know the real reason Hank had focused on her father. The only ones who did were him and Dunc, and Judge Marvin Sedstone. And probably Sedstone's wife, because the spouses always found out eventually. The judge had started an affair – with Marian McCleary, which would make Duncan a murder suspect in anyone's book, even his son-in-law's. Once the case was over, Dunc begged Hank not to ruin Maggie's regard for her mother by divulging what she'd done. Hank had flat-out refused. Telling Maggie about the affair was the only way he could explain why he had Duncan interrogated. The only way he could save his own marriage. And he point-blank told the old man that.

But then Duncan fled, running off to his sister's place a few hours north. And Hank decided – since the old man wasn't a constant presence in the middle of their marriage anymore – he would try to fix it without ruining Marian in the eyes of her daughter.

Sitting here today, Maggie still had no idea. Dr Hernandez, on the other hand, had suspected something was up for quite a while. She cleared her throat softly.

'You're right, Maggie, that you're lucky to know. But that doesn't mean it hasn't affected you. It has, and that's OK. For you, and your dad.'

Maggie looked across at Hank. 'And you, too, honey. I know that.' That was progress. He nodded.

'So,' the therapist continued, 'what if we found a new normal?'

'I just don't want to cause Dad even more pain by asking him what his plans are,' Maggie said.

They both looked at Dr Hernandez. She put her notepad on the table next to her chair. 'Look, this is hard. And sudden. I'm not going to pretend it's not. But from what you've both said, Duncan is pretty tough. I don't think he's going to melt if you bring up the subject. Plus, he knows it's there, too. It's not going to be a surprise to him when it gets brought up.'

They both sat silent and motionless – refusing to engage, if Hank were to use therapist-speak. Which he wasn't going to do, because if he stayed quiet, maybe Dr Hernandez would move on to a different topic.

'When *you* bring it up,' she said, pinning them with a look that said: *You both need to grow a pair.* At least that was Hank's interpretation. He didn't dare look at Maggie to see what she might be thinking. Hernandez pressed on.

'You two are in the position of power. It's your home. You're the ones who invited him back. He thinks that anyway, even if it was Maribel who actually sent the texts.'

'So we need to do it,' Hank said after an excruciatingly long pause that Maggie did nothing to alleviate.

'So you need to do it,' Hernandez echoed. 'Let's talk about how to broach the subject.'

It took the rest of their hour session, but they came up with a plan that centered on the kids' need for stability and their desperate desire to know if Grandpop would start driving the carpool again. And, most importantly as far as Hank was concerned, they decided Maggie would do the talking. And that the conversation would take place as soon as possible. Maggie shot him a look.

'I know. I'll be home tonight, I promise,' he said. 'We can do it after the kids go to bed.'

The clock chimed softly and Dr Hernandez walked them to the door. Hank was the last to leave. She eyed him critically. 'I have a colleague. I can give you his number. In case you wanted to talk about anything. Things that maybe you're not saying here.'

He gave her a noncommittal nod and hustled Maggie outside into the rain before she realized the therapist had said something. He walked her to their minivan, holding her umbrella over them and then handing it to her.

'Keep it,' she said. 'You've got farther to walk.'

He'd parked far down the street. It wouldn't do to have the sheriff's squad car sitting in front of a marriage therapist's office. 'No, it's fine. I have one in the car.' He kissed her goodbye and pulled away slowly, breathing in the scent of her skin and touching a strand of her hair that had curled in the wet weather. He wanted to wrap her in his arms and make them both forget about everything and everyone. Instead, he pulled away and jogged the long block to his car. By the time he got there, he was soaked and no closer to an answer for the question Hernandez hadn't known to ask.

If Duncan really was back for good, would Hank follow through on his promise and tell Maggie exactly why he'd been a suspect?

THIRTY-TWO

S am was now finally the owner of the Subaru, and a car loan from Central Bank. It was better than a sedan, and better than dealership financing. Otherwise, he was not excited. The car felt tiny, even though it was really no smaller than his Bronco had been. Just differently arranged, which would take some getting used to. It did have working air conditioning, something so foreign to him that for a split second he thought something was wrong with the fan motor. Then he turned it on high and ran it all the way home, even as his windshield wipers struggled to keep up with the chilly autumn downpour.

The rain had probably filled that muddy hole in the woods by now. It would be a nice little pond, with any evidence at the bottom now ground down into whatever archaeological strata were underneath the newly formed hapless-deputy-and-Ozark-trespasser-body-imprint layer. Or if the mud had ended up filling the hole, instead of continuing to slide down the hill, there would be no pond – just layers upon layers and an apoplectic tweed-elbowed professor. He could hear Alice Randall laughing now.

He pulled into his driveway and limped-ran into the house, wishing for the thousandth time that he had a garage. He closed the front door behind him and thought about the woods and the podcast and the deluded searchers and their hopes of gold. He called Sheila and after he told her about the catalytic converter thief, he brought up what was really on his mind.

'When you talked to the guy at the beginning, the one who was lost for all those days, did you find out if he actually ever found Murder Rocks?'

'Mingo Culver? Yeah, he said he didn't. That the only thing he found was Alan Takama's hatcheted body. Course, we didn't know it was Takama until yesterday,' she said. 'Why?'

'And he wasn't working with anybody, right?'

'No, he was on his own.'

'But Takama had a partner?'

'Yeah, kind of. They'd never met. He'd been texting to meet up with that Cheryl Maclin woman.' She paused. 'What are you thinking, Sammy?'

He looked down at his muddy shoes. He still stood dripping on the doormat. 'I don't know. It just seems like if they were going to meet up, why wouldn't he wait for her?'

'Aside from straight-up greed, I have no idea. There's . . .' She stopped, and he heard the rain on her end of the phone line get louder. 'I tell you what, you call Takama's roommate and ask that question. You won't even have to leave your house with your bum leg. I'll text you the guy's number. And see if he knows anything about relatives. I haven't been able to find any family.'

She was already hanging up as Sam agreed to do it. He stared at his phone thoughtfully. It wasn't like her to give up an interview that potentially significant just so he could have something to do. He slipped out of his shoes and padded over to the bookcase, where he dug around until he found a notepad. He went into the kitchen for a pen and, since he was there, a sizable hunk of raisin bread. He took both things out to the couch and made himself comfortable. Then he dialed.

'Yeah, this is Ahmed Bashar. You're a cop from where?'

Sam identified himself again, this time with a geography lesson.

'Huh. That's the middle of nowhere. I guess Alan did need all that equipment.'

'You saw his equipment? Can you tell me what he took when he left your condo?'

A backpack with a strapped-on sleeping mat, some fancy water bottles, a folding shovel, a normal-sized shovel, a tent, a camera, and some kind of microphone.

'A microphone?' Sam asked.

'He said he was going to record his treasure hunt, so that when he found it, he could be a guest host on whatever that podcast is.'

Mingo told Sheila the same thing. It seemed that everybody wanted to be a podcast star. Takama's equipment hadn't been in his car, which they'd tracked down at a Hollister tow yard once the body was identified. An annoyed landowner a few miles from the Fackrell property asked that it be hauled away a week ago. A tent and a full-sized shovel were in the trunk. Everything else was still missing.

'How long have you lived with Alan?'

Mr Bashar snorted. 'Too long.'

'So why do you live with him?'

'He owns the condo and needed a roommate to help pay the mortgage. For me, it's a good location and the rent's reasonable for this area. I was pretty excited to find it. Then I moved in.' He paused. 'Be careful what you wish for and all that.'

'Why do you say that?'

Silence. 'He is . . . he was . . . a windbag. A know-it-all. Any topic that came up, he knew all about it. Even when he really didn't.'

Takama worked in IT at a hospital, doing basic computer maintenance stuff – a job where he didn't really interact with many people. Mr Bashar figured that was by design, once the bosses got a taste of his pomposity.

'He was an expert on military jets, on paleo diets, on global warming, and of course on surgery, since he worked for a hospital. You name it, he thought he knew something about it.'

'Did he pack up like that and go off on trips often?'

'Kind of, I guess? He'd go to conventions and stuff, on different topics. But I think this is the first time he was actively going somewhere. Does that make sense?'

It did. Going to a fan convention and listening to speakers was a lot different than striking out on your own in a flat-out race to find something before your competitors did.

'He was active in a *Hidden Hoards* chat room. Did he ever talk about that? Or about the podcast at all?'

Alan had talked about it – a lot. He'd been late to the party, only discovering the show after the end of the first season. He was practically giddy when he found out the second season would focus on domestic treasures.

'That's when he went out and bought the shovels. We don't even have a yard,' Mr Bashar scoffed. 'I told him it'd be the same as hunting for some ridiculous fantasy pirate treasure. It's still bullshit, only this time within driving distance. He said he was ready to pounce when something nearby enough came on season two.'

'Did he talk about anybody else? In connection with the show or the chat room?'

'Not to me.'

'Could you see him teaming up with someone?'

Mr Bashar thought about that. 'In the context of treasure hunting? Yeah, I could see that. If it benefited him in some way. Someone who had better access to the search area, maybe. Or someone who knew more than he did.'

Someone like a Civil War history professor. 'It seems he did form an alliance with another chat-room person. They were texting back and forth and had plans to meet when they both got to Branson.'

'Did that person get killed, too?'

'No. They never actually met up. Alan went into the woods before she got into town.'

'Lucky her.'

Sam bit back a chuckle. If only Cheryl Maclin deigned to look at it that way, she might not be quite as upset about sitting in a nice safe jail cell. He ran the professor's name past Mr Bashar, who didn't recognize it. 'What about *FoundIt72*? Or *FortunesFave*?'

'Are those screen names? Let me guess – he was *FortunesFave*, wasn't he?' Mr Bashar sighed. 'It's not that he was a bad person, you know? It's just that he always saw himself as being at the top of the heap. And he never was.'

'Do you think that's why he didn't wait for Ms Maclin? Even though he said he would?'

'Oh, definitely. He must've gotten everything he thought he needed from her. So no need to wait. Especially since he believed there was treasure at the end.'

Sam thought about this next question carefully. He'd been thinking about the order of things ever since he traipsed through the woods with the amazing Roscoe. *Who did what when?*

'And if he came across someone else in otherwise empty woods, what do you think he would do?'

'Um . . .'

Sam winced. 'What I mean is, what would his reaction be?' He was trying like the devil not to commit one of Hank's cardinal sins – asking a leading question.

'I guess it would depend on who the person was.' Mr Bashar still sounded puzzled. 'Like, if it was the guy who owned the woods, he'd probably try to wheedle his way into getting permission to search. Or lie about what he was doing. Although, to be fair, I bet he wouldn't be the only searcher doing that.'

Sam kept quiet.

'Oh, do you mean if he met another treasure hunter?' The silence lengthened as he waited for Sam to respond.

'Let's say he did,' Sam finally said. 'Do you think his reaction would be different if it was a treasure hunter instead of a landowner?'

'Yeah, I do. I think there would be an argument.'

Interesting. 'Even without knowing anything about the other treasure hunter?'

'That wouldn't matter. Alan would talk and talk and not back down and just keep pushing. So unless the other guy flat-out turned around and walked away, there would be an argument. Hell, it'd be likely he'd follow the guy who's walking away so he could continue to make his case.'

'When you say "just keep pushing," do you mean that in terms of pushing forward on a verbal argument, or literally like pushing? Getting physical?'

Mr Bashar started laughing. 'Dude, definitely not. Alan was a lot of things, but he was not, not, not somebody who could back up his talk with action. He would say – and I've witnessed this – that the conversation was suddenly no longer worth his time, and he'd get away before someone could throw a punch.'

The roommate's mirth stopped abruptly. 'It was funny those times, because people would just roll their eyes or stomp off in the other direction. But that's not what you want to know, is it? You want to know if Alan could make someone he just met so mad in that moment that they'd kill him.'

'It's not a question I normally ask, but yeah.' Visions of hatchet wounds danced through Sam's head. 'Do you think it's possible?'

'Possible, probable, likely. Whatever word you want to use. He absolutely could drive someone over the edge.'

Especially someone who was also hopped up on dreams of Civil War gold. Like Philip Garvan.

The rain lessened the farther north Sheila went. Thank God. It was bad enough that she'd be in a car for four hours. She didn't need a torrential storm to up the difficulty level even more. As it was, she'd grudgingly bowed to reality and brought her donut seat cushion, her back brace, her cane, and three extra doses of Advil. She hoped to leave them all in the car when she got to St Joseph. No need for Jordan Fackrell Markham to know he was being questioned by an invalid.

Her final concession had been the hardest. She was sitting in the passenger seat. A delighted Deputy Ray Gillespie was behind the wheel. He'd jumped at the chance to play chauffeur, mostly because of the promise of participating in a suspect interview when they got to St. Joe. She glanced at him out of the corner of her eye. She'd definitely brought along a driver and not extra muscle. He was in his thirties, slim and of below average height, with glasses and dusty brown hair much shorter than when she'd met him in his capacity as property manager of a strip-mall-turned-crime scene. The investigation had so fascinated him, he had applied to the department and Hank had hired him. She'd been skeptical, but he was turning out to be fantastic at dealing with the public and knowing the ins-and-outs of local businesses.

They sailed through Springfield and she dialed Judge Sedstone after Ray turned off I-44 and north onto Route 13. She'd be much obliged if he would approve the search warrant request her records clerk had delivered to his office. He put her through the usual twenty questions and then signed it. She heard her email ping as he sent her the official copy.

'Before you go,' the judge said, 'Wanda mentioned that you attended the change of venue hearing.'

That woman got on Sheila's last nerve. She was the information equivalent of a broken fire hydrant, oblivious to who got soaked in the process. Sheila made some noncommittal sounds and tried to hang up the phone. The judge rolled right over her.

'How do you think it went?'

She didn't know how to respond to that. He filled the silence. 'I'm just wondering if I'm going to need to give up my courtroom for a trial in addition to all the preliminary matters.'

'Ah. Well, he seems even-handed. And he said he'd issue his decision within the next week.'

'I read that about the timing in the paper. I do approve of a speedy jurist.' He paused. 'And remember, Ms Turley, that even with everything that's going on, you've still got friends.'

Everything going on? Did he mean his secret beef with Hank? Commissioner Fizzel, Sr and his influence? What was he referring to?

'You be careful out there in the rain.'

She assured him they would and, after a close call with a semi-truck and a flooded intersection, they mostly complied. They hit the McDonald's drive-thru in Clinton and the car still smelled like French fries two hours later as they entered St. Joseph. She dialed the cell phone of the city police officer assigned to watch Markham's apartment.

'Sorry, we're at Biggins. Well, not together. I followed him to Biggins.'

'What is Biggins?'

'Oh. Uh, sorry, ma'am. It's a sports bar. On Hickory Street. Great tenderloins. Anyway, the suspect left his apartment just a little bit ago, at fifteen hundred hours, and has been here ever since.'

Sheila thought for a moment. They could wait for him to return home and do the interview and the search at the same time. Or they could start the search right now. And conducting one without a loud, protesting suspect nearby sounded lovely. She asked the St. Joe officer to stay on Markham and directed Ray toward the apartment neighborhood. She just hoped they could find the landlord to let them in. She and Ray were not well suited for busting down a doorway.

They parked and Ray, no dummy, immediately made himself scarce and thereby avoided witnessing the ten minutes it took Sheila to get out of the car and force her legs to start working. She was standing next to the squad car in the sprinkling rain when he returned with the landlord. He let them in and stood in the doorway as they started to work. It was a small apartment and didn't take much time. Of note, there was a newer looking .22 hunting rifle and a collection of large dark-colored hoodie sweatshirts. There were not any aviator sunglasses or big hiking backpacks.

Garvan wasn't killed with a rifle, but seeing it in Markham's home at least meant he was familiar with firearms. Sheila put it back in the closet as Ray finished looking under the bed. They walked back to the little living room and an unimpressed landlord. 'It's more exciting on TV.'

'Yes, sir,' she said, stripping off her nitrile gloves. 'When you don't find what you're looking for, it can get boring.'

'So you're done?' He looked puzzled. Sheila stopped with one glove still on her hand. Ray looked up from dusting off his knees.

'Should we not be?' she said slowly.

'There's still the storage closet.'

'Is there really? We would very much like to see that.'

All three of them, brimming with hope for different reasons, hustled around the back of the building, where an overhang shielded a row of doors with cheap hardware-store mailbox stickers that matched the apartment numbers. The lock on Markham's door was twice the size of the others and brand new. One look at Ray and he was running back to the squad car for the bolt cutters. She admitted to herself she was glad she'd brought him, and then called

Judge Sedstone for a warrant that would piggyback on her original one and let her search the separate closet for the same reasons she wanted to search the apartment.

Ray made short work of the lock and the landlord held the door as Sheila stepped inside and he reached for the lightbulb pull chain. It was definitely closet-sized, about four feet square and crammed with assorted crap. A mountain bike hung from the ceiling by its front wheel. And wedged behind it—

'Ray, go get the giant evidence bags. And sir, if you could help me lift this bike down?'

Fifteen minutes later, they had two large hiking backpacks in the trunk of the squad car. A half-hour after that, they had the entire contents of the closet spread out on the building's back lawn. For all they knew, Markham had tucked the nine-millimeter handgun that killed Garvan in with all this junk. An hour after that, they determined that he hadn't. There was no gun and everything, including them, was wet. The only one not tired and annoyed was the landlord, who was tickled pink to get his own copy of the receipt Sheila left to tell Markham they took the packs.

Sheila waited until he was gone before folding herself back into the car. She hurt so badly she could barely do it. Ray busied himself with the evidence in the trunk until she was settled.

'We'll ask to borrow an office at the police station so we can go through the backpacks,' she said as he started the car. 'But first, I'm in the mood for some bar food. What do you think?'

THIRTY-THREE

Sheila was gone. Her cane was gone. Her squad car was gone. Hank swore to himself and stomped down the office hallway to find Wanda.

'Yeah. She left with that new deputy. Little nerdy guy with the glasses.' Ray Gillespie must not do anything gossip-worthy, otherwise Wanda would've learned his name by now.

'Do you know where they went?' He was soaked and tired and emotionally exhausted, and now standing in a cubicle overflowing with Precious Moments figurines and file folders. And Wanda. Her chair protested loudly as she shifted back to better consider his question.

'Don't know for sure, but I got a good idea.'

'Can you share with me what that is?' he said after waiting in the hope she'd continue on her own.

She spun around faster than he would've thought possible. Her chair creaked alarmingly. She pulled a crisp new file from a cabinet and turned back to Hank. She presented it smugly, saying without words that she knew she was bestowing a gift, even if he didn't. He forced a smile and flipped it open.

There were a lot of words on the page. The only ones he read were *Fackrell* and *St. Joseph*. He looked up and stared unseeingly at the filing cabinets. It'd be nice if his investigative partner would act like one.

'She dictated it to me from the road and had me walk it over to Judge Sedstone. Have you ever seen his office? So fancy. I dropped it off and then went back once he signed it. He said he'd already emailed it to her, so I didn't need to scan it.'

He looked back down at the search warrant application and said nothing. Wanda smiled indulgently and pointed at a spot further down the document. 'The address is right there, see?'

Oh, he saw. He saw a lot of things – about the Fackrells, and about his second-in-command. He was dialing Sheila before he was even back in the hallway, the folder bent in his clenched hand. It went straight to voicemail.

He did not leave a message.

Instead, he went into her office and sat down at her desk, so ticked off at her leaving that he ignored good sense and messed with her chair until it accommodated his ten-inch height difference. Three pages deep into her stack of papers were the notes from Jean Utley. Thank God for Sheila's neat handwriting. He looked at the Fackrell family tree and thought about the gun Leo had said he kept for his grandson. What else did he do for young Jordan?

He wanted to immediately go back out to their farmhouse, but he knew it was useless until he had a report from Sheila. He tried again – her phone was still off. He dug around her desk until he found Ray Gillespie's cell number. Ray didn't answer. No one picked up a call to the squad car's radio. He was shuffling through the rest of her paperwork when he heard very big footsteps unevenly squeaking down the hall. A wet Sam limped in and gasped in surprise.

'She's gonna kill you for sitting there.'

'No, she won't, because I'm going to kill her first. For going all the way up to St. Joseph when her still-injured self can barely handle a drive to the grocery store.' He glowered at Sam. 'And what did I tell you? You're supposed to be recuperating, too.'

Sam held up a notebook. 'I wanted to type up this interview. It seems that Alan Takama had a gift for pissing people off.'

Hank pushed away from Sheila's desk and offered him the chair. 'If we're already in trouble, you might as well do your report here.'

'"We?" No way. This is all on you.'

But he took advantage anyway. As he turned on her computer, he told Hank about the roommate's interview. They talked it through as he typed and Hank paced his usual circuit around her office. He noticed he was starting to wear a track in the carpet. He shrugged and kept going. The rain intensified and he stopped at the window. There were several cars in the lot, but no little red hatchback.

'How'd you get here?'

Sam got up and pointed to the blue Subaru. 'Got it this morning.'

'You don't sound too happy about it.'

'Eh. It's OK.'

Hank thought about the beloved Bronco. He wondered if Sam had been forced to sell it for scrap. Was that why he looked so miserable?

'It looks like it'll hold all your gear,' Hank said carefully. 'Maybe as well as the Bronco did?'

Sam shrugged. 'Probably. It's just more than I wanted to spend.'

Hank looked from his deputy back to the SUV. It was nice, but it looked to be about eight years old with only standard options. Sam made almost decent money, especially for this area, and never seemed to spend any. This kind of used car shouldn't be a bank buster for him.

He deliberately kept his gaze on the parking lot. 'Everything OK?'

Sam shifted and slouched more than he already was. 'Yeah.' He looked down at Sheila's desk and the murder investigation paperwork. And chuckled, to himself more than anything. 'Seriously. Everything's fine. Especially compared to . . .'

Now he was trying to put things in perspective. That definitely meant something was up. 'Your parents all right?'

He straightened. 'Huh? My parents? Yeah. Why?'

Not that, then. 'You and Brenna doing OK?'

Bingo. Sam's face flamed red from collar to hairline. Hank watched out of the corner of his eye, and waited. He wouldn't press. It technically wasn't any of his business, but he did care about the kid and wanted to see him happy.

'We're fine.'

His tone sounded truthful, not like he was trying to dissemble his way out of the question. So – Brenna plus money worries. Hank bit back a huge smile. He couldn't resist. 'More than fine?'

Sam startled, then sighed in exasperation. 'Yes. I want to buy a ring.' He crossed his arms and glared at him. 'It was going to be a secret.'

Hank quickly held up a hand and swore he would tell no one. 'I can see where needing a new car came at a really bad time, then.'

'Yeah. I've already put a deposit down on the ring. So I have nothing in savings, and then the Bronco dies. I've still got the last repairs and tow trucks on my credit cards so I'm at my limit. And I was lucky to get the loan for that thing.' He pointed out the window. 'I don't know how I'm going to come up with the rest of what I need for the ring.'

Hank considered that. He didn't know how much money Sam was talking about, but he had a feeling it was more than necessary. In his opinion, at least. He leaned back against the windowsill, blocking view of the offending Subaru.

'I don't know Brenna all that well.' He paused. 'But I'm fairly confident in saying that I think she'd want you financially solvent more than she'd want another carat worth of diamond.'

Sam shoved his hands in his jeans pockets.

'And I think that's what makes her special.'

'That she'd settle for a small ring?'

Shit. 'God, no,' Hank said. 'That's not what I mean. Just that she seems, to me, to be a person who values things like friends and family, and helping people and being kind. Not material things. That what matters most to her is you. Not how much you're able to spend on a ring.'

He asked and Sam admitted he could switch the deposit over to a different ring. The jeweler had others in the same style, so that wasn't an issue. That would make it much easier, but Sam clearly didn't see it that way. He sank down into Sheila's chair, shoulders still slumped. 'What did you do?'

Hank laughed. 'We were so poor. Maggie had just finished med school. I'd just got on with KCPD. We were living together, so that helped with expenses. But still. It was rough enough to even pay the bills every month. I squirreled away a little money every paycheck until I had enough to pay for about eighty percent of it, then I charged the rest. Paid it off as fast as I could. If I'd gone for a huge diamond, I would've been in debt forever – then add that to her huge med school loans. We never would've gotten out of that hole. Neither of us wanted that.'

'Brenna does want to go back to school,' Sam said slowly. 'That's one of the reasons I want to propose now. It'll be easier for her to go back if we're married. I can take more of the living expenses and she can put more of her salary toward school.'

'I think that's a great plan.'

'If she says yes.' He smiled weakly.

Hank had seen the way she looked at Sam. He wasn't worried.

THIRTY-FOUR

'Hello, Jordan.' Sheila sat down at the table's one vacant chair, wielding the cane as if she were the dowager countess of Downtown Abbey. The young man froze, burger halfway to his mouth. His companion choked on his beer.

'Let's talk about your last trip to Branson.'

Jordan stared at her for a hard second, then dropped the burger and bolted. His chair went clattering across the floor as he darted toward the back. Ray left his post by the door and scrambled after him, and the other guy's spit-take sprayed lite beer all over Sheila.

She sighed. Then she levered herself to her feet, rapped the cane handle hard next to Beerman's plate, and told him not to go anywhere. She made it out the front door as fast as she could, hoping Markham would circle around to the front parking lot to get to his truck. She'd spotted it in a corner space when they arrived. She hurried down the length of the shed-like building and waited, cane at the ready. She'd tried the English gentry method with it. Now it was time to go Roadhouse.

She heard running footsteps and prayed it wasn't Ray, otherwise she was going to have a lot of apologizing to do. Then she swung like she was aiming for a low fastball across home plate.

She hit Markham right across the middle. His momentum kept him stumbling forward for several yards, then he collapsed on the pavement. Ray skidded to a stop and looked at her in shock.

'We can do that?'

She shrugged. She had Ray and the St. Joseph officer cuff and search him while she went back inside and had an unproductive chat with Beerman, who worked with Markham at the construction site but didn't really know him. They'd met for a beer only because work was rained out. By the time she came back outside, it was raining again and the paramedics were there. The St. Joe guy looked apologetic and muttered something about procedures and regulations. She nodded.

'I hate to tell you this, but he is going to need to go in.' The lead paramedic was a burly Latino in his fifties. 'He could have abdominal injuries. They'll probably want to do a scan.'

She'd figured as much. At least it would give her time to take her Advil. She was going to need a double dose after all that activity. She hobbled over to the St. Joe officer, a tall white kid who carried himself like he just came out of the military. 'Yes, ma'am. Marines, ma'am. Corporal. Or I used to be, anyway.'

He'd been on the force only eight months and was perfectly content to do a little scut work by babysitting Markham at the hospital. That let Sheila and Ray head straight for the police station to hopefully borrow an office big enough to inventory the last earthly possessions of two unlucky treasure hunters.

The watch commander took one look at their wet, bedraggled asses and gave them a spacious conference room and two cups of coffee instead. Sheila stood there sipping as Ray slipped the packs out of the evidence bags. He poked at the blue Osprey brand that had to be Takama's, based on the amount of blood soaked into a strap and along one side. 'This zipper is open. And this one over here.' He gingerly opened a pocket to find nothing inside. The rest held jumbles of clothes and equipment, as well as Takama's wallet. As if someone had rummaged through it already.

'You know what isn't here,' Sheila said as she surveyed everything, now individually bagged, tagged, and photographed.

'His phone.'

'Yeah. And paperwork.'

Ray looked at her quizzically.

'It just seems like he would've had treasure paperwork of some kind. Printouts, or a map, or something. I guess it could've all been on his phone, but he seemed like the kind of guy who would overprepare, be prepped for a loss of electrical power, have lots of stuff to show off how much he knew – based on what Sam told me the roommate said.

'And we sure didn't find anything like that in Markham's apartment,' Ray said.

'So did he go through the other one, too?'

They both looked down the length of the table, where a slightly smaller pack sat, a dirty nylon lump of straps and zippers. Sheila put on a fresh pair of gloves and pulled it toward them. Every pouch and compartment on this one was closed tight. Ray gave her a look as he reached out and tugged at a drooping side loop.

'Seems like that could've held a hatchet at one point, doesn't it?' Sheila said.

Ray took a breath and opened the main compartment. It was fairly neat. Food, clothing, blanket – all in place. Ray moved on to a specialty side pocket and pulled out Garvan's wallet and a phone. He moved to the other side. And out came another phone.

'Two? That seems excessive.'

'Unless one of them's not yours.' Ray jiggled the second phone and Alan Takama appeared on the lock screen, kneeling next to a golden retriever puppy.

Now they were getting somewhere. Sheila was almost smiling. Someone ransacked Takama's pack and stole his phone. It seemed unlikely to have been Markham because why would he have searched only one pack? So Garvan must've taken Takama's pack. Which led to one very sharp-bladed conclusion.

'Keep going. Are there papers in there anywhere? Something to tell us if Garvan was working with anybody?'

Ray was already zipping and snapping and pulling. 'There's a million pockets on this thing.'

Several grumbles later, a thin interior sleeve yielded five sheets of neatly folded paper. Three more zippers and he found nine additional pieces crammed into another slot. 'I betcha these were Takama's. Garvan took them in a hurry and stuffed them in quick as he could.'

Sheila nodded in agreement. Things were playing out right in front of her, a terrible game of Clue. Who did what to whom and in what order. And Jordan Fackrell Markham at the end of it. The last one standing – on land owned by his family for generations and soaked in blood even longer than that.

She watched as Ray made his way into the depths of the pack. He turned it over to access the back and a loud thunk stopped him. He rotated the whole thing and pulled at a few straps until he found the right access. He reached his hand inside and stopped, sucking in a breath and staring at Sheila.

'What?'

'I think this is . . .'

'For chrissakes, what?'

He pulled out his hand. Nestled in his palm and staring at her with its unblinking and – please God – all-seeing eye, was a GoPro camera.

* * *

They stared at each other from opposite sides of the kitchen. Hank by the door and Duncan by the stove, where something dubious bubbled in a pot.

'She got called into work. An accident out on the Strip. Multiple injuries.'

He laughed. It was all he could do. If it wasn't him, it was her. They could never get the timing right.

'Yep. Nothing's changed. One of you always missing dinner.'

And tonight, missing a promised conversation, too. Hank laughed again. He'd gladly kick that can down the road because there was no way he was going to bring up the topic without Maggie. He moved toward the living room, stepping over dog toys and picking up a dropped unicorn backpack on the way. Dunc had turned back to the stove, the kids were watching cartoons, and the dog snored under the table. No one was scrambling to find a babysitter, or calling for pizza delivery. It all felt like what normal used to be.

He stopped. Yes, everything around him at this moment was back in place. Even him and Dunc, sort of. But him and Maggie? No. And so all this around him right now – the lovingly, haphazardly constructed edifice they'd built together – would never be truly solid again without its core foundational strength. Their marriage.

He turned around.

'I need to tell you something.'

Dunc looked up from the stove. 'Yeah?' He met Hank's gaze and then calmly put down the stirring spoon. 'OK, shoot.'

'While Maggie's not here . . . I need you to . . .' Duncan had done so much for them, Hank felt he at least owed the old man a heads-up. 'I want you to know that I'm going to tell her. About Marian and the affair.'

Duncan nodded slowly. 'I figured you hadn't. She would've said something to me if she knew. Maybe not. I don't know much of anything anymore.'

'Me, either.'

They stared at each other across the cluttered countertop.

'I've tried,' Hank said finally. 'We've tried. We can't get past . . . she's very protective of you.'

Duncan scoffed softly.

'She's the same about you, boy-o. Believe that.'

'I need her to know why. Because we aren't getting past it.' And there it was. Admitting the marriage problem. Laying it out to the person he least wanted to know. Stripping himself bare in his own damn kitchen, his only armor a rainbow unicorn. He should've just stayed at work.

Duncan settled the pot more firmly on the burner. 'I want to protect her, too, you understand? And there's two directions to go, I know. Protect her marriage or protect her memories.' Resignation and heartbreak tugged his mouth into a slight, unexpected smile. 'And we can't have both, can we?'

Hank shook his head. Duncan nodded his.

'I cede it to you. It's your call to make. Always has been.' He paused. Hank kept quiet as the stew bubbled. He knew there was more. 'And rightfully so. We got to live in the present, don't we? And the present is them.' Dunc waved toward the living room and the giggling kids. 'And you. And Maggie. Moving forward.'

He picked up the spoon and bent over the pot, his part in this conversation finished. Hank could leave now with a win. A solid, relief-swooning win. But wins didn't feel like this awkward silence. Wins felt like noisy, crowded kitchens and strange cooking smells and the security of children thriving in the care of someone who would quite literally do anything for them. And just had.

'And you, too.'

Dunc looked up in surprise. Hank repeated it. 'And you, too. Moving forward. You have a present – and a future – too. However you want to do it.'

Dunc bit at his lip. The pot boiled over. And Hank moved to clean up the mess.

THIRTY-FIVE

'Under arrest? For what? I didn't do anything.'

'Mr Markham, that is ridiculous. And I don't have time for ridiculous.' Sheila stared across the interview room table at the young man. He was white, blond, average height, and compact, likely recruited for the wrestling team in high school. 'We're going to take you down to Branson, where you'll be booked into jail until you have a bail hearing.'

He gaped at her, then looked over at Ray Gillespie, who sat in the corner of the little room and wouldn't meet his gaze. He turned back to Sheila. 'You can't extradite me.'

'We're in the same state. That's not a thing.' She tried not to laugh at him. 'You're under arrest. We get to take you where we want to.'

'Again – for what?'

'Theft. We found two stolen backpacks in the storage closet of your apartment.'

She waited while he thought about that.

'They weren't . . . I didn't steal those. I found them.'

'Oh. OK. Where?'

'Where what?'

'Where did you "find" them?'

He picked at a thumbnail.

'I was on a hike in the woods.'

'Where? Which woods?'

'Down near Branson.'

'You know that area. Surely you can be more specific than that.' The thumbnail started to bleed. 'My grandfather's land.'

'Who's your grandfather?'

'Leo Fackrell.'

'OK. And where in his woods did you find the backpacks? Were they together or in different places or what?'

'Together.'

She was a dentist pulling teeth. She kept at it.

'Describe where you found them.'

He shrugged like a petulant teenager. 'On the ground.'

'Near a campsite? Near a creek? Near people?'

His gaze slid over to Ray again.

'He ain't gonna help you.' She clunked her elbows down on the table, redirecting his focus back to her. 'You need to answer my question.'

'Just on the ground. By themselves. Two backpacks. So I picked them up. Brought them home.'

'Now that's curious to me. Why would you bring them all the way up here to St. Joe when you could've just walked them over to Grandpa's house and gone through them there?'

Another shrug. 'I guess I didn't think of that.'

'You don't strike me as quite that stupid, Jordan.'

He straightened indignantly. 'I . . . I didn't want to bother him. So I just put them in my truck and brought them back here.'

'And did you go through them?' Had he been the one to rifle through Takama's belongings? She watched him carefully.

'No.'

'Why not?'

He thought about that. 'I stuck them in my storage space and kinda forgot about them. So . . . yeah.'

'You forgot about big expensive packs, one of which was soaked in blood?'

'I've been busy.'

They went through what he'd been doing, where he worked and how often he visited his grandparents.

'And are you in the habit of using a rental car when you visit?'

What little color he had drained from his pale face. 'What do you mean?'

'You seem to know exactly what I mean.' She wished she'd brought the photos from the Springfield Airport surveillance cameras. It would've been nice to slide those in front of him. 'You returned a rental car that wasn't yours, obscured your identity, caught two different Ubers, and then disappeared from a Best Buy parking lot.' She made a *poof* gesture with her fingers.

He shrugged again, failing completely at nonchalance. 'That's where I left my truck.'

'Why were you in the rental car?'

'I found it.'

'Where?' She really did want to kick him.

'Out by Grandpa's.'

'And you just got in and drove away?' Her voice was getting louder, she couldn't help it.

He flopped a hand on the table. 'OK, look. I found the packs. One of them had car keys looped to it. I found the car. I thought it would be nice to turn it back in.'

'Why would you think that was necessary? Why wouldn't the person who rented it return it themselves?'

Silence. They stared at each other.

'I was just trying to help.'

'Tell me.'

He slumped, finally bending to the reality that she already knew. 'He was dead. There was a dead guy and two backpacks. I took the packs and found the keys and got out of there.'

'And you didn't call 911?'

'Obviously not.' He went at his thumbnail again as she glared at him. 'I was freaked out. So I didn't. And then it got to be . . . too late? I didn't know how I'd explain it to the cops.'

Maybe he was that stupid. But she didn't think so.

'Where was the body when you found it?'

'I told you.' His voice rose in pitch and volume. 'In the woods.'

'Where exactly? Describe the terrain.'

Trees. Rocks. Weeds. She gave him a dirty look. He shrank further down in the chair.

'It was flat. A clearing kinda spot. Not very big. He was lying there. Both backpacks were there, too.'

'Did you move anything?'

'Just the backpacks.'

She considered that. If he was telling the truth, then someone else dragged Garvan's body to the outcropping and pushed him off.

'Did your grandfather know that you were there? Had you been staying with him?'

Any way he answered this question was bad news for someone. Either Leo Fackrell deliberately didn't mention that his grandson was visiting at the same time that two people were murdered nearby, or Jordan hadn't told Grandpa he was in town and was secretly skulking around on the family land.

'I was going to, but I hadn't gotten up to the house yet. I just wanted to walk around, chill out a little first. Before I had to go stay in Mom's old bedroom, you know?'

That was a fairly good explanation, she had to give him that. She waited.

'Then I saw the guy, and I freaked out, and I left.' He stared at her, looking as exhausted as she felt. 'I'm sorry. Take the bags back. Please. I'll just go home.'

'We'll keep the bags.' She gestured to Ray. 'But you're still going to have to come with us.'

His breathing was heavy and labored; the sound rasped in his ears and frightened small animals in the underbrush. He was a stranger both to exertion and to these woods. The compass was hard to read through the sweat stinging his eyes. It confused him more each time he looked at it. He did not know which way to turn.

This was not how it was supposed to happen. He had prepared well and was on the side of righteousness. Of understanding. No one else knew the full story. The story that included him. But there would be no happy ending if he couldn't find it. He turned again, trying to orient himself and stop the sniffling that threatened to rob him of the little breath he had. He stopped and stared down at his feet until he was back in control. His gasping quieted and let him hear other things. Other footsteps. He spun to the left, where trees were not as tightly spaced, and saw a flash of movement. Tall, bipedal, fast-moving. Competition.

He sprinted after the man, yelling random words as he stumbled over logs and uneven ground. The competitor turned in surprise. 'Are you looking, too? You're the first I've seen.'

He shook his head, talking almost to himself. 'No, this is mine. I have the family connection.'

'That's ridiculous. Nobody's got a claim. That's the whole point. I listened, same as you. And I did research. Professional level research. I've even got expert reinforcements coming. I bet you don't. You're out here totally by yourself with no clue.' He stopped to catch his own breath and smirked once he did. 'You pretty much got a neon "I'm lost" sign flashing over your head. And for all you know, I've already found it.'

It went on. They both got louder and angrier. And closer together. He stepped forward, now less than five feet from the man, out of breath with outrage. 'I have proof. Genealogy proof. I'm a Finnegan.'

A scoff. 'The money belonged to the bank, not the Finnegans.'

'No. They were the last to have it.'

The man smirked. 'Alf Bolin was the last to have it. You gonna say you're related to him, too?'

He shoved, so quick there was no time for thought. The man pushed back, hard. There was yelling and swearing and incoherent shouting. He struggled with his pack and there was a scrape of metal and he swung his hatchet. The sheathed broadside hit the man in the shoulder and bounced off. The next swing did not. The naked blade sank into the man's arm just as he raised it to shield himself. The competitor staggered back as the blows continued. He hunched and turned just as the hatchet came down again, sinking in where the neck met the shoulder.

They both screamed. He tugged frantically and stepped away. The competitor slowly toppled over, eyes locked on him the whole time.

It had taken no more than thirty seconds.

He fell to his knees, staring at the bloody tool. Then he reached for the man but his shaking hand stopped, hovering over the sightless eyes. A benediction. An apology. It was hard to tell. He lurched to his feet and looked around wildly. He found the sheath with its broken strap and turned to flee but stopped after a dozen steps. His hyperventilating overwhelmed every other sense for too many minutes, until he finally turned back and filled his vision with the other man's pack. Neither his hands nor his breath would stay steady enough to unzip it, so instead he tugged until it slipped off the bloody body. And then he ran.

He staggered along with double the weight, clutching the stolen bag in front of him without realizing it blocked his view of the ground. He didn't see the rock and went down hard, his knee cracking against the stone and the bag tumbling down an incline. He scrambled after it, this time looping his arms through the straps. He pushed himself to his feet and ran, swinging his head from side to side as he tried to get his bearings. The trees danced dizzily around him.

Finally they opened up and he saw a patch of sky. It was a small clearing. He dropped both packs and sank to his knees. He used the edge of his T-shirt to wipe the sweat and tears off his face. A pause and he swore at himself, tugging a headband off his head. The view tilted widely as he unzipped his own pack. And then the world went black.

They all stood there, in front of the conference room screen that was linked to a laptop that was linked to the GoPro that was linked to the murder. Which they had just watched.

No one sat the entire time, even Sheila. It didn't seem proper, when they were watching Alan Takama die. It also didn't seem proper they all had hoped to see another one die, too.

Hank raked a hand through his hair. 'Why couldn't Garvan have left his GoPro on?' He waved at the screen. 'Because that was it, right? That clearing is the same one Roscoe the dog hit on, and the same one where Markham says he found Garvan's body and the packs?'

'Yeah, that's where Roscoe first stopped,' Sam said.

'And yes,' said Ray, as Sheila finally lowered herself into a chair. 'What's on the video is just like Markham described.'

'He described a lot of things. It seems like the only one he left out is that Garvan was alive when he found him,' Sheila said. They all turned and stared at her. 'I think Markham killed him.'

'Look,' she said in the taut voice Hank knew meant she was in pain, 'why would someone do that whole cockamamie Uber-hopping bullshit? With a disguise on? That's an awful lot for just stealing two backpacks. I think he killed him, dumped him and took the backpacks. And he returned the car to make it look like Garvan had finished his Branson business and left town. He covered the entire thing up. Pretty successfully, too. No one would've known there was a body in the woods at all – except for the fact that somebody reported *another* body and the dogs found them both.'

'OK. So what do you think?' Hank asked. 'We take another crack at him?'

'Oh, hell yes.' She paused. 'But not until we hear what Old Man Fackrell has to say.'

'Agreed,' he said. 'I find it hard to believe his grandparents didn't know he was in town.'

'So do I,' said Sheila. 'And if it weren't one o'clock in the morning, I'd be at their door right now. As it is, I think a nice early wakeup knock is in order.'

Ray's eyes got wide. Sam chuckled.

Hank appraised her, sitting disheveled and stiff in an uncomfortable office chair. Sheila on four hours' sleep after a day of painful long-distance driving and being forced to move faster than her doctor recommended in order to catch a fleeing suspect? The Fackrells had no idea what they were in for. 'I'll pick you up at six,' he said. He was looking forward to it.

THIRTY-SIX

There was finally a break in the weather. The rain wasn't over – Sam could still smell it, just on the other side of dawn, waiting for a few degrees more warmth to start up again. Which was why he was out here in the gloom, with a powerful flashlight and a willing but probably useless suburbia-raised Ray Gillespie. They sludged their way into the woods and back to the skeleton's final resting place.

'Damn, you surely did make a mess.' Ray wouldn't even hazard a guess as to where exactly the hole had been, it was that completely filled. And the ground a dozen feet in all directions was churned into six-inch-thick, boot-sucking muck. They steered well clear as Ray scooped up the remaining tarp and Sam oriented himself.

'Womack came from that direction. By the time he got to me, he wasn't carrying anything.'

'OK,' said Ray. 'If we spread out we can cover more ground. But – is it just his camping equipment?'

'You mean, why am I so interested in retrieving random personal property? Before the sun comes up?' He sighed. 'There's gotta be a reason he was over here instead of the area around Murder Rocks. I think there's all kinds of things he's not telling us. Who knows what he found while he was out here all that time until I caught him.'

'"Who knows what he found?"' Ray repeated. 'You think there is treasure?'

Sam shrugged. 'I don't know. I don't think so, I guess. It would've been found by now. Especially all that supposed bank money. Somebody would've stumbled across it by now. I really just want to know what Womack was trying to pull. What he was going to say about this area. Honestly, I wouldn't put it past him to plant something, to make it look like he discovered bits of the lost hoard.'

Ray's eyebrows shot up.

'Or maybe I'm just tired of people coming down here and taking what they want with no regard for anything,' Sam said. 'I think people come down here and don't know what they're getting into.

They've always thought they did. It's just a bunch of hills and hollers, how hard could it be? Take what they want and move on. But this place doesn't work that way.

'We're not like a city, that chews you up and spits you out and you get to go crawling off back home as a failure. The lesson you learn here is your last one.'

'Like Bolin with his head on a pike?'

'Yeah, exactly. When you fail here, you fail permanent.'

Ray nodded and turned to the east. Sam went west, into thicker stands of trees still coated in darkness. Which of course was where Womack had been hiding. The backpack lay tucked against a large, uprooted tree that had long ago fallen onto a boulder and cracked clean in two. The halves were rotting now, decomposing nicely into the soil. Sam tugged the pack loose and saw it wasn't as big as it had been in the hotel surveillance video. The sleeping bag was missing. And the shovel. He dropped the whole thing and started searching the length of the tree.

Ray arrived and looped around to the other side of the flat-topped boulder. It took him all of two seconds to call Sam over. They both stared down at the large, freshly dug hole next to the rock. Sam picked up the shovel and they poked around for a few minutes. They found no treasure.

'Why do you think he chose to dig here?' Ray said. 'Out of all the places in the woods that he could?'

'That's a damn good question.' Sam stepped back and took in the whole landscape. Then he walked back around the log to the other side and did the same. Then he took Womack's shovel and started to dig.

'My grandson?'

'Yes. When was the last time you saw him?'

'Sometime after Christmas. February, maybe?' Leo Fackrell was still blinking sleep out of his eyes.

The Fackrells both stared uneasily at Hank and Sheila, who'd hung their dripping raincoats on the back of their chairs. 'Why do you want to know?' Darlene asked.

Hank leaned forward and put his elbows on the kitchen table. Relaxed, friendly. They weren't buying it. Darlene crossed her arms and scowled. Her bathrobe had threadbare patches on the sleeves. Leo was halfway dressed, with an untucked shirt and Bass Pro sweatpants and hair that looked like it'd been combed by one of his goats. The few lights they'd turned on flickered as the power bowed to the whims of the wind.

'Why do you want to know?' she repeated. 'Especially at this hour?'

Hank ignored her. 'Are you sure? You haven't seen him since February?'

'We're not answering any questions until you tell us what's going on.' Darlene's scowl was fearsome.

'Mr Markham has taken some things that weren't his. And—'

'Jordan's not a thief.'

'Well, Leo, we're less concerned with that than we are with his whereabouts during the past week or so.'

Now Leo scowled, too. 'I got no idea. He lives in St. Joe.'

They both glared at him. He kept himself loose as he pressed them. They hadn't talked to him on the phone or texted since July. He was a busy kid and a hard worker. They were proud of him for making his own way.

'Did he spend a lot of time with you when he was growing up?'

'Big chunks of his summers, yeah.' Leo said it cautiously, worried he was giving something away that would hurt Jordan. But the kid had already done enough of that himself.

'And he played in the woods?'

Darlene smacked a hand down on the table. 'He was a kid in the middle of nowhere with two old people. Of course he went out and played in the damn woods.'

Sheila looked unimpressed. Hank kept his face blank and watched their expressions carefully as Sheila spoke.

'The first time we were here,' she said, 'you mentioned that one of the rifles in the house belonged to Jordan. Are there any other guns that you consider to be his?'

Leo waved in the direction of the gun cabinet in the hallway. 'They'll all go to him eventually. He's the only grandkid.'

'That's not what I'm asking, sir. Does Jordan have a handgun?'

'Are you talking about that fella in the woods?'

'Oh, this all comes back to the fella in the woods,' Sheila said. 'Because Jordan found the fella.'

They both did a fairly good job of looking confused. Hank was skeptical. And he knew Sheila wasn't believing it at all. He leaned back, ceding the table to her and the file folder she opened with a sharp flick.

'This is a surveillance photo of your grandson carrying the backpacks of two dead men.'

Nothing. No sound, no reaction.

'You can't tell who that is. You can't even tell if it's a man or a woman.' Leo pushed the photo back at Sheila.

'Oh, he's admitted that it's him. And he's admitted that he took the backpacks from Mr Philip Garvan, who was indeed the fella shot in the woods.' She looked straight at Leo. 'Then he returned Mr Garvan's rental car to the Springfield Airport and did a spectacular bob-and-weave in order to get back down to Branson. To you.'

The last two words came out so sharply, both Fackrells jerked back in their seats. Hank didn't allow them time to collect themselves.

'We don't think Jordan would've made that kind of discovery and not told you,' he said. 'You're his beloved grandfather and a natural person to confide in. And also, the murder victim was on your property – purely as a landowner matter, you should be told.'

Leo raised his hand a few inches off the table with a slashing motion, like a politician making a point during a speech. But no words came out. After a moment, Darlene took his hand and held it in both of hers.

'I don't believe any of this,' she said. 'Anything he told you had to be under duress. You can't confirm those backpacks were those people's. You can't prove that's Jordan in that blurry picture.'

'We have the backpacks,' Hank said. 'And we have your grandson.'

All the color left her face.

'He's currently locked in a jail cell, and he's about to be charged with murder.' Hank rose to his feet.

'Sweet Jesus.' Leo pushed back from the table, horrified. Darlene just stared at them.

'I want to see him.' Leo was starting to shake. Darlene laid her hand over his. 'You have no proof,' she said.

'We have a significant amount of proof,' Hank said. 'Did he tell you that he was in town? Did he tell you what he found?'

'I'm not saying a word. You can't make me.' Leo waved his arms angrily and hefted himself to his feet. 'Now get out.'

The Fackrells protested Jordan's arrest the entire way to the front door, and then slammed it behind Hank and Sheila once they were outside in the rain. They walked to the cruiser as quickly as they were able with Sheila's limp.

'Why do you walk with me?' she said once they were in the car.

'You could be sitting in here ten times drier if you'd ambulated like a normal person.'

He just gave her a smile as water dripped down his nose. She rolled her eyes and pointed at the house. 'You agree with me now?'

'Today? Yes,' he said. With the rain and the dark clouds and a flickering light in the living-room window, it did look like a horror movie.

THIRTY-SEVEN

Sam dropped Womack's pack onto the evidence room table with a splat. Alice Randall glared at him. 'I'd better be looking for something besides dirty underwear.'

He shrugged. 'Hopefully a murder weapon. Nine-millimeter pistol, to be precise.'

She told him he was an optimistic fool and then made him help pull everything out. There was no gun. Just a lot of recording equipment, a soaked and probably ruined laptop, some rumpled clothing, a wallet, and a three-ring binder.

'If I'm cataloging this under Stanley Womack, then who the hell is Victor Hardwick?' Alice said as she bagged the items.

'Same person. That's what he calls himself as the podcast host.' Sam handed over a Hardwick Productions, LLC, credit card from Womack's wallet, along with a bent business card that identified Victor as president and 'Chief Fortune Officer.' Alice looked at it and scoffed. Sam nodded and stepped out of her way. She could do this much faster without his fumbling help. He pulled up a chair and sat down with the binder.

Every page was in a plastic sheet protector. The first papers were internet photo printouts of Civil War-era coins, with typed analysis and comparisons. Then came handwritten letters. They were clearly Xeroxed copies, but definitely seemed to be from the same time period. He started to read.

'Hey, Sammy.'

He looked up, startled.

'Lord, child. For the third time, I need to mark that.' Alice pointed at the binder in exasperation. He sprang to his feet, winced as his left leg bore weight, and moved back to the table.

'You've been sitting with it for ten minutes. What's so interesting?'

'Letters. The ones he quoted in the podcast.' He laid it on the table. 'I don't know why he wouldn't just have pictures of them on his phone, though. It'd be a lot easier to carry.'

'Maybe because some people think actual paper is still the best,' she said, in a tone that clearly implied she was one of them. Sam grinned and flipped through a few to show her. She pointed at the last page. 'That one looks real.'

It did. A small, yellowed sheet, floating in its plastic protector. Sam squinted at the delicate writing, smaller than the enlarged photocopies of the other letters. But written by the same hand. He leaned closer. Then he swore and picked the binder up again. Alice barely got it in an evidence bag with a chain of custody sheet before he was out the door. He speed-limped down the hallway looking for Sheila. He found her ferociously adjusting her desk chair.

'He knew more. He knew more than he told us. Look at this letter. This one wasn't on the podcast.'

She stopped, pushed away the chair, and grabbed the binder. Hank peeked out of his office. They both waited while she read.

'He knew where to dig. *He knew where to dig?*'

'Yeah. It's a pretty specific description,' Sam said.

Hank emerged and read the letter. 'It sounds a lot like the terrain around where the skeleton was found.'

'It also could describe the spot where I found Womack's backpack. And where he was digging a hole. Same kind of boulder and rocky outcropping. Same uphill slope.'

Sheila grabbed her cane. 'I'm going to have another conversation with that little weasel.'

Neither he nor Hank wanted to miss that. They all marched over to the jail. Once they were in the interrogation room, Sheila went to work.

'Stanley, we've discovered that you weren't honest with your podcast listeners. And more importantly, you weren't honest with me. You didn't tell me you still had an original Mary Louise letter – what seems to be the most important letter.' She read the location description. Womack's cheeks got very pink while the rest of him turned pale. 'And you've been using this information to do some prospecting. You didn't tell me that, either.'

He groaned and lost what little starch his spine had left, slumping forward in defeat. The days in jail were wearing on him. 'It wasn't relevant. Where other people were looking was relevant. They were the ones going after each other.'

'And whose fault is that?'

Silence. Hank, leaning against the wall in the corner, eventually cleared his throat.

'What I don't understand is why you did the episode in the first place. If you had all these letters, go search on your own with no one knowing about it. You could've found "treasure" with no competition. Instead you let loose every crazy fortune hunter with a podcast app and made your own search a hundred times harder. Why?'

More waiting. Finally Womack gave in. 'That bastard came out of nowhere and ruined the entire plan.'

'Who? Philip Garvan?'

Yeah, him, Womack muttered. The guy who claimed to be related to the Finnegan family and the one who threatened to review-bomb the podcast if Womack didn't hand over the letters. He'd used portions of the letters in the episode, but not everything. He'd kept some things to himself. But now, with possession of the letters, Garvan suddenly had the same information Womack did. It was completely unexpected and forced Womack to move up his entire timeline.

'What timeline?' Hank's words were almost as clipped as Sheila's.

The plan was to air the episode and have people flock to Murder Rocks. They'd search, word of mouth would explode, his ratings would go up, social media would be set ablaze. Then, toward the end of the week, he'd swoop into town with the information in those letters, and find the treasure. He'd break the news on a subsequent episode – or maybe even in the mainstream media – and look like a genius. Because he could find what others could not.

'And because he ruined that plan for you, you killed him.'

He stared at Hank in horror. Or pretend horror. Sam still considered him a prime suspect. He watched closely as Hank pressed.

'You shot him to death to eliminate your strongest competition.'

'No, no, God no. I didn't even know what he looked like. And I sure as hell didn't stalk him in the woods. I don't even know how to shoot a gun.'

'You were in those woods when he was killed. You had more motive than anyone else to want him dead. If he was gone, you could go back to your original timeline.'

Womack was shaking and trying to hide it. 'If I killed him, wouldn't I have his stuff? Wouldn't I have taken the letters back? Or hell, wouldn't I have buried him? I clearly have no problem digging holes.' His deep radio announcer voice was gone, his words now high-pitched and scared. 'I didn't, didn't kill him. I swear.'

He looked at all of them with wide eyes. Sheila waited a beat, then pushed the binder into the middle of the table. 'Let's go back to this last letter.'

Sam had a feeling she'd changed to an easier subject so Womack wouldn't decide to stop talking and ask for a lawyer. He fought back a scowl.

'How do you come to still have an original?'

'I didn't use it in the podcast, so that Garvan guy didn't know it existed.'

Sheila placed a gentle hand on the sheet protector. 'Why didn't you use this letter in your podcast? It's the best one. It's heart-wrenching. You could've just omitted the part where she talks about the location.'

'The location's the only important part. Nothing else in that letter has anything to do with the treasure. I wasn't going to use up podcast time with it.'

Sheila shut the binder with a snap and looked at him with contempt.

'And have those treasure location descriptions helped you?' Sam tried not to sound mocking, but failed spectacularly. Out of the corner of his eye, he saw Hank fight back a grin.

'I don't know,' Womack said in a tone that mirrored Sam's. 'I haven't finished digging yet.'

He was exactly what Sam hated. Coming in and thinking he could take anything he wanted and then waltz right on out again. 'Yeah, you mean that hole near where you left your pack? Not very big, is it? I did poke around a little, made it bigger.'

He almost leaped out of his seat. 'Did you find anything?'

'You don't hear my pockets jingling, do you?' he snapped.

Sheila tapped a fingernail on the table, reclaiming their focus. 'Where else have you dug? How many places?'

Womack hemmed and hawed until a glare from Sheila set him counting on his fingers. He started listing them, with pretty poor descriptions of where in the woods he'd been. Sam stood quietly, trying to place them on the topographical map in his head.

'Wait a minute,' he interrupted. 'You dug over by what looked like a dry creek bed? And did the slope have a big oak tree on it? And the boulder there is flatter, and tilted?'

Womack nodded hesitantly, unsure whether he was helping or hurting his case.

Sam stepped closer to the table. 'When? What day?'

'Tuesday, I think?' He wouldn't meet Sam's eyes, which was curious.

'That's right near where Garvan was shot. Did you see anything around there? Did you see a body?'

'No. God, no.' He reflexively pushed away from the table, but the bolted chair wouldn't let him move. He sat there, stiff arms gripping the table like a life preserver, and stared at them.

'So what did you see?' Sheila said.

'All I wanted was to break out my podcast. I'm so close to hitting the top twenty.' His voice started to crack. 'The whole plan, all the timing went to shit. I was just trying to salvage everything.'

Sheila leaned forward. 'We. Don't. Care.'

He slowly slumped down, arms turned to rubber and dangling at his sides. 'I saw another person. At first I thought they were hunting, like me, so I stayed where I was so they wouldn't see me. Competition, you know. But they weren't equipped at all, no shovel or gear or anything. Just out there searching in the bushes. All around, like they were panicked.'

'And what did this person look like?' asked Hank, still leaning casually in the corner, but now with a deadeye stare that Sam knew meant he was out of patience.

'I did not want to get involved with this.' His voice got higher and faster. 'They could've been there for any kind of reason. I didn't know there had been murders. By the time I did . . . what use would I be?'

Hank straightened and Womack fell silent. He looked from Hank to Sheila and did a quick calculation that had him at zero.

'It was a woman. Older. Kinda stocky. Long gray hair in a braid.'

Sam couldn't help but look over at Hank. That description only fit one person.

'Did you see them find anything?' Sheila said.

'A gun. Some kind of handgun. Off in the weeds. She found it and took off.'

'Which direction?'

'Away from me, thank God.'

Sheila pushed herself to her feet. 'I wouldn't thank Him just yet. You're not coming out of this unscathed. Not by a long shot.'

And neither, Sam thought as he watched Sheila leave, was Darlene Fackrell.

THIRTY-EIGHT

Hank pounded on the farmhouse door. It swung open to reveal a still disheveled Leo Fackrell.

'What on earth are you doing? You were just here.'

'And now we're back. With a bit more information we'd like to talk about with you. And your wife.'

He stepped inside without invitation, Sheila right on his heels. The wind was picking up and blowing the rain straight at them. Leo struggled to close the door. Once he did, everything plunged into gloom and shadow.

'Is your power out?'

'Yeah. It's always sketchy during storms.'

Hank glanced around. The front room was dark and the fireplace cold and empty. Leo saw him looking. 'I can't kneel so good anymore. Laying a fire's out of my capabilities now.'

'Darlene isn't able to do it?' Sheila's tone was carefully neutral.

Leo turned toward the kitchen. 'She's upstairs right now.'

They filed into the kitchen, where a battery-powered lantern sat on the counter and candles flickered from the table and the sideboard by the window.

'Can you ask Darlene to come down, please?' Hank said.

Leo eyed him. 'Why don't you tell me first what you want?'

'I want to talk to your wife.'

'You were here two hours ago accusing my grandson of murder. Now you come back and what – want to accuse her of something, too?'

Sheila tapped Hank's shoe with her cane and then stepped forward. She asked again about Darlene as Hank slid back toward the hallway. She was giving him the opportunity to go upstairs. He made it only three steps in the flickering light before Leo noticed. 'Don't you do that.'

Hank kept going. 'Mrs Fackrell? Darlene? We need you to come down, please.'

'No. You stop.' Leo shuffled after Hank, reaching for his arm and hollering. 'Darlene, you don't have to.'

'Mrs Fackrell?' Hank's voice would've rattled the windows if the wind hadn't already been doing it. As he finished calling out, a loud crash came from above. They all froze for the barest second. Then Hank took another step. Leo swatted at him and moved to stand in his way. Sheila went to the left to act as a buffer at the same time Hank raised a placating hand and Leo swung out to block his path. Leo's arm hit the candle on the sideboard and knocked it into the curtains behind it. Seemingly as old as the house, they ignited instantly.

Hank raced to the sink, searching for anything that would hold water. All he saw was a flower vase on the table. He dumped the bouquet and filled it to the brim. The fire was crackling higher, almost to the ceiling. The other half of the curtain pair was starting to smoke. He threw the water on it and turned to Leo, yelling for a fire extinguisher. The old man didn't hear, waving his arms and screaming for his wife. Sheila started shoving him toward the door. He pulled away, heading for the stairs. Sheila grabbed his arm and used her whole body weight to propel him toward the front of the house.

'Yes. Get him out of here,' Hank yelled. He spun back around and wrenched open the cabinet under the sink, pushing aside cleaning supplies until he saw what he needed. He pulled out the extinguisher and positioned himself in front of the curtains. And nothing. The device was a dud. Expired, broken – it didn't matter. Same disastrous result either way. He dropped it and picked the vase up again. He had no idea if this was a good idea or a very bad one. He said a prayer, and heaved it through the window.

He could barely hear the glass break over the noise of the fire, which was making short work of the second curtain, too. Wind blasted through the hole and with it, rain. But not enough. He looked around frantically and his gaze landed on the stove. Three seconds later, a cast-iron frying pan went flying. The single-pane window disintegrated and the rain let itself in.

He abandoned the kitchen and stepped into the hall to see Sheila close to getting Leo out the front door. He turned to the narrow flight of stairs, which hugged the hallway wall all the way up. He took them three at a time and ended up in a short hallway with two bedrooms on either side. Only one had light underneath the door.

He burst in to find Darlene with her own broken window, one that led out onto the roof. She'd been trying to open it. A pane of glass lay on the floor. She stood there with a bloody palm.

'Where were you going to go, Darlene?'

'I don't know. I don't know.'

'Well, you need to come with me now. Your kitchen's on fire. We have to get out of here.'

'Fire?'

'Yes. Come with me, and we'll get you someplace safe.'

'But I'm not safe. It hasn't been safe here for a hundred and fifty years.'

Hank stepped closer and held out his hand. 'Darlene, you need to come with me.'

She looked down at her bloody hand and back at Hank. 'What was I supposed to do? I thought he'd found something. Two big bags he had. We're the ones who need money. All I wanted was the bags.'

The wind whistled through the hole in her window and pellets of rain sprayed them like buckshot. He grabbed her wrist. 'Walk with me now.'

They moved toward the door. 'All those people. All those damn searchers all those years. And to think there actually could be something there. I thought he'd found it.'

They reached the hallway. Smoke was coming up the stairs. Little puffs that didn't look too bad. It was only when he got to the top of the stairs and looked down that he could see the billows pouring out of the kitchen and the back of the house. He didn't know if they could make it through to the front door. Darlene was already starting to cough. A sharp crack sounded from somewhere in the downstairs hallway, and Hank swore.

He pushed Darlene back into the bedroom and over to the window. He peered out, trying to judge the slope of the roof.

'It wouldn't open all the way,' she yelled over the rain. She showed him her sliced hand. 'I was going to go. I don't know. I heard you downstairs and I didn't know what to do.'

He grabbed her shoulders. 'I need for you to stay with me. I need you to be that lady who doesn't take any shit for just a little bit longer, OK?'

She stared at him. He let go, not knowing if that registered, and grabbed the bedspread. He wrapped his arm and busted out the rest of the glass. Then he laid it over the sill and took her hand. He worried that if he went first, she would just stand there inside and not follow.

'I need you to climb out the window. Can you do that for me?'
She snatched her hand away. 'I was trying to do that anyway.'
She climbed out slowly, her hair whipping in the wind. When she
was out, but before her hand left the sill, Hank grabbed her wrist.
There was no way he was going to let a distraught suspect stand
on a precipice with nothing to hold her back. He climbed out, his
fingers like a manacle. She shot him a look of confusion and then
outrage. He didn't care. He straightened and looked around. The
roof sloped downward at an angle that would've been merely
moderate were it not for the slick shingles and gusting rain. Those
turned it into what felt like a downhill ski jump.
   'We're going to crawl down to that corner,' he yelled.
   'Let go of my arm.'
   'No.'
   He dropped down onto his ass, pulling her with him. They scooted
across rough shingles as Hank tried desperately to see the ground
below them. Finally there was a flash of movement. Sam shifted
into full view and started waving his arms at both of them. Then
he cupped his hands around his mouth and hollered.
   '. . . have . . . faster. Go . . . faster.'
   They looked at each other, not more than a foot apart and soaked
through.
   'I'm not dying in this Goddamn house.' The wind sent her hair
snaking around her head like a Greek myth. 'Come on, Sheriff.'
   They scrambled to the edge, twenty feet off the ground. Sam was
directly below, guiding the parking of a squad car under the eaves.
Ray hopped out and the two of them clambered onto the car's roof.
   'OK,' Hank yelled, grabbing her other wrist. 'You're going to
face me and go over feet first. I'm not going to let go of you until
they have hold of you down there. Got it?'
   She nodded and gave him the slightest smirk. 'Got it.' It made
him sad. He liked this woman. She'd carved a place for herself in
an old family and done it well. And gone too far in trying to keep
it all together. He lay flat on the roof as she dropped her bottom
half over the edge. He inched forward as more and more of her
went off the roof. Finally she was swinging in the wind, her whole
weight held only by his hands. His arms wanted to rip out of their
sockets. He could see Sam and Ray trying to grab her. Then he felt
them succeed. The weight miraculously disappeared. He lay his
forehead on a splintered shingle and breathed through the pain.

'You've got to get down,' Sam shouted. 'The fire's almost out the back, right here.' Hank raised his head to see the Pup pointing frantically. He cursed the gods of fire and rain and got to his knees. Then he swung off the roof by his tired, shaking fingers, and prayed they would catch him.

THIRTY-NINE

They sat in a squad car and watched the house burn. They couldn't get down the driveway with all the fire trucks blocking the way. Sam had the heat on in an attempt to dry them all. It didn't seem to be reaching Darlene Fackrell, huddled into a ball in the back seat and peering out the window. Hank wondered if he could reach her in another way.

'What happened, in the woods?'

She didn't look away from the window and the flames. Firefighters brought out another hose. Hank waited.

'I went for a walk.'

Men yelled and worked, and the flames continued. In the driver's seat, Sam started to fidget.

'I knew about the podcast. Somebody told me about it at church that morning. So I went home and listened to it.' She paused. 'And I knew we were in trouble.'

All three of them thought about that.

'All those years,' she finally said. 'Nodding and chuckling at the people who came traipsing through. It was funny. Because there was nothing. They all went home dirty and tired and with nothing to show for it but a case of poison ivy. Then this radio show. Saying a bank's worth of gold tipped over in our dirt. I knew they'd be coming in droves. Thinking they had a right.'

So she went out to see if there was a way to mark the property line. Leo had always insisted it was too much bother. It was only a few people a year, so who cared? Well. Now Leo was old. Old and past the days when he could patrol the land and solve problems and hang on to the way things had always been done. So she grabbed her own father's Smith & Wesson Model 39 and a stack of signs that said 'Private Property,' and took a walk.

She found him in a little clearing; young, slightly pudgy, and sitting with two big bags. He had to have found something. Why else would he have two? He'd just put something in the bigger pack. He looked up and saw her.

'He was . . . something was wrong with him. His face was beet red and his eyes were huge. He was breathing like he'd just sprinted a mile. He stood up real quick and told me I needed to get back.' Her tone made clear what she'd thought about that. 'I said that he was on my land and needed to leave.' Her voice turned small. 'Then I looked at the bags. Why would he have two? He must've found something. That bank gold information, I couldn't get it out of my head. It was so unexpected. That there might be real facts that would lead to real treasure. It would solve everything.'

She fell silent. Hank thought about pudgy Philip Garvan and stayed facing forward in the passenger seat, deliberately not turning around.

'What happened next?'

The beating rain was the only sound. He repeated the question.

'I told him to get away from the bags. He started laughing at me. Not like "ha-ha." More like, "this is nuts." Then he said no. So I pulled out the gun.'

She told him to back away. He wouldn't. He reached to grab one of the bags and she ordered him not to move. He was shaking and looking around like he'd lost something. Then he started shouting about some Finnegan family and everything being part of his heritage. *His* heritage? This was Fackrell land, going back generations. She'd barely earned the right to subsist here, and she'd lived on this property for thirty-four years. For someone from God-knows-where to come in and insist that something taken from this land was his?

So she shot him. At him. She shot at him – to scare him, to shut him up, to get him away from the bags. She hadn't intended to hit him. But, in retrospect, she should've waited until he wasn't shaking and moving so much.

'Even then, I'm not going to lie, I would've been fine with getting him in an arm or a leg. But he stepped to the side at the same time I fired.' Her voice was a flat blend of remorse and exhaustion. 'He went down like a bag of rocks.'

She ran over. He died within what felt like seconds. And she fled.

'I was surprised at myself later. I would've thought I'd do better in a bad situation – that I would stay, figure it out in a calm fashion. Not panic and run. But that's what I did. My mind just seized up. I went straight home and didn't breathe a word. I finally decided that I would leave him where he was. More podcast listeners would

be coming, and someone surely would find him. Then the cops
would know and his family could be notified. But it wouldn't point
back to me.'

She thought about the bags. She wanted to see what was in them.
She might need to take them, might not. But she had to go through
them. By this point it was dark, so she set out the next day after
waiting until Leo was busy feeding the goats. When she got there,
the clearing was empty. No body. No bags. All that remained were
her scattered 'Private Property' signs and the gun she'd dropped in
the bushes.

'And that was all I knew, until you showed up earlier talking
about Jordan.' She dropped her head in her hands. 'What was I
going to do? Stay quiet and have my grandson get convicted, but
then I'd be there to take care of Leo for the rest of his life? Or turn
myself in and leave Leo on his own, because that boy isn't ever
going to step up. Then you were at the door and I just wanted to
run again.'

The car had turned humid with their confined breath and drying
clothes. The heater, still on high, was making Hank's head hurt. He
looked out the window. They were getting the fire under control.
Small favors, he thought. In a world of big sins.

If Jordan had seen the dropped private property signs, it wasn't
a leap of logic to conclude that he thought one of the two people
who lived on that land was responsible for the murder. So he did
indeed step up – returning the rental car, taking the backpacks, and
most likely moving the body, too. To protect Grandpa and Grandma.
Elderly, declining Grandpa.

'What would the bank gold solve, Darlene?'

She lowered her hands. 'What?'

'Earlier you said the bank gold would solve everything. What
did you mean?'

'Leo keeps doing worse. His daddy lived to a hundred and one.
So Leo's probably got a lotta years left, and they're not going to
be high quality. We don't have enough money to deal with that. So
if there is bank gold? Yeah, it would solve some things.'

FORTY

Jordan Markham found himself in a suspiciously comfortable interview room with a smoke-grimed chief deputy. Jordan looked confused, and scared. Sheila knew the poor kid's emotions were only going to get worse.

'You're right – this isn't an interrogation room,' she said. 'Because this isn't an interrogation. You're no longer a suspect in the murder of the man in the woods.'

Jordan sagged forward, relief all over his face. He took a few deep breaths, then looked at Sheila and down at his jail scrubs. 'But . . .'

'All I have is one question, that I need you to answer honestly. Then I can explain to you why.'

'Do I need a lawyer?'

Now he asks? If he was smart, he would've asked for one up in St. Joseph. Sheila tried to push away the ache in her temples and keep a neutral expression. 'You can have one. Although we're not charging you with anything new. No matter what your answer to this question is.'

He eyed her skeptically. She didn't blame him. She tried to look trustworthy and doubted it worked, with her wild hair and dirty uniform. He sniffled a bit and then slowly nodded. 'OK.'

'Did you move the body?'

They stared at each other. He blinked. She tried not to smell her own clothing. Finally he spoke. 'No more new charges? At all? No matter what?'

'Yes.'

He traced a pattern on the table in between them, watching his fingers instead of her. 'Yeah. I did.'

'Thank you. That helps us out a lot. Can you explain to me why you thought that was a necessary thing to do?'

'No.'

That fit with what she'd expected. 'Now it's my turn to keep my end of the bargain.' Now he looked at her full on, his gaze sharp. She went on. 'Your grandmother has confessed to killing that man.

His name was Philip Garvan and he was a treasure hunter. She shot him and left him. When she went back the next day, he and the two backpacks were gone.'

'No . . .' It came out like a sigh. 'Grandma?'

'Why did you move the body?'

'I saw the no trespassing signs. I thought Grandpa did it. And if I got rid of everything, no one would know.'

She reached out her hands. Not far enough to touch him, but enough to settle him down. He was a decent kid who did something stupid on the spur of the moment. 'I can't promise all your charges will go away, but for right now, we're going to release you on your own recognizance.'

She got up and left the room. When she returned, a soot-covered, broken old man was with her. 'We'll process and release you, but I thought you and your grandpa needed to see each other first.'

She left them wrapped in a sobbing hug. She didn't need to stay, and there was nothing she could do that would make any of it better. She set off down the hall, wishing it were otherwise. And glad she wasn't the one having to book Darlene Fackrell into jail. She turned toward her office but stopped when her phone buzzed. Where are you? The judge is about to issue his decision.

Damn it. She noticed several other texts from Oberholz as she switched direction and hurried across to the courthouse as fast as she could, silently berating both herself and the Bootheel judge. She smoothed down her hair as best she could and slipped into the courtroom as quietly as possible. It didn't work. Everyone turned around and stared, even more blatantly than folks usually did when she entered a room. Fine. She would own it. She straightened and dowager duchess-ed her solitary Black self into a seat in the front row. Lanton Decker beamed at her.

'Ma'am. Welcome.' The judge turned back to Dolores Jacobsen. 'You may continue.'

Eddie Junior's attorney sniffed disapprovingly without bothering to look at Sheila. 'As I was saying, that is our motion for pre-trial release, Your Honor. My client will agree to an ankle monitor and submit to regular check-ins.'

Decker's bristle-brush mustache bent down into a frown. 'Oh, he'd "agree" to it, would he?'

Jacobsen backpedaled so quickly Sheila barely had time to laugh. Decker waved the lawyer quiet. 'Doesn't matter. I'm not releasing

him. That decision's already been made by an esteemed member of
the Branson County bench and I see no reason to revisit it. He stays
in custody until trial.'

Sheila was delighted she'd made it in time for this. Jacobsen
looked like she'd eaten a lemon and Junior looked like he was about
to cry. An overall excellent outcome.

'Now to address the other motion – the people's request to move
the trial out of this locality. I've gone through the newspaper
clippings and TV broadcast exhibits submitted by Mr Oberholz and,
while I do agree that there are a great many of them, I don't think
they add up to unduly prejudicial influence in regard to jury
selection.'

It took Sheila a second to parse through the thicket of words.
Oberholz was quicker. He leapt to his feet. 'Your Honor, we very
strongly feel that—'

'Sit down, Mr Oberholz. I'm not finished.' He shuffled his papers
and continued. 'This case is unusual in that it's the prosecution
instead of the defendant asking for a venue change. Nevertheless,
the court finds there is not enough pre-trial publicity to harm either
side. The trial will stay in Branson and as such . . .'

Decker went on, quoting sections of state law, but Sheila didn't
hear. Her ears filled with static and her vision grew blurry. She
blinked several times and things came back into focus – including
Eddie Junior. She looked him straight in the eye. He smirked at her.
She smiled right back, and kept at it until the hearing ended. She
would've kept on doing it, except Oberholz practically picked her
up and carried her out of the courtroom.

'This is . . . this is . . . unfortunate,' he said once they were safely
alone in the small workroom down the hall. 'But it's not
insurmountable. I don't want you to think that.'

She wasn't. 'I know you'll do your best.'

He sighed. 'That's your way of saying the fix is in.'

She gave him a smile – a much more tired, world-weary one
than what she'd shot at Junior. 'I might not go quite that far. Yet.
But I got faith it'll happen.'

'Faith we'll get an impartial jury?'

She scoffed. 'Hell, no. I got faith that the fix'll come riding
around the corner at the last minute. It's just whether we can run a
wire across the path and trip it up so bad that it's critically injured.
You know, like Eddie Junior did to me.'

FORTY-ONE

We dragged poor Tommy away as the bandits fell upon the gold. Billy and I could hardly move him, his body so heavy without the lightening lift of his soul. Mother was able to rouse Father from his insensibility, and he stumbled along beside her as we fled. Darkness was falling and we hid among the trees and crags. And then Billy went back. He said it was for a horse, but I worried otherwise. I feared that the gold glittered for him still.

We huddled together, the three of us living and the one of us dead. A rock outcropping afforded us the barest shelter. The ground sloped down from there and formed a slight indentation. I told my father what we must do. He was still not fully of clear mind and did not move to assist. So I began on my own. I was sixteen and had not dug a hole in the entirety of my life. And to this day, I never have again. Any gouge in the dirt reminds me of my dirty hands and the sound of earth hitting my beloved brother as I covered him with it.

I wished Billy had stayed with us. The job would have been easier and we could have continued our escape directly after the prayers we said over Tommy's grave. Instead we were afraid to move, lest Billy not be able to find us. It was a full day before he returned, in much a worse condition. A sharp wound festered in his leg and he had been pummeled about the head by someone's fists, although he insisted the bruises came from a simple fall. He had no horse.

Mother and I insisted we all leave at once. Billy wanted to head down along a nearby creek, a route that would not take us toward Forsyth and safety. He and I argued until finally he confessed that he had hidden a pack along the creek, beneath an overreaching boulder on a sharp slope. He had filled it with coins scattered during the ambush and overlooked by the bushwhackers. I asked him why he had not searched for our spilled food rations instead. He laughed at me and patted my head. I am not ashamed to say I then kicked him in the shin and started off in the correct direction. He did not follow.

*We three walked in silence and made it to Forsyth days later,
surviving only on eggs stolen from a farm's chicken coop. Billy
appeared a day after us, looking even more poorly than before.
His wound was infected and he had not found his pack full of
gold. He stayed with us for the rest of the journey to Springfield,
but he and I were never the same again. I did not trust that he
would not go running off again in search of riches. And I was
sadly correct – as soon as the war came to its bloody conclusion,
he left to find his precious treasure. I do not know if he was
successful. He always refused to say.*

*But I will tell you that he always had enough money for drink,
a tragedy – as poverty might have provided an impediment to his
whiskey-buying and the speed with which he used it to ruin his
life. I wonder now – if I had been more charitable toward his
folly as we argued next to Tommy's grave, would he have sunk
so low in later years? Is his downfall my fault? Family is a tricky
thing. If only ours had not been forced into such circumstances
as that journey north from Carrollton. If only we had not encountered Bolin and been swept up in his rampages and greed. We
would be intact. Instead Billy is in a grave of his own these past
ten years, and Mother and Father buried well before that, broken
and penniless. How all of our actions in that time – family and
killers alike – still haunt me. Old sins throw long shadows, dear
cousin. I pray you will always find the light.*

Mary Louise Finnegan O'Grady

Sam booked Darlene Fackrell into jail and left Hank to deal
with her and the lawyer she'd called. Sheila was on the phone
to Philip Garvan's sister, asking for the research he said showed
their family was related to the Finnegans. She was also requesting
permission to test the dead man's DNA against that of the skeleton.
If the bones and Garvan turned out to be related, it was a virtual
certainty that the man buried in the Ozark dirt was Tommy Finnegan.
Sam doubted the sister would refuse. It would be nice for her to
find out her brother was right about something, even if he was so
misguided about everything else.

He spent a minute in the parking lot reflexively looking for his
Bronco before he remembered. He sighed and trudged over to the
Subaru. He fired it up and sat for a minute, letting the heater take
the edge off his wet clothes. It worked as well as the blissful air

conditioning. Maybe he could get used to a car with fully functioning systems.

By the time he got home, both windshield wipers miraculously working the entire time, the rain had lessened and he'd dried to a clammy, clothes-sticking damp. He pulled up to see a red hatchback in the driveway. Brenna climbed out and waited for him. He parked behind her and met her on the lawn.

'Why're you smiling so big?'

She stuck her hands in the pockets of her raincoat and shrugged. 'I . . . I did something.'

Her smile had a little nervousness to it. And a little excitement.

'On a rainy Friday afternoon?' he said. 'What?'

'I registered. For classes.'

He stepped back in surprise. 'At the college?'

'Yes, at the college. Where else?' She pursed her lips as rain dripped down her nose. 'I decided that I'm just going to do it. Registration opened for spring semester, and I have enough saved to pay for it and I'll shift my hours at the coffee shop and I'll figure out how to be in school again after seven years since high school.' She said it in a rush and ended with an emphatic exhale. She wiped rain out of her eyes and shrugged again. Sam took her hand.

'I'm really proud of you. I know you've been wanting to.'

She smiled – that smile that was just for him, that made everything all right, that he wanted to keep for the rest of his life. And he found himself kneeling in the grass.

'What are you doing? Are you OK? Did you get hurt at work again?'

'Brenna Cassidy.' He looked up at her and took her other hand so he was holding both. 'I love you. Will you marry me?'

He couldn't believe this. He didn't have a ring. He'd done no planning. They were both getting soaked. He stared up at her. And what he thought before was a smile transformed into something even more. Light and love and the future.

'Yes. Yes, of course, yes.' She pulled him to his feet and kissed him. He tasted tears mixed in with the rainwater.

He pulled away, just barely. 'I don't have . . . I haven't bought yet . . .'

She cradled his face in her hands. He tried to keep talking. She kissed him again. 'I don't care. This is perfect. You're perfect. I love you.' The next kiss was deep and long. 'Now stop talking and take me inside.'

And so he did.

Hank made it home in time for dinner. It was the first time he'd seen Maggie since their therapy appointment. All three adults behaved themselves over spaghetti and meatballs while the kids chattered about their day at school. They dragged Duncan down the hall for bedtime stories, leaving their father with nothing but the dirty dishes. He grumbled as he scraped the food scraps into Guapo's bowl and started to load the dishwasher. Even his wife had disappeared.

He was wiping off the table when Maggie came in from the living room. 'Hey. Come here.' She tiptoed toward the bedrooms and stopped before the trio in Benny's room could see them. 'Listen.'

He fully expected to hear Duncan's gravelly rasp spinning tales of Roman gods. Instead, the Maya god of death was causing trouble for a young hero. They snuck away and stayed quiet until they were back in the kitchen.

'I don't get it,' Hank said. 'The kids vetoed that book.'

'Dad said if they wanted him to be the one reading to them, then it had to be the series on Central American myths. And they both fell in line.'

He chuckled. 'If they refuse to listen to me, at least they're listening to somebody.'

'You think we should make it Grandpop's job to get them to eat their vegetables?' She shot him a wry smile and he pulled her close.

'Nah. I think there's only so much one man can do.' He rested his chin on the top of her head and decided he'd wait until the weekend to tell her. No need to ruin a Friday night he knew she wanted to fill with nothing more than mindless TV and an early bedtime. They were still standing like that when Duncan came out. He looked at Hank, Maggie in between them, and cleared his throat.

'I've got something I need to talk to you about, sweetie,' he said. Maggie turned around and stiffened when she saw the look on his face. She started to say something, but Duncan shushed her and guided her over to the table. Hank gaped at his father-in-law. There was only one topic that rated this level of intensity. He quickly turned to leave.

'You stay. If I'm going to own up, I might as well do it in front of the other party.' Duncan waved him to an empty chair. Hank sat and tried to unobtrusively scoot himself into a corner.

'What the hell's going on?' Maggie said slowly, her hopes of Netflix and a cup of tea slipping away. Dunc gave her a sad smile.

'I need to tell you something. I thought it would iron itself out, especially if I wasn't here to get in the way. But I guess it hasn't.' He carefully avoided looking at his son-in-law. 'I don't want you and Hank to be angry at each other. I don't want your marriage to suffer for something that neither one of you did.'

Maggie squinted in puzzlement. 'Dad, I'm sure whatever it is, it's fine and—'

'No. Stop. Please.' There was the slightest tremor to his voice that Hank knew wasn't due to old age. It took a lot for the old man to be doing this. Guts, fortitude, sheer orneriness – whatever it was, Dunc was finding a hidden reserve.

'I know you were upset they treated me as a suspect in your mom's case.'

Maggie scowled. Dunc patted the table. 'And I know – especially now that I'm back – that you've been upset at Hank. And I don't want you to be.' He turned to Hank. 'I let Marian outweigh you two.' He gripped his hands together tightly. 'It's hard to balance the interests of those you love, you know?'

Hank knew.

Dunc turned back to Maggie. 'So I want you to know it wasn't a knee-jerk suspicion on Hank's part. He had reason to suspect me – standard, justifiable police reason to be looking at me more than anyone else. I don't blame him, and I don't want you to, either.'

'Now you're agreeing with him?' Her voice rose with each word as she flung an arm toward Hank. 'What the hell?'

Hank fervently wished he were somewhere else.

'Can we leave it at that?' Duncan's fingers were intertwined in prayer, but he kept his voice from pleading. Hank was proud of him and exasperated at the same time.

'Hank did nothing wrong. So please don't be angry with him.'

Maggie leaned back in her chair and crossed her arms. Both men tensed at the expression on her face. 'So just like that, I'm supposed to be happy, be accepting that everything is OK? That you two are fine? Bullshit. Because what about me? If you both are fine, why has it taken this long to say so, Dad? And you,' she said, her gaze swinging to Hank, 'what the hell are you not telling me?'

Dunc unwound his fingers and pressed his palms on the table. The praying hadn't worked.

'I didn't want to tell you because I thought I could save you from it. But all that's done is hurt you in a different way.' He looked over at Hank and then back at his daughter. 'So we'll go for the whole truth here. I need to explain about me and your mother.'

The old man began to speak. Hank quietly slipped out of the brightly lit kitchen. He stood in the darkened living room for a moment and then walked away. There didn't need to be a witness to this new wound. Just someone to help with the healing. He'd be ready.

Acknowledgements

Murder rocks is real. As was the lawless anarchy in this area of the Ozarks during the Civil War, where civilians were left to fend for themselves against guerrillas, bushwhackers, and even soldiers. For the purposes of this novel, I've deliberately changed the topography and details of the area. I also added the treasure. Trust me when I say, there's none out there. Carrollton was a real, thriving town at the onset of the Civil War. It had many successful businesses, but the First Bank of Carrollton is entirely fictional – as is the content of its vault. I consulted many sources, including wonderful letters and diary entries from civilians and soldiers. Two scholarly works deserve special mention. "Murder Rocks: A Historic Site," by Marilyn Perlberg, editor of The Society of Ozarkian Hillcrofters, gives a wide-ranging look at the many years of history swirling around Murder Rocks and the wagon road from Harrisonville, Arkansas, up to Springfield, Missouri. And the indispensable *A History of the Ozarks: Volume 2, The Conflicted Ozarks*, by Brooks Blevins, gives this area the attention it deserves as one just as brutal as regions more well known to Civil War history.

While writing about the past, I was lucky to have plenty of support in the present. I always do, but this time it was especially meaningful. My sister, Aimee, was my partner in the most difficult thing I've ever had to do, and my brother, Kenny, helped with the initial brainstorming of this book during a time when I really needed it. Betsy Wheelock and Shannon Walters were there with long distance hugs and support. Capitol Crimes, my local Sisters in Crime chapter, is the most creative, fun, and encouraging group, and I'm so thankful to be a part of it. And none of us would be anywhere without wonderful bookstores like our local Face in a Book and all the other independent bookstores throughout the country. Thank you for your support of so many authors.

Carol Adler, Paige Kneeland, and Mike Brown continue to read each book before it goes to my publisher, and their knowledge and high standards have made every single Hank book so much better. I'm also tremendously lucky to have Laurie Johnson as my editor at Severn House, along with the team of Jo Grant, Rachel Slatter, copyeditor Penny Isaac, and cover artist Jem Butcher of Jem Butcher Designs. One of my favorite parts of these acknowledgements is getting to thank my agent, Jim McCarthy. It's something I've been fortunate enough to be able to do with every book I've written. Once again, a huge, heartfelt thanks, Jim.

Lastly, and always, none of this would be possible – not this book, not this career – without my family. Joe, Carolyn, Meredith – thank you.